THE DUMB SUPPER

All the best
Jack Pertue

First published in paperback in 2024 by Sixth Element Publishing
on behalf of Jack Pentire

Sixth Element Publishing
Arthur Robinson House
13-14 The Green
Billingham
Stockton on Tees
TS23 1EU
www.6epublishing.net

© 2024 Jack Pentire

ISBN 978-1-914170-58-4

British Library Cataloguing in Publication Data.
A catalogue record for this book is available from the British Library.

This is a work of fiction. Names, characters, businesses, places, events and incidents are either the products of the author's imagination or used in a fictitious manner. Any resemblance to actual persons, living or dead, or actual events and places is purely coincidental.

All rights reserved. No part of this publication may be reproduced, stored in a retrieval system or transmitted, in any form or by any means, electronic, mechanical, photocopying, recording and/or otherwise without the prior written permission of the publishers. This book may not be lent, resold, hired out or disposed of by way of trade in any form, binding or cover other than that in which it is published without the prior written consent of the publishers.

Jack Pentire asserts the moral right to be identified as the author of this work.

Printed in Great Britain.

THE DUMB SUPPER

JACK PENTIRE

CHAPTER ONE

At sunrise on Friday June the sixteenth, in the year of our lord sixteen hundred and forty-seven, the West Country was uneasy. For the long years of the English civil war, most of Cornwall had been untouched. Of course, the rumours and stories of battles 'up country' and the gains and losses of either side penetrated, even here, where the main language of daily communication was still Cornish, and the doings of those 'to the north' had little relevance to the day-to-day life of the people.

There were exceptions. In Falmouth, the siege of the old king's gun platform of Pendennis Castle was in its late stages, and it was becoming obvious to even the most ardent royalist, that soon the castle on Pendennis Head must either surrender, or else be resupplied by sea. Out in the clear waters of the bay, Parliament's picket boats were stationed, standing ready to seal off that option. There were sporadic bursts of gunfire, but, by then, they were few and far between, as powder and shot ran low on both sides.

Even that full scale military operation had no great impact outside the curve of Falmouth Bay. The only obvious effect was the increasingly entrenched encampment of the soldiers of Parliament's New Model Army who formed a small, temporary, tented village of their own on the heathland to the west.

As the sun crawled up out of the eastern sea that morning, Simon De Montfort, hereditary owner of a mighty estate, whose only major asset was a little good grazing, and a few dozen tenant farmers who scratched a living from a thin and unkind soil, awoke to an all too familiar pain.

The early morning sunlight, filtered by the heavy bed-hangings to a few bars of blood red, lay across the bed in luscious stripes, but he was past appreciating the new day. The pain in his jaw was a solid chromium band of agony, that tightened like a vice. Every heartbeat was punctuated by a bright flash of light from somewhere behind his right eye. In this age, there was no real help for rotten teeth.

Even for the rich, pain did not discriminate. In the end, he knew that the inevitable visit of the local smith with his iron pliers and hefty muscles would put paid to the problem, but still, he procrastinated, trading short term agony for long term suffering. He pulled the covers around himself and willed the day not to come. The dawn was unmoved, and cared not at all for the middle-aged man lying on a soft bed, with the stink of old farts trapped inside his bed curtains, and his throbbing jaw.

Presently there was a familiar rap on the chamber door and his man servant came in with hot water and towels. The steel razor glittered on the tray, and the reflected light jammed fresh daggers of pain into the tender meat of his brain. The new day was starting, and pain or not, he had duties that could not easily be avoided. Rank had advantages, but it carried duties.

At the same moment, two miles away from the manor house in the coastal hamlet of Tregadrew, the inhabitants were already up and doing. Most of them lived by fishing, earning a precarious living from the sea, and their day started and ended with the sun, and followed the endless, relentless, run of the tides. The only real exception to the rule, aside from the great feast days of Easter and Midsummer, was the occasional bounty of the seas, if an unlucky ship happened to be caught by a south westerly gale in the bay and driven ashore.

This particular morning, however, was special. In the little crypt, under the church that formed one side of the village square, old Goody Penrose was waiting to discover her fate, waiting, along with the rest of the village, for justice, of a sort, to be done.

Goody and her like had been a vital part of village life since time out of mind. She was one of the 'cunning folk', and was the living repository of the village's history, and its folk memory. She remembered the history of the various families that made up the small community. She remembered, at least by her own account, the great storm of 1600, when the wind had destroyed half the village and brought the church tower crashing down.

She remembered all the old tales of the 'little people', and of how old Freddy Pascoe had spent three whole nights 'Pixie led', out on the open heath, before he had staggered home to the village with his hair shocked white by the experience.

She knew of the secret uses of the plants that grew all around in the fields and hedge boundaries, and she was often to be found wandering the clifftops on the moonlit nights of high summer, picking the herbs that she used to help the people who came to her, seeking relief from the many ills that beset the poor rural folk of that region.

It was said, in whispers, that Goody Penrose seemed to know far more than the uses of herbs. Perhaps, they said, she was possessed of darker secrets. If a man was afflicted with the inability to please his new young wife, Goody had a charm that would restore him to youthful vigour, and, again, if a young girl was pregnant out of wedlock, Goody had potions that would release her from her predicament. The old people of the community swore that she attended secret gatherings of those who followed the old religion, gatherings that were held at the stone circle, which was, according to legend, the remains of nine maidens caught dancing on the sabbath. It was said of Goody Penrose, that in her long-ago youth – and she was so old by then, that no one living could remember her being young – on one midsummer night, she had gone to the Logan Stone, and there, by the light of the full moon, she had made her vows to the old Gods. In their turn, they were said to have rewarded her loyalty with powers far beyond the normal.

Thus far, Goody Penrose was no more than a wise woman, one of hundreds of 'cunning folk' who lived throughout Cornwall, but then, events, far to the north, broke onto the peaceful rhythm of Cornish life.

As the war dragged on, and people died in increasing numbers on both sides of the argument, the ideals of the Parliament, the concept of rule by the people, under the rule of law, gradually eroded, as those noble ideas have ever eroded at such times. As the code of law no longer held true, older, darker, currents in society came to the surface.

Perhaps the most florid example of those dark turns of events sparked off in the village of Manningtree, far to the north, in the low country of East Anglia. A certain master Matthew Hopkins, a lawyer of sorts, joined forces with his murderous supporters, John Stearne and

Mary Phillips. Jointly, they began a crusade, not simply against the political opponents of Parliament, but – at least according to his own claims – against the pervading, insidious influence of the Devil incarnate. The time of the witch trials was come.

Hopkins' insanity spread like a brush fire, filling the void that the collapse of law and order had left behind. His easy certainties, and his simple solutions to a society on the verge of collapse, quickly gained a solid following.

Witchfinding, with its endless rounds of torture and summary executions, stalked the land. Hopkins and his crew profited in a very real sense, by charging the local dignitaries a full pound for every poor wretch that they accused, tried, and then assassinated.

Hopkins killed at least three hundred people, or so they said, and included at least one ordained priest among his score. The travellers who brought the news of his crimes to the south, cited the number of killings as proof of the insidious nature of the enemy, either supernatural or earthly. The seeds of religious insanity, thus sown, grew well in the fertile ground of the folklore of the South West.

In Tregadrew, the trouble really started with Millie Tresize, poor, idiotic Millie, whose left eye wandered where it would, and whose speech was slurred and scrambled. It was Millie who claimed to have seen Goody Penrose with a gathering of other people, dancing naked by moonlight at the old stone circle. She claimed that the Devil himself, in the form of a huge, red eyed, jet-black billy goat, appeared and watched over the gathering.

The fact that the scene she described was identical,

in every detail, with a picture in a book that the parish priest delighted in showing to those local children who he considered 'naughty', was ignored.

Goody Penrose was dragged from her hovel, a tiny one roomed rubble stone cottage, where smoke from the fire hung in the air at all hours of the day, and whose beams were hung with herbs drying in bundles. Once out in the square, she was stripped naked in front of the whole village. She shivered in the light, warm though the early summer sunlight was, the long empty sacs of her breasts and the pouch of her wrinkled belly hanging, as she tried in vain to cover the iron-grey thatch at her crotch with her crossed, liver spotted hands. The villagers, most of whom had been her customers themselves at some point, shifted mood from respectful petitioners to baying mob, in a moment.

They blindfolded her, and, with a sailmaker's awl, they pricked her body, searching for the Devil's mark, a spot where the old stories claimed that a witch, having been touched by Satan at her dark baptism, would be forever insensitive to pain. Sadly, for Goody, she bore on her left thigh a broad, pinkish-white stripe of scar tissue, where many years before, she had suffered a scald that had very nearly cost her life. For a week she had hung in the balance, before, finally, the dead skin and flesh that the heat had destroyed sloughed off, leaving a wrinkled pink patch that was vaguely in the shape of a map of England. The tissue loss, and the associated nerve damage, had left a broad scar of skin that was as unfeeling as a plank of wood. The bodkin sunk in a half inch deep, and she did not, could not, react.

With 'proof' of her guilt thus established, she was

secured in the old crypt below the church, there being no other place in the village that was secure. So, confined with the ancient dead, alone in the semi dark, and breathing in the slight stink of corruption and ancient piss that always hung around the place, the old woman awaited her fate.

Simon De Montfort, in his role as the local magistrate, was responsible for administering justice. It was a part of his role he normally enjoyed, sitting behind the long oak table with the drawn sword – his symbol of authority – laid in front of him. The run of local offenders were mostly nothing more serious than domestic disputes between spouses, or the odd case of poaching, as often as not on his own land. In practice, the penalties for such things were mostly trivial and humiliating, rather than seriously dangerous. The village had a set of stocks, and those who found themselves confined there between the hours of sunrise and sunset, would, as often as not, be ignored by the passing villagers. The odd, unpopular, member of the community might be mocked, or pelted with rubbish, as the mood was, but there was little crime anyhow, and the cases that came before him were rarely serious. If a malefactor was accused of some serious crime, he was normally referred to the Bodmin Assize, where the travelling circuit judge dispensed more severe justice.

The war had disrupted that easy pattern of life, as it had disrupted so much else. Most of the judiciary were Royalists, and if a Royalist judge was to sit in a court in an area loyal to Parliament, or vice versa, the possibilities for disturbances, if the sentence was unpopular, were endless. For the duration of the war, the local magistrates dispensed justice as they saw fit, and, if that justice involved the death penalty, as it often did, the local smith, or even a sturdy local sailor, skilled in the use of ropes, could be called on to do the honours. The results were generally slow strangulation, while the victim kicked and choked their way to eternity.

Executions were not edifying, though a hanging always drew a good crowd, but they were believed, by the ruling elite, to act as a deterrent to the dangerous classes, and the hangman made a good, if intermittent, sideline, in selling portions of his used ropes. They were thought to act as a cure for everything, from childhood rickets to worms in the gut.

All of this was well and good for the most part, but witch trials, involving as they did the workings of the Prince of Darkness himself, had complications outside the usual run of events. Principal of them was the involvement of the church. Religion was a desperately contentious issue, quite apart from the war, and the inclusion of the local priest was a ticklish matter of fine judgement, liable to bring down the wrath of various authorities, especially those of a variant religious belief. All of that was complex enough, but any legal involvement with the church was dangerous, especially when the local priest was of the stripe of the very Reverend Ivor Thomas.

Cornwall was solidly Royalist, and so dedicated to the old church of Rome, that to attempt the introduction of any suggestion of the new Church of England ritual was to risk violent disagreement. Ivor Thomas fitted this situation admirably. His rituals were solidly, and unrepentantly, Roman Catholic. He was raised in a family on the Welsh borders, where the mass was still said, even in the days when the officiating priest travelled at night, and under cover, and then hid in foetid, specially built cavities in the masonry, constantly in fear of his life. That was the time when the mass was furtive, and celebrated with improvised ritual objects, in private rooms, and the risk of the martyr's stake was ever present.

As a child, and then through a troubled adolescence, Ivor's favourite books were, firstly the bible of course, and then an old and precious book of hours, with bright coloured illustrations. He was taught religion at his mother's knee, and her god was the foul tempered, unpredictable, capricious tyrant of the Old Testament.

There was one other book that he loved from the moment he could read it. That was 'Demonolatry' by the renowned French witch hunter Nicholas Remy, who, a hundred years before, had personally tortured and burned at least four hundred people. Remy's book had fed the growing boy's imagination with a hundred images of demonic manifestations. As a twelve-year-old, Ivor was already planning to join a seminary, over the water in solidly catholic Spain. He read avidly the accounts of witch's sabbats and their revels. He gazed, for hours at a time, at the woodcut images of naked celebrants of the black mass, lying, legs spread, before the horned devil, who sat on a low altar sporting a hyperbolic erection that reached nearly to his chest.

The young Ivor would gaze at that picture for hours. As an adolescent, he would masturbate over the book, vicariously enjoying the delights of the sabbat. At first, he imaged himself kneeling before the horned devil in the firelight, enjoying the willing favours of a dozen different partners and, afterwards, in a frenzy of remorse, he would lash himself with an improvised multi-corded whip, until the blood flowed. By the time he was finally ordained, he was already thirty-five, and long set in his ways. And, if he had once held mass with blood soaking through the back of his cassock, after an especially vigorous session of self-flagellation, well, among his loyal flock, that was thought of as no more than an expression of his extreme holiness.

At a time when people were routinely ready to die for their faith, and when the dispute between King and Parliament was often couched in religious terms, his piety was not thought to be unusual.

The priest's presence at the trial of Goody Penrose for witchcraft was unwelcome to Simon De Montfort in his capacity as representative of the secular arm of the law, but it was a legal requirement. A representative of the church was required to oversee, and, if need be, to advise on the theological aspects of the case.

The manor's great hall was cold that morning, even though the sunlight flooded the village square outside. Simon De Montfort sat on a chair at the head of the hall that was mounted on a raised platform to emphasise his superior status. From his vantage position, he looked out at the assembled people and wished that this was over. His jaw throbbed, as the abscess under the big molar on the right-hand side steadily bored away at the bone of his jaw. In three weeks' time, the erosion would finally point up and burst, releasing a flood of foul tasting pus into his mouth, but that rough relief seemed a long way in the future that morning.

Ivor Thomas sat beside him, his chair slightly lower than Simon's. The priest was so close that Simon was extremely aware of his body odour, a strange mix of old sweat and incense. It was as if he carried an aura around him.

The gathered villagers were excited, bubbling with anticipation of the spectacle. The atmosphere in the room was closer to a feast day gathering than a court of law.

Finally, the doors at the end of the room slammed back against the wall with a sound like a tuneless drumbeat, and the two members of the village watch, puffed up with their own temporary importance, came into view, dragging Goody between them. They were holding a scrawny arm each, and getting through the door, three abreast was a small, undignified struggle. They dragged her in backwards, facing out, so that she would have no chance of casting her evil eye and thus influencing the judgement. Once inside the room, they forced her to an isolated three-legged stool that stood on the flag stones in front of the bench.

Simon de Montfort, seeing the accused for the first time, was impressed only by how insignificant she seemed. She was just an old hag, undernourished and filthy, with ingrained stains on her elbows and knees, and wasted muscle hanging loose on her upper arms. There was a rough covering of dirty cloth around her middle, though whose modesty that was intended to preserve, God only knew.

Her hair was straggling about her shoulders in rough dirty coils. Simon noticed a heavy brownish/blue bruise on her upper thigh. Suddenly, he was overwhelmed by the outright stupidity of the whole business. This was no witch, no servant of the Powers of Darkness. Surely, if he needed to employ mortal help, the Devil could find better recruits than this sad old woman.

Still, Simon was not such a fool as to go against accepted wisdom, nor would he fly in the face of the crowds. He was only too well-aware of stories of those justices who had refused to find a witch guilty, only to find themselves accused in their turn.

Simon said, "Who brings evidence against this woman?"

Millie Tresize was pushed forwards, her wandering eye gazing off to the left, and a thin stream of drool hanging from her loose lips under the stress of the moment.

"Now child," said Simon solemnly, speaking as though he could really take the word of this poor idiot for anything. "Tell me what you saw."

Millie was tongue-tied at the sight of so many faces all turned in her direction.

"Speak up, Child," he said, in what he imagined was a kindly voice.

"I seed her at the old Stone circle," said Millie. Her voice was high and trembling with the stress of the event. "It were near dark but there were a moon, so I could see. One night, she were there with lots of others, all different people. I don't reckon I ever seen them before, they none of them got clothes on, and there were this thing on the big stone in the middle."

"What kind of thing, Millie?"

"Like a goat. A bit like old Tommy Herring's goat. But it weren't standing up. It were sitting on its arse, like."

The child's accent was so thick under the stress of the occasion that Simon had trouble following her, but he said, "Now, you are quite sure, Millie, about what you saw?"

"I seed it, Sir. I seed the goat and the people, all of them with no clothes on, and there was an old man there as well. He was playing the pipes, Sir."

"I see. Is there anything else? Is anyone else bringing evidence against this woman?"

And then there came the endless recitation of village gossip. The old woman had bewitched Jimmy Pascoe's good pig so that it took sick and died. She had cursed the pedlar who had insulted her last summer, and he had fallen from the cliffs at the Devil's Cove and smashed his head on the rocks, so his brain was splashed over the sands in a hot, pinkish grey splatter.

She had, by all accounts, bewitched a dozen village girls and aborted their pregnancies, whether they would or no. And, last winter, she had called up a great storm that drove the Royalist ships away from the relief of Pendennis, and that was sure to cost King Charles his last castle in the West Country.

There was no doubt, at least in the collective mind of the community. Goody Penrose was a witch.

Simon intended, up to that point, to pass a sentence that would satisfy the village, but absolve him of the need to shed blood.

'A flogging should do it,' he thought. With the convicted witch tied to the baiting stone in the square, the watch would take turns to beat the old woman with whips. With luck, she would survive with nothing worse than a few more scars to add to those she already had on her aging hide. Father Thomas, of course, had other ideas.

"If I might address the court," he said in his cracked voice that always sounded to onlookers as if it came from a stone trapped under a door.

"If you must," said Simon with a heavy heart. The pain in his jaw was worse than ever by then, and the bright green pinpoints of light were back in his vision.

"This woman has committed the worst of sins against her creator," Ivor began in his cracked voice. "She has willingly chosen to link hands with the powers of evil. As long as she lives, our community will never rest."

There was a rumble of agreement among the crowd.

"It is your contention that she should hang?" said Simon, more coldly that he had originally intended.

"It is my contention, Sir," said Ivor, "that she should burn. Fire alone will atone for her infamy."

The crowd rumbled again. This was an exciting diversion from the norm, and Simon knew very well that there was very little he could do to change the course of matters at this point. He made one last try, even so.

"That sentence is beyond my powers to apply," he said. "I am minded to refer her to the next assize for sentence."

A rumble rose from the crowd, a single collective voice of disapproval. This witch was theirs to dispatch and they would see her end. In better political times, Simon might have stood out against them, but he was aware of the realistic limits to his powers.

He said, "Is this the punishment required by sacred, as well as cannon law, Reverend Thomas?"

"It is. The law is clear, Leviticus says it clearly: 'Thou shalt not suffer a witch to live'."

Simon opened his mouth to object but suddenly the pain in his face, the pressure of office, the crowd, and the danger of the bad feelings of the mob, were all too much. He wanted this farce done with, so he said, "Very well. Goody Penrose. You have been found guilty of the crime of witchcraft, of consorting with the Prince of Darkness, of killing by magic, and of destroying the unborn. Your sentence is that you be taken from here to a safe place, there to be held until the time is right, when you shall be taken to the village square and burned until you are dead. After that, your ashes shall be scattered to the ocean depths. I will not commend your soul to God. You have already chosen another master."

For the first time the old woman responded. She gathered herself up, stood in front of the bench, and spat in Simon's face. The two members of the watch who were supposed to be escorting her recoiled as if she were some dangerous animal. Wiping the warm slime from his cheek, he glanced downwards and saw that Ivor Thomas had an erection tenting against the cloth of his surplice.

Death by burning was outside the expertise of the local watch, those worthy part-timers who were responsible to Simon De Montfort for maintaining law and order. Billy Hawkins, the local smith, and the strongest man in the village, had carried out three hangings by the orders of the court since the war had wrecked the local system of law and order, but burning was something foreign to him. In the end, he co-opted Arthur Hardy, a local labourer who was no more than a strong back for hire, to act as his assistant.

Hanging a man is comparatively easy. A stout rope, a stool and a strong beam were enough, and the victim's hands and feet were tied so there was no chance of resistance. At a push, even the branch of a sturdy tree would serve as a gallows.

Burning was much, much slower, and intended to be so. Prolonged suffering was the aim of the punishment. But a victim of the fire could escape and break away from the flames, unless some way of restraining them could be found to hold them to the spot while the flames rose around them. Ropes, themselves susceptible to the fire, would obviously not fit the bill. Chains would not burn, but of themselves, simple lengths of chain would hardly hold the victim long enough for the fire to do its work, unless they were fixed to something solid. A stake as such, like those used in the short, violent reign of Queen Mary Tudor, who had burned protestants with great abandon, would suit, but a wooden stake was out of the question. The old queen had used iron beams driven into the ground, but that would take time to prepare, and time was short.

It was Arthur Hardy who suggested using the old baiting block in the village square.

Animal baiting, once a popular spectacle, was less popular by then. The old granite block, set with a rusting iron ring where a bull had, once upon a time, been tethered, while dogs had worried at it while the rowdy crowd shouted encouragement and placed bets, had sunk into the surface over the years, until only a few inches of the granite cube showed at the surface. Even so, the block of granite was solidly immovable. For that day's event, all that was needed was a length of chain, and a quick scout around the blacksmith's workshop would provide that. There remained only the matter of the fire.

They settled on gorse branches, cut from the local heathland and tied in great bundles. On top of them, they intended to use poles of scrap wood, and the old, dry and rotten roof beams, taken from what had been Jenny Keith's old cottage before she had died and left it to rot five years before. By that evening, the stack of fuel was ten feet high, and there was a feeling of expectation on the wind. It was like the evening before the May eve festival.

Excitement was in the air, hot and sooty, as if the flames already burned. During the final preparations, in the pale light of the new dawn, Reverend Thomas inspected the pile of fuel and blessed it, sprinkling it with holy water, sanctifying the fire to come.

They kept her for a second night in the crypt while three village women watched by candlelight, hoping for the appearance of the witch's familiar. Anything would have served, a stray cat, a barn rat, even a passing cockroach, but aside from the condemned woman, nothing stirred through the night. Her impromptu escort, three worthy village matrons, were at first deliciously excited by the possibility of witnessing the workings of evil at first hand, then bored with waiting. One by one, they dozed in the small hours of that final night. It made no difference to Goody. In any case, she was already guilty and sentenced.

At dawn the next day, they came to take Goody Penrose out to die. Two men held her hands out in front of her, wrists crossed, while they chained her wrists together, cold riveting the links of the chain, and leaving a trailing tail of iron links to fix her to the stone.

At first light they took her out into the new morning. The sun was already well up in the sky and the air was fresh and clear. She walked out, with her head up, ignoring the crowd, who once, a few days before, had been her neighbours.

Goody was shoved down into a rough crouch while they fixed the loose chain to the ring. The chain was shorter than it might have been, so that, with the chain fixed, she could no longer stand completely upright, there just wasn't enough slack in the tether. So, she crouched as the men piled the bundles of gorse around her. The next layer of fuel, the larger kindling, grew around her in a pile. In the end, only her head, shoulders and upper body were exposed at the top of an untidy cone of wood. A fire licked in a rough brazier close at hand, and three torches, wooden sticks with oil-soaked cloths wrapped around them, stood ready to hand. There was a moment of expectant quiet. In the stillness, the small crackling sounds of the brazier were clear.

Ivor Thomas held the big brass cross that he had borrowed from the altar, in front of him, offering it to the condemned woman to kiss.

"Your body is forfeit, woman," he said in his cracked and broken voice. This was, as he saw it, a great theatrical moment. "Still," he said, "acknowledge God and you may yet save your soul from the pains of Hell."

Foe the first time that morning, Goody Penrose, convicted witch and cunning woman, spoke.

"You, Priest," she said, and she made the title sound like an obscenity, "are no more known to your God than I am. I will soon be gone to whatever waits all of us at the end, but I promise you this: for what you will do today, the echoes will ring down through time. Long after you are no more than an empty memory, and your false god is forgotten, today's work will still be remembered. So, do your worst, little man. Your power is of this Earth. Your fire is nothing to me… but my fire, and my power, will go on through all eternity."

Reverend Thomas recoiled as if he had been suddenly threatened by a snake. He nodded to the two men waiting by the brazier.

"Proceed," he said.

They had chosen gorse as the main fuel for the fire with the best of intentions. Billy Hawkins, though he was the chosen executioner, was not by nature a cruel man, and his thinking, as he gathered fuel for the pyre, was that gorse flared into an instant hot burst of flame within moments of catching fire. Nothing, he thought, could survive that first quick burn. Goody Penrose would be gone almost before she realised what was happening.

There was a problem with this thinking. True, gorse bundles caught easily. True, they flared into bright hot flame in an instant, but even though the flame that gorse produces is hot, it burns briefly. As they lit the fire, that morning, the flames flowered into life, hiding Goody from view in a sheet of white flame. That done, with massive surface burns inflicted on most of her body, the fire began to wane a little.

She had instinctively held her breath as the flames rose, and that had the effect of protecting her airway and lungs from the heat. The end result was that, though the first, bright burst of fire caused her excruciating agony, leaving most of her exposed skin scorched to a bright slippery pink, it failed to either kill her, or even render her insensible to the next phase of the execution. By then she was writhing and making a high-pitched mewling noise like an animal caught in some cruel trap, but the chain that held her to the baiting stone refused to give a millimetre, and no matter how she threw herself from side to side, she could not escape the dreadful grinding agony.

Billy Hawkins, appalled by what he had unleashed, went in close to the flames and tried to throw a cord around her neck from behind, intending to strangle her to death, but there was no chance of that, as the heat drove him back, again and again.

The crowd, most of the village population, simply watched in silence and horrified fascination. Simon de Montfort was as shocked as anyone else, and he sent his man to fetch a pistol from the armoury in the great hall so that he might finish the job with a one-ounce ball, but even that small measure of mercy was not to be. The armoury was securely locked in these uncertain times, and, while his man could see the guns neatly racked up behind an iron grille, there was no chance of reaching them, and even less chance of loading the cumbersome muzzle-loading flintlock in time to be of any help,

Meanwhile in the square, the spectacle went on and on. Five long minutes after the fire was lit, finally, after what had seemed an untold time in agony, Goody Penrose, cunning woman of the parish, slipped into unconsciousness.

After she slumped against the restricting chains, she folded forwards, so that her face was concealed by the burning fuel. The rest was simply a visceral horror, and in a country village, the crowd were well used to the sight of blood and gore. Even the bursting of her belly wall that released coils of slippery gut that cooked and hissed in the flames, was nothing that they had not all seen before, as the endless pattern of raising and slaughtering livestock went on. Even the stink of the greasy black smoke that smelled of a nauseating mix of singed hair, rotten meat, and shit, was familiar.

The fire threatened to go out before the body was wholly consumed, and there was a final element of dark farce, as the men had to go to fetch more wood, but eventually, three hours after the flames were first lit, there was nothing left but a pile of wood ash and blackened, cremated bone. Goody's skull with a few startlingly white teeth was still quite recognisable among the shards of bone.

In the end, Billy Hawkins fetched a ten-pound hammer from the forge and pounded the remaining bone to unrecognisable ash. They gathered what was left and scattered it in the ocean, reducing Goody Penrose to no more than a drifting dusty scum of grey, floating on the sea. The village square, the baiting stone, and the old houses were all unmoved by events. The granite stone was a little scorched by the flames, and blackened with ash, both gorse and human, but all that would fade soon enough when it next rained.

That night, the summer weather, that gorgeous, endless, harvest summer weather, broke in a violent storm that filled the air with white streamers of light and crashes of thunder. The superstitious crossed themselves, and swore that Goody's vengeful spirit was angry, but by morning, the sea was settling into a rough semblance of its normal self.

Within a few years, the whole episode was forgotten by everyone, except the old folks who whispered the tale darkly on winter nights, and swore that, though the old witch Goody Penrose might be dead, she was far from at rest.

"Eventually," they said, "sooner or later, there will be an account to settle."

CHAPTER TWO

The morning meeting at the Tregadrew medical practice was an informal affair. In many ways it had to be, as the practice only boasted two doctors, and one of them was old and edging gently towards retirement. The surgery was set a little back from the market cross, where, for many years, a small agricultural market had met to serve the needs of the local populace every Thursday.

The surgery was an early twentieth century building, created in the days when Edwardian gentlemen demonstrated their status by the size of their residences, and the original house had boasted five bedrooms, two in the third-floor attic spaces for the live-in servants. Downstairs were three generous rooms, a scullery and a kitchen. The rambling nature of the place was admirably suited to the sort of lazy, rather old fashioned, medicine that Dr Eric Francis, the elder of the two partners, had practised there ever since the fifties, when new evidence-based medicine and the nascent NHS was starting to infiltrate even here, in the depths of the far western reaches of the country. Like many tiny rural practices, the surgery served as its own dispensary. On occasions, a patient who might need some treatment outside of the usual run of syrups for coughs, or antibiotics, might be left waiting for the drug to be delivered, before it could finally be dispensed, but the extra NHS money that the dispensary brought in just about kept the practice afloat.

Old fashioned it might be, but the practice served the two thousand or so villagers and the outlying farms well enough. Of course, every now and then some visiting townie from 'up country' would complain about this rather laid-back arrangement. Strangely enough, the most vociferous complainers were always those with the most trivial complaints.

That morning, Eric Francis was sitting on one side of a rather fine mahogany table that would not have looked out of place in a Victorian gentleman's drawing room. He was one of those tall men who look somehow stretched, and he had a hook nose and a mane of white hair that he wore rather longer than most men of his generation. Among the villagers there was a standing joke that, with a long blue robe and a staff, he might have doubled for Gandalf. The two laptops on the polished table's surface were the only modern touch, and they looked odd and somehow out of place, like a telephone in a Rossetti painting.

On the other side of the table sat his partner, Dr Jonathan Wilde. Forty years Eric's junior, Jonathan was one of those men who gave the impression of always being about to spring into rapid action even when he was at rest. He was slim, of medium height, and dark haired. He was a graduate of Queens in Belfast, and an especially savage junior internship during the florid IRA bombing campaign. For a junior in a busy A&E department, it had been a baptism, almost literally, of fire. Starting out with the intention of specialising in emergency medicine, Jonathan had become a GP not initially from choice, but almost by default.

He had loved the constant edginess of emergency medicine but after a few years, he was introspective enough to come to know that a lifetime spent on the very edge of acute emergency medicine would destroy him as a human being.

He was far from alone in that. Few people who choose emergency medicine as a calling come away completely unscathed. In the end, it was a matter of learning to accept the carnage that routinely came through the department doors or learning to ignore the realities of the fanatics who wielded the knife, the Armalite and the Semtex, all this without losing track of humanity.

CHAPTER THREE

It had all come to a head, in the warmth of a late summer, when the department's windows were open to a balmy evening, and the warm air filtered past the netting that was placed there to foil the casual grenade. All seemed well with the world until a bomb, consisting of three kilos of CO-OP mix with a five-hundred-gram plastique booster, enveloped a quiet, mainly protestant district and caught a small catholic family who were committing the ideological crime of sleeping peacefully in the front bedrooms of a small, terraced house. The blast, with its mighty over pressure, and a massive ball of flame, first smashed into the room, and then enveloped the inhabitants of the house in fire.

Twenty-three minutes later, the long, sad procession of smashed bodies began to come through the doors of A&E. The first two brought in, both of them teenage girls, were beyond all hope. The third, their younger brother, cleared triage and was directed to cubicle three of the major accident side of the emergency room.

As it happened, Jonathan Wilde was the junior member of staff on duty. His senior that night, a much older and more experienced doctor called Stephen Williams, was asleep in the rest room, three floors away, and only available – in theory at least – at ten minutes' notice, having pulled a straight thirty-hour stint earlier in the week. For the first half hour of the developing incident, Jonathan was the responsible attending physician.

The kid was maybe seventeen and he was as skinny as a lawn rake. Lying on the resuss couch, every rib showed under the fish-belly white skin where his bare chest was exposed to the merciless glare of the examination lights. Jonathan Wilde went through the initial examination mechanically. Check the pulse, clear the airway, check for bleeding, clip the oximeter to a finger to check for O2 saturation, listen for the chest sounds and observe respiration. The old routine, the old relentless pressure.

Jonathan pressed the cup of the stethoscope to the pale skin. On the boy's left side there was an ominous silence. No breath sounds, no air moving in the restless tide of life. Jonathan ran one gloved hand flat against the boy's rib cage feeling for the fractures that he already knew were there. Later, if there was a later for this boy, there would be time for the portable X-ray image, that is, if they could rouse a radiologist in time to do any good.

Jonathan Wilde, resting his right hand against clammy white skin, knew that the X-ray would tell him nothing that was not obvious to the touch. There was a large patch of chest wall on that side, that moved independently of the boy's increasingly spasmodic breathing. Flail Chest, the result of massive blast injury. A section of the rib cage had been smashed loose by the explosive pressure wave, effectively negating the boy's breathing efforts.

Reacting now to events, and well into the well-oiled routine, Jonathan was not thinking, not really needing to take time to think. Calling for the airway, he stood at the lad's head, looking downwards towards his feet, easing the mouth open and reflexively noting the trickle of blood, bright red blood. Bright, vivid scarlet blood, loaded with oxygen, so it was probably from the lungs, maybe a tear, maybe just diffuse pressure injury from the blast. Easing the long, bluntly curved blades of the laryngoscope into position to depress the boy's tongue, Jonathan visualised the vocal cords and the entrance to the trachea. The vocal cords were relaxed. He eased the tube of the endotracheal airway into place, and held one hand out to the nurse beside him for the syringe that she held. It was already filled with saline.

He eased the liquid in, pressing the syringe plunger gently to fill the cuff of the airway, sealing the tube to the trachea wall, and called for the nurse to note the time of intubation. This kind of intubation has a shelf life, left in situ for too long, the pressure of the inflated cuff can cause ulceration.

Jonathan took the rubber Ambu bag and connected it to the airway. He gave it a gentle squeeze and noted that the chest rose in response. So far, so good. He spared a quick glance to check on the oxygen saturation readout. Eighty eight percent – not good by any standards, but not catastrophic. The pulse readout was flickering, unsteady. He watched as the blood pressure, according to the reading from the cuff, was down and falling. Somewhere inside, the lad was bleeding out. Jonathan ran an educated hand over the smooth skin of the abdomen. There was no clear swelling, and still the BP was dropping.

Almost for the first time, Jonathan spoke.

"Staff," he said to the nurse who was standing close by. "Page Mr Williams again and make it urgent this time. I really don't like this kid's vitals."

"Still on his way doctor."

Suddenly, Jonathan Wilde felt very alone. The heart monitor abruptly started its rapid beep, an audio warning that the heart rhythm was outside its electronic understanding of normality.

"Get the ressus trolley ready, Staff," he said. And part of him knew it was already too late.

The trolley was beside him in seconds, the defibrillator was already charging, the whine of the capacitors rising in pitch towards the high point.

Just at the second that the trolley arrived, the lad's heart finally stopped. The green line that had kicked every second or so, flatlined. The monitor started its one note high pitched audio warning.

Someone said, "Shit," in a quiet voice.

Staff said, rather unnecessarily, "He's arrested, Doctor."

Jonathan peeled the backing from the adhesive conductive patches, sticking them to the skin where the first purple bruising was starting to show, knowing that that bruise would probably never have a chance to develop to maturity.

"Clear," he shouted, making sure everyone was safe from the shock.

There was a heavy dull thump as the paddles discharged six hundred joules into the boy's chest. His body arched in automatic response, then let go and relaxed, falling back onto the trolley.

Right after the shock, there were a few brief moments of frantic electrical activity on the monitor screen, a jagged mesh of bright blue lines, but other than that, there was no response. The glowing flatline stayed flat, other than one feeble upwards twitch that was gone as soon as it was there.

The Asiatic nurse at the head who was still squeezing the Ambu bag, filling the lad's lungs every few seconds, had a shocked look in her eyes.

Repeated exposure to the realities of human mortality

never does soften those first few seconds where, at first, a life is there, and then, gone. Jonathan pressed the recharge button, working on training routine alone, acting more out of hope than expectation, as he listened to the whine of the capacitor recharging. The line of LED lights turned green, indicating the machine was ready to discharge again. He took the paddles in his hands and laid them on the patches.

It was two hours before they finally wrote the certificate and released the kid's body, as a victim of a terrorist act, to the coroner's officer.

CHAPTER FOUR

Afterwards there was a good deal of speculation among the hospital staff as to why the promising young house officer, who everyone regarded as the coming man, should have quit so abruptly.

The truth was that not even Jonathan Wilde himself could have really articulated his reasons, but that last night, when a youth died under his care, had shifted something in Jonathan's psyche. It was not simply the death itself... having come so far in training, he had already developed a tough carapace for such things, but it was more than that. That single death had seemed, for Jonathan, to make the whole, carefully choreographed, treatment process seem futile, and without the motivation of the certainty that ultimately it was all worthwhile, there suddenly seemed to be no point in going on with the work at all.

In a way, it was a crisis that would have been very familiar with the religious leaders of old. A promising novice, already wise in the ways of the church, would suddenly, and for no apparent reason, lose the will to continue. A kind of malign transubstantiation took place where wine became nothing more than soured grapes, and the communion wafers were transformed into stale bread. With the miracle turned to ashes, there was no point in ritual for its own sake.

Those long-ago religious leaders put such things down to the working of the Devil. In the enlightened twenty-first century, the Devil is no longer held responsible. God being dead, there is no need of his involvement any longer, and the authorities simply call such dark nights of the soul 'burn out'.

Jonathan, given a semi-compulsory medical leave of absence for six months, spent endless days walking in the lonely countryside, and on the empty seashore, encountering nothing more challenging than a few dog walkers and a succession of sweaty, gasping joggers, who nodded in passing to acknowledge another human being who was crazy enough to venture out in such a place, and at such a time.

On one such lonely walk, by the grey waters of the Irish Sea where the distant misty mountains created a severe backdrop to the seascape, he met Sally Johnson for the first time.

At least it was the first time that they had actually spoken. For her part, she had seen Jonathan on several occasions. He had become one of those people who you barely notice in passing, registering them almost subconsciously, logging them as a known figure, and then pretty well forgetting.

She was petite, slim, dark haired, and fair skinned with Irish blue eyes that would light up when she smiled, and that was often, for she was a smiling girl. That late morning, she was wearing a blue track suit that emphasised, rather than concealed, the small swell of her breasts.

Jonathan was sitting, looking out to sea, on a bench that was grey with long exposure of its timbers to the sea air and the sun. He was wearing jeans and a camo-green anorak that came to his knees and was half-way zipped up at the front. She sat on the bench beside him, leaving just enough space between them to not create discomfort by her proximity.

Jonathan said nothing, so she said, "It's a gorgeous view, isn't it?"

"Yes," he replied. "It must be great on a bright day."

"A bright day? You're not from around here?"

"I'm at Queens, or at least most of the time I am. I'm on leave of absence."

"Lucky you."

"I suppose."

"What brought you here? You don't have a local accent."

"A course. I'm a medic, or, I was, before… Well, you don't want my bloody life story."

"Not if you don't want to talk about it. I'm sorry, I didn't mean to pry."

"It's not that," he said. "It's just that…" and, with that, he found himself pouring it all out, baring his soul to a stranger, as if it was the most natural thing in the world.

As he talked, the sun crept across the sky and headed towards the western horizon, then, suddenly, it seemed it was a great ball of red and gold in the west, and the sea looked as if it were on fire.

Jonathan suddenly realised how long he had been talking, and he said, "Christ, I'm sorry. You didn't need to hear all that."

She said, "That's okay. You needed to say it. I'm sorry that it had to be to a stranger, but maybe it's easier that way. I don't even know your name."

"It's Jonathan Wilde. And yours?"

"Sally, Sally Johnson."

"You live here?"

"My parents did once. I was brought up a few miles away from here, but they had to leave and go to the

UK a few years back. It was during the first part of the troubles, you know?"

"Sorry, I didn't mean to pry."

"It's okay. It's funny really, my family have lived all over the place. My dad's people came from here, but they are all dead now. My mother was from Cornwall. When I was just a kid, she used to tell me all the old stories about it. That's always been where my real roots are, I think, well, I've always thought that I'd go back there, sooner or later. Somehow, it's never happened, at least so far. I suppose that, doing what I do, I could move anywhere. I'm a freelance researcher. I do archive historical research for people who can't find all they want on the net. You'd be surprised how many still need a real live person to do the donkey work."

As if it were a sudden event, he realised that it was growing colder as the heat of the sun went out of the day.

He said, "I've kept you talking too long. I'm sorry."

"Maybe I'll see you again?"

"Yes. I'd like that."

And just like that, a chance encounter on a windswept bit of shore became the start of the most important relationship in his life.

CHAPTER FIVE

Jonathan had never really given any thought to actually living in the South West of the UK. He had always, as he climbed steadily up the greasy pole of qualifications, assumed that, at some time in the future, he would meet someone who would become a long-term partner. That done, he vaguely expected that there would be a fixed base somewhere.

Sometimes, though, he seriously wondered if any normal woman could ever stomach the killing hours and endless shift changes, to say nothing of the abrupt changes of hospital without any hope of acquiring a place to call home. The changes of location, intended as a way of giving trainees wide hospital experience, were notorious for destroying relationships almost before they were properly begun. In the meanwhile, there was an inevitable series of short-term partnerships. One of them, with a pretty, brittle, blonde American girl called Suzanne Harris, had even seemed as if it might lead to something more permanent, before the demands of the job took her to a hospital three hundred miles off. The women were, all of them, very well in their way, but those relationships were no more, on either side, than satisfying a mutual sexual itch. Coming from that background, the effect that Sally Johnson had on him was strange and unfamiliar.

Jonathan, up until then, had never been in love. In fact, he had regarded the whole idea as probably no more than a romanticising of a simple biological drive. Sexual desire was one thing, he understood that very well, but this intense emotional bond, instant, and so intense that it took over much of his waking life, was a new thing.

Even then the logical, rational, part of his mind thought that there might be no future in it. After all, he hardly knew the girl. Even so, the very idea of uprooting this love, so recent, and yet so seemingly permanent, never occurred to him, beyond a passing fantasy. It would, he thought, be like flying unaided, or reversing the passage of time.

He found himself wandering the shore, where he had first met her, at odd times, even when the weather was, as it often was in Ireland, foul and damp. At odd times, when he was alone, reading a book, or half watching some vapid offering on TV, her face was suddenly in front of him in his mind's eye, as if projected there by some strange alchemy.

Finally, on the fifth day, as he was starting to think the whole thing was, after all, no more than a product of his own inner longings, she was finally there, wandering the shore, alone. Suddenly, faced with the reality of her presence, he was almost afraid to actually approach her, reluctant to risk the magical fantasy by exposure to the cold reality of everyday life.

Finally, he simply walked up to her and said, "Hello, I was hoping that you'd be here."

And then, he inwardly cursed himself for being too forwards in his approach, seeming too needy, maybe.

If she felt that way, she didn't show it.

She just said, "I was sort of expecting you. I'm glad you're finally here. How are you?"

He said, "Good, thank you, and you?" and inwardly cursed himself for the stilted formality.

"Oh, I'm well thank you." She shook her head as if mentally squaring up to a difficult task, then she said, "To be honest, I was really trying to make up my mind on something. Walking here by the sea helps sometimes. It's nothing really, I can't expect you to be interested, but I'd really value an open-minded opinion."

"After the last time we met, I'd say I owe you that one, wouldn't you? Go ahead. How can I help?"

"I've finally been offered the chance to move back to the mainland. To Cornwall."

Jonathan felt a level of dismay that he wouldn't have thought possible a few days before. She was leaving, and he might never see her again. The prospect hurt more than he would have believed possible.

He said, "You mentioned that you have relatives there."

"Yes. But things have changed. Well, what it is… is, my aunty June died suddenly three days back."

"I'm sorry."

"No," she said, shaking her head in negation. "There's no need to be. She was old, ninety-four, would you believe? And the last few years she had been, well, less able. I think she was ready. Besides, we were never that close."

"Okay. But it's never easy. When it happens, I mean."

"Oh, of course you must have seen it more than most people in your work."

Images of a pale torso under bright lights flashed briefly into his mind. He grimly forced the mental picture away.

"Yes," he said.

She said, "Well, I always thought that I would like to make the move to the mainland. After the peace agreement, well, we all thought things would be better right away. They are better of course, but it will be a long time before the scars heal. I think I'd rather live in a place with less history. After all, the job I have here, in the library, and the research stuff? Well, the library is alright, and I can do research anywhere. Ireland, well, it's okay but I can't say I would really miss it. And now Aunty June's house is mine…"

"Sounds like a no brainer to me," he said, and the words were like ash in his mouth.

"It would be, but there's something come up that changes everything."

"Can I help?" he said.

"Christ, this is silly. Look, I'll say it out loud if you won't. After all, if you don't feel the same way, well, I'll be gone in three weeks and that will be an end of it, but if I don't say something, I'll wonder about it forever, I know I will, and I'm making such a bloody mess of this." She broke off, trailing into silence.

"Sounds ominous," he said, but there was a lump in his throat as he said it.

Sally took a deep breath. "After I met you the other day… well, I've just never connected with anyone like that. Since that day I can't think straight. I keep wondering if you feel the same way, or maybe I'm just reading all the signals wrong…"

She broke off.

He said, "It's all okay. I know just how you feel. It's weird, isn't it? But it's okay. Really it is. I feel that way too."

And then she was in his arms and her warmth was against him and he had never felt so absolutely confident before, that here, finally, was the path through his life he was searching for.

He said, "Looks as if I'll be moving to Cornwall then."

"I can't ask that of you. You've got more than a job. It's a career, a vocation even."

"I'm done with A&E. Even before I met you, I knew that."

"What will you do?"

"For a living?" he said. "Well…"

She said, "There's no problem to start with. We'd have somewhere to live. The house is there for the asking, and I already have a job lined up, but eventually… well you'll need something."

"I can locum as a GP anywhere, at least at first," he said. "It means stepping down two grades but the money isn't that bad. Every other day I get e-mails from the agencies. There would be enough money, if you'd be happy with a GP as a partner."

"Husband," she said, almost before she knew she was going to say it.

"Sorry?"

"Husband, not partner. I'm old fashioned that way."

He said, "Shouldn't I be the one to propose?"

She grinned and said, "Not that old fashioned."

Later that evening, in the big old double bed that the health trust had hired, along with the rest of the furnished rooms that went with his job, they exchanged confidences, far into the night. The small details of their lives, the people and the places, the stuff that binds people together far more tightly than the sex. By three thirty the next morning, when they finally slept, enjoying the mutual heat of warm bodies in the cool dark of the night, while a westerly gale ruffled the sea into a foam and the wind rattled the sash, they were already an established couple.

CHAPTER SIX

Six years after that night, at the morning meeting of the medical practice, Jonathan Wilde was already a well-established figure in Tregadrew. Of course, some of the old people in the village still regarded him as the 'new' doctor and, Cornwall being Cornwall, it would, he fully expected, be nearly time for his own retirement before he might be fully accepted. For now, he was regarded by most of the population as competent and caring. He would, they thought, probably become an asset to the community – when they had had time to assess him properly. Maybe another fifteen years would be about right.

Eric Francis had no such reservations. During Jonathan Wilde's first week at Tregadrew, with Jonathan still working as a locum through an agency that employed him on a day-by-day basis and rented him out to the practice at a vicious mark up, in that first week, a call out had come to attend at a neighbouring farm. It was one of those nasty accidents that often happen when farmers, with a cavalier attitude to health and safety, operate heavy machinery. This time, it was a beet grader that had been modified to lift and grade second year daffodil bulbs before riddling off the loose soil, ready for their biennial inspection and sulphur dusting.

That grader was a monstrous bit of kit, eight feet wide with a set of rotating splines that churned up the soil, and a wide stainless steel mesh belt to carry the freshly raised bulbs to the hopper at the rear. Given that the thing was twenty years old, and modified from a potato grader from the start, the machine had far too many unguarded drives.

The steel conveyer belt was tattered, with exposed bits of wire mesh that stuck up as sharp as small razors.

A young farm hand called Harry Pengelly had reached across the moving mesh belt to clear a stone, clotted with earth, that had threatened to spring the whole issue off its rollers. Sadly, for him, a stray bit of torn cloth from his overalls caught fast in the drive shaft that turned the whole contraption and hauled him neatly into close proximity to the whirring PTO shaft from the tractor.

By the time Harry's father had managed to kill the diesel and bring the whole issue to a halt, Harry's right arm was broken in two places, with two fingers of that hand partially degloved, exposing yellow white bone, and twisted around the now motionless drive shaft. By sheer luck, WiIde was a on a house call only three farms away and he was on the scene within ten minutes or so.

Harry was still in that first phase of shock when the reality of the pain was masked by the endorphins flooding into his blood stream. He was pale with that clammy, sweaty, 'shock flesh' look that heralds hypovolemic collapse.

By the time the familiar rattle of rotors overhead signalled the approach of the air ambulance, Jonathan had disentangled the shattered limb from the shaft and the damage was swathed in pristine white gauze that only betrayed the damage underneath by seeping bright red in a few places through the dressing. The effect was like a brightly coloured Ink Blot test.

It was a routine job, the kind of thing that Jonathan would have done any night of the week in the Queen's casualty unit, but because it was his very first week as locum, and the dressing and stabilisation job had been carried out with impressive alacrity and efficiency, that simple industrial accident did more to cement his reputation in Tregadrew than months of careful work at the surgery in the village.

Eric Francis was bowled over by his new practice partner. Jonathan was young, energetic, and, best of all, the people accepted him from the start. He was popular with the villagers, and his popularity with the female section of the local population was not exclusively confined to the young and nubile.

Eric had, for the last three years or so, been increasingly aware of advancing years, and he was finding that night calls and walk in surgery on six days out of seven were increasingly a strain. The matter of a fresh partner had long been at the back of his mind. He had idly considered it, really, since old Jimmy Gooch had died four years before, leaving him sole practitioner. Jonathan, who came like a gift from the gods, fitted the bill perfectly.

That morning, Eric was running through the list of patients who required special attention with the younger man.

"Gerry Pascoe," he said, "is coming to the end of it. Poor soul has fought late onset Parkinson's for eight years now, but I think that this week will see him gone. There will be no rush to certify, Jon, especially if he goes at night, but if you're the one on duty, there's no problem with signing him off as senile decay and Parkinson's. Now, on a happier note. Gill McBrea is in the last trimester, of course. The twins are due in the next few weeks. She's such a little thing that I wouldn't be surprised to find her an early starter. She's keen on a home delivery, but given that it is a twin pregnancy, we might well need to do an emergency admission to the GP unit. You are okay with that?"

"Yes," said Jonathan. "There should be no problem there. If there were to be any complications, where is the nearest full Obs and Gynae unit with availability?"

"Truro, from here," said Eric. "Penzance might be willing, but Truro is favourite. If there's a problem, even if it looks straightforward, let's get her shifted asap. Gill is a dear girl, and she's really keen on home delivery, but I'd feel easier if she was in a unit just the same. Still, we can't force her if she really wants it that way."

"Do we have a community midwife available in any case?" asked Jonathan.

"Yes, Jenny Benbow is on call for the next week or so."

"Good."

"Yes," said Eric, "Jenny is a good girl. She's probably forgotten more about emergency delivery than most of us ever learned. Jenny's the kind you wish would be on hand to deliver your own kids if you have some someday." Eric blew thorough pursed lips; it was a conversation filler with him. He said, "Okay then, I think that covers the extras. On to the morning surgery?"

Jonathan was on his feet almost before the older man had finished speaking.

"I was as keen as that, once," Eric said, "I remember it well."

Jonathan grinned. "Well, I'm still the new kid on the block, Eric. How long will I be the 'new' doctor, do you think?"

"Janet tells me they are already asking for you when they ring for an appointment. We were lucky to get you, Jon."

"I was lucky to come here."

Old Gerry Pascoe was eighty-seven, and patriarch of a dairy farm that his family had run since the days of doorstep delivery and churns. Sixty years before, when he had taken over the farm tenancy from his own father, the tiny pocket handkerchief fields had been dotted with pale fawn jersey cows, whose mild, dark outlined eyes and pale coats gave them a look of local beauty queens on a day off.

They had shipped the rich, heavy butterfat milk out to the surrounding district and sold it direct from the churn, scooping out each measure into the blue and white enamel jugs that the customers brought to the cart to be filled.

Later, as the sale of raw milk had gradually declined, and the big, centralised dairies had come into being, churns were replaced by glass lined, stainless steel bulk tankers, and, as the fashion for high fat milk had waned, the Jerseys had gone, replaced by large, heavy, black and white Holstein crosses.

Gerry, missing the old ways, had found himself an anachronism, but he was still businessman enough to realise that times change and the man who fails to change with them rapidly becomes a footnote to history.

Then, eight years ago, he had begun to notice worrying symptoms. Small things at first, a transient weakness in his left hand, and a tremor in his limbs. It was nothing that you couldn't put down to simple aging initially. Then the disease had gradually progressed, robbing him of voluntary movement first, and then of the power of coherent thought, until, finally, he had become bedridden, lying in the same quiet back room where his own father had died in 'thirty-eight'.

Now it was coming to his time, and he knew it. That

morning, he lay quietly, waiting for a visit from the new doctor who old Eric had hired to help him out.

'No one escapes this,' Gerry thought in one of those rational periods when thought was still possible. 'No one gets out of it. There's no ducking destiny, we all face the same end.'

Recently, he had been troubled by a strange fancy that something was reaching out from those parts of his thinking brain that he had thought long defunct.

The disease itself had caused odd periods of strange mentation but this was different. It was as if another being was taking hold of his mind and reducing him to a bystander inside his own head. Recently these episodes had happened more and more frequently, almost to the point where he had begun to wonder who the rightful tenant of his body was, and who the interloper.

That morning, for a time at least, he was himself again, but there was a new thing. That second personality, the interloper in his head, was strong, very strong, today. He supposed that he was dying, but the thought held no great terrors for him. What did frighten old Gerry that morning was not even the 'stranger' as he referred to the new being inside him. What really scared him was the total alien strangeness of that second personality.

CHAPTER SEVEN

Every summer, millions of tourists flock to cross the Tamar and many of them marvel at the feeling that another country lies south of that simple crossing. There are modern touches of course. Virtually on the county line, there is a vulgar McDonald's, peddling junk food to the passing trade and, further along the expressway, there is a Cornwall 'services complex', whose traffic system confuses even those who know it well.

Thus far, the twenty-first century has touched the South West, but Cornwall still retains the feel of another country, living life at its own pace, on its own terms, and in its own way.

Those who visit in spring and autumn, at the turning points of the old Celtic calendar, marvel at the complex and mysterious folk rituals, ranging from frankly Victorian copies like the Helston Flora, to the more mysterious, and far more honestly pagan, Padstow 'obby oss' ceremony. The spring is welcomed into Cornwall in the way it has always been and the turning of the seasons with lengthening days saluted as it ever was.

At the end of the year, there are fewer outsiders left to watch as the days shorten towards winter. They might gather the harvest with a combine today, but the old timers still 'cry the neck', as the last stand of corn in a field that was once believed to hold the spirit of the fertile field is cut, not by the big machine, but by hand, as it has always been. Those last precious few stalks are gathered to be woven into a complex corn dolly that is saved, and the grain is carefully replanted in the following spring, to maintain the fertility of the soil from one year to the next.

The old ways and the West Country are very old bedfellows indeed, and, despite the rise of the fundamentalist Christianity of the Wesley brothers, the Cornish have ever tolerated older undercurrents with amused acceptance.

Today, not a few practising Christians attend church on Sunday, after spending their evening at a Celtic Nos Lowen the night before. This happy tolerance extends across the narrow sea to Catholic Brittany where the same 'live and let live' atmosphere remains to this day.

In the village of Tregadrew, the most overt symbol of this relaxed attitude was the old circle of standing stones that stood a few yards outside the official village boundary.

There were nine stones in the circle, set a bare half mile from the old dolmen which marked the grave of some long-forgotten iron age chief. Each stone was different, though they were all formed of rough cut, Cornish granite as tough as the bones of the county itself, weathered and lichen encrusted, with the yellow stained patches of growth that only develop where the air is clean and pure. The stones were far from a random circle, set in an exact alignment that framed the rising and setting sun at the time of the solstices.

Some long expired, and very straight-laced, Victorian curate, finding that his flock had accepted the old pagan ways a little too enthusiastically, had renamed the stones 'The Nine Maidens' and explained them, by saying that they were the mortal remains of nine local women who had followed a visiting piper to the old dancing place on the sabbath, and been turned to stone for their temerity.

Two of the stones were inscribed. One had a complex intaglio of spirals and swirls illustrating, said some, the complex relationships of the sands of time. Another, less poetically, had a mysterious Latin inscription carved roughly on its surface that had defied translation, until a local antiquarian had discovered, to his chagrin, that the mysterious message from the long past read: *Marcus Priscus has got a cock the size of my strong right arm.* The truth of that translation had remained hidden in that worthy gentleman's notes until long after his death.

The Nine Maidens was a place to go on an early summer day to picnic and enjoy the sun, sheltered as it was from the prevailing south-westerlies. Jonathan and Sally had adopted it very early on as 'their' place, a spot to go and sit in the sunshine and eat an alfresco meal and share a bottle cooled in the nearby stream. Had they but known it, in its previous incarnation, a thousand years before, that little watercourse had been a holy well, sacred to the local Celtic goddess of the stream.

That spring morning, the sun was already gaining its summer strength in a sky the colour of old, faded denim. There were a few fluffy white cumulus clouds floating by. The birds were singing, and the first flush of spring flowers was breaking through the rough grass, scattered like tiny multi-coloured jewels, against the green velvet of the sward.

They were completely alone that mid spring morning. Eric was taking morning rounds and, with surgery done, Jonathan, for once, had a precious few hours to appreciate the glorious place where they lived.

They ate in companionable fashion, talking a little, simply enjoying the place, relaxing in the warmth of the day. Jonathan was still, after all those months, coming to terms with the near miraculous turn that his life had taken.

The practice was just big enough to offer challenges, Eric was the perfect working partner, and Sally was, simply, perfect.

His attention was briefly drawn by a Holly Blue butterfly, out early in the season and searching for a mate. It settled on a wild thyme plant that was sticking up out of the grass and folded its small jewel-like wings in a neat triangle over its back.

The air was so clear Jonathan could appreciate every tiny detail. It was like taking a low dose of some fabulous hallucinogenic drug, but with none of the blurring effect that goes with weed. For a brief time, it felt as if they were completely alone, in a new made world. Not really thinking, but simply reacting to the wonder of the day. They reached for each other, and the heat of the warm sun on their skin was softened just a little by the gentlest of breezes that blew across the clearing between the stones.

They made love, at first hesitantly, and then with increasing urgency, and for a time nothing else mattered but their warmth and the sweet summer smells of wildflowers. Every touch was heightened, every sensation carried to the extreme. Each exquisite touch was a new experience, every tingling nerve ending was hyper-alert and responsive.

Presently, sanity returned. The circle was still deserted, aside from the two of them.

Sally brushed the last fragments of dried grass off her clothes. "God, that was incredible, but, Jon, what if someone had seen us?"

"They didn't," he answered, grinning, still making no especial attempt to cover himself.

She said, "No, but you're the village doctor. You may think it's okay, but some of the older people might be really shocked."

"Well," he said in a considering tone. "We aren't making a habit of outdoor sex."

"No?" She gave him an arch look and stretched in the sun, enjoying the warmth on her skin. "Pity."

The Holly Blue fluttered past again and finally settled like a tiny gemstone on the skin of her shoulder. The wings were a deep blue purple on the upper surfaces, and patterned with a complex, black outlined, checkerboard pattern of browns and golds on the underside. Looking at the tiny creature, Jonathan was suddenly aware of every detail. The antennae were quivering a little in the soft breeze, two tiny clubs, the colour of deep violet with darker swollen tips.

The strange hyper-real quality of the afternoon was very slow to fade, normality seemed reluctant to return, but, even so, despite the extraordinary detail, neither of them noticed the tall figure outside the stone circle. That was maybe not so hard to understand, as the figure itself flickered in and out of existence, as if it was a badly projected 3D image produced by a laser projector with a faulty cell.

This apparition watched the lovers impassively, and finally, when it was all over, and they started to dress, it seemed to emerge as if from some deep reverie. With that, and at that moment, the stones were clearly visible behind it. As it verged on invisibility, it flickered one last time, and finally vanished.

Twenty minutes or so later, when Kevin Tremaine drove his chain harrow past the place, he was mildly surprised to see the new doctor and his wife giggling like teenagers as he passed them. He raised a hand in acknowledgement, and the doctor returned the gesture.

'Odd,' Kevin thought, but then again, her people might have been from round here to start with, but he was, of course, from 'up country'.

Sally missed her period just twenty days later.

CHAPTER EIGHT

Old Gerry Pascoe's bedroom had the same sour smell of dying that all such rooms have at the end. Jonathan Wilde had seen maybe three-hundred people die in his time as an emergency medic. Sometimes it was quiet, gentle, almost. Often it was medically aided, deliberately or not, by morphine, following the sacred sophistry of the principle of 'double effect'.

Sometimes it was a violent and bitter battle as the patient went unwillingly, fighting every inch of the way. It was never easy to witness. It never really got easier, perhaps because, in the final analysis, every death was a mirror held up to the mortality of everyone who witnessed it. Human beings are the only creature that, as far as we are aware, live every day in the certainty of their own approaching death.

Every language, every culture, has unique ways of describing that moment of ending. In the godless twenty-first century, the supernatural is not regarded as a real runner in the mortality stakes by the vast majority. Still, we talk of 'passing', as if there was, in reality, another phase of existence waiting beyond this one. In Cornwall, where the sea is a constant, and sometimes capricious, companion to everyday life, many of the phrases used to describe death are maritime. A man is said to have 'slipped his cable', to have 'gone round the land' or, perhaps to have 'gone out with the ebb'.

On the night when old Gerry finally came to the edge of existence, the ebb tides, according to the observatory tables, peaked at twenty-three eighteen and, with a full moon, the tidal range at Tregadrew was eight feet at the harbour wall.

Gerry was easy with his coming ending. Long before the tide turned that day, he had known, as all living creatures that are even marginally self-aware must know, that it was time. He lay on the ageing bed that his own parents had died on, resting on a monster of a mahogany bedframe that was a relic from Victoria's reign.

By the time Jonathan, with his neat black bag of drugs, arrived, Gerry was already far down into the long passage towards the end. Gerry was mildly, and pleasurably, surprised to find that his mind and his inner awareness, was as sharp as ever. He had half expected that the realities of the room around him would fade into shadows, but instead he found the opposite. His vision had been gradually softening over the last two years, and more and more, recently, he needed to wear his glasses to produce anything more than a sort of dreamy half focused view of the world. Now, each tiny detail was in sharp focus, like some cinema trick from the French realists of the nineteen fifties, but this was in full colour, not film noir black and white. Every little detail stood out. He could see the fine, hairline tracery of cracks in the old lime plaster of the ceiling. It had been skimmed time and again after the original damage. That was a legacy of a stray German parachute mine, jettisoned by a lost raider, unable to locate Falmouth docks in forty-three. His parents had actually seen the thing, a sinister black cylinder hanging from a cone of sheer white silk that had trapped itself in the old ash tree at the end of the lane. When the timer had finally ticked down to detonation, that blast had sounded like the wrath of God, and afterwards, those cracks in the old bedroom ceiling were the least of the damage. Every window on that side of the house was blown in, and the curtains had fluttered like a flag of surrender in the sea breeze. Now, after nearly seventy years, the cracks were still there, or rather their ghosts were, defying modern restoration work.

Gerry saw the young doctor come into the room and would have greeted him, as a civilised man should, but somehow speech was an effort too far, and instead, he lay there, an observer at his own death bed, watching as Jonathan took one scrawny, blue veined arm and felt for the radial pulse. Although Jonathan said nothing aloud, Gerry heard the doctor's thoughts, almost as if he had spoken, 'Not long now. His heart is failing.'

Gerry could hear, in his head, that clear inner track of Jonathan's thoughts, accepting this ability to read the other man's mind, as if it were something that he had been able to do all his life. Jonathan was thinking, 'Best to let him go easy. He'll make it by himself – or should I maybe help him over?'

And Gerry, secure inside his head. responded, 'No, let it go as it will, doctor. This is natural. This is easy. Just let me do it in my own time.'

He saw Jonathan accept a mug of tea from Winnie, his daughter, and knew the young man didn't really want it, just glad to give her something to do.

He heard Winnie say, "Is he going, doctor?" as if it was a journey he was on.

He heard Jonathan say, "Soon, I think. I doubt he'll last more than another hour or so."

Then, in this strange hyper-real state, came the voice of the other. As if a couple of massive rocks rubbed together and had learned the power of speech, the voice in Gerry Pascoe's mind was as inhuman as a dog's bark.

"Before you go, old man," it said, "pass on the message."

Gerry wanted to be left alone, to do what he had to, and he said, inside his head, "No, leave me to die in peace."

"Not until you pass the message on, old man. You want to do that. You know you do, Unless…"

Suddenly, his vision clouded with a nightmare of misshapen vile creatures, surrounding a deep open shaft, and from the darkness of the open pit, came an aura of such terror that Gerry's very core trembled at it. Anything, anything at all, was better than to face that. To the other, he said, "What do you want me to say to him? Quickly, there's no time left…"

As Jonathan sipped his unwanted tea, and waited, Gerry's respiration took on a hitching uneven pattern. Jonathan had seen this often enough to recognise that the end was finally here.

Then, just as he was reaching to take the pulse for a final time, the old man took a last deep breath. His chest rose, and his eyes opened, and they were suddenly, fully aware. After a moment, he spoke.

Jonathan Wilde was well aware of the oddities that sometimes interrupt the smooth transition out of life, but even so, for Gerry Pascoe to speak to him at that moment, in a perfectly normal conversational tone, as if they were guests at a dinner party, was a new thing.

"Be careful, doctor," said Gerry, as if he were discussing the chances of another storm that might stir up the ocean. "There's no more that they can do to me. This reality of yours is no more than a dream of a dream for me, but be careful, doctor. This one is old, very, very old, and has no good intentions for this village. There is still a debt to be paid, you see, and it has crossed oceans of time to collect the dues. For your own sake, take care, for the sake of your unborn daughter take care. Most of all, for the sake of your living soul, take care."

Just for a few moments a strange change had come over the dying man's features. It was as if he was the world's best mime artist. His face had taken on the look of another persona entirely. The shift was subtle, hardly more than a brief rearrangement of the muscles of the face, but the overall effect was to expose an altogether different personality. The old man's eyes that had been clouded with the approaching end a few moments before, were suddenly bright and alive, and full of a being that meant no good for the rest of the world.

Jonathan Wilde felt that he, for the first time in his life, was looking on the face of true evil. Then the old man's features rearranged themselves again. The monster was gone, and Gerry Pascoe, the innocent and dying old man, was back. His voice, when he spoke for that last time, was clear and sharp, as he said, "I must be away. They are calling me, and I can't delay longer, but remember, doctor, for the sake of the help you gave me, for the love of humanity that you showed, listen well…"

And then he simply stopped, as if some hand had flicked the off switch. Gerry Pascoe's body relaxed. His bladder emptied, and his face took on the blank empty look of all dead faces everywhere.

Jonathan Wilde opened his bag, and the small 'snap/clicks' of the latches was loud in the silence. He took out the pad of green certificates and wrote: Myocardial infarct resulting from senile decay. Then, as a secondary cause, he wrote: Late-stage Parkinson's Disease, and he signed the form.

Winnie was suddenly standing in the open doorway to the landing as if she was afraid to cross the threshold. She was holding a striped tea towel in her hands and twisting it into tight little knots. She said, "Is he…?"

As if not naming death would somehow banish it.

Jonathan said, "Yes, a few moments ago. I'm truly sorry for your loss, Winnie."

"There'll be papers to sign?" she said.

Jonathan produced the certificate, tearing it off the pad along the perforations. The last few hung up and tore the corner of the certificate.

He said, "The undertaker will want this before they can accept the body. Are you okay with that, or would you like me to call them? I expect that you'll be using Jimmy Tresize?"

"Yes," said Winnie, in the flat, wondering tone of voice that the newly bereaved use. "They did my mother, and my gran."

"Good," said Jonathan. "Is there anything else I can do? Would you maybe like a tablet to help you sleep tonight?"

"Thank you, doctor," said Winnie, "but I need to contact the rest of the family. They'll want to be here. I'll need to be up early in the morning."

"Well, I'll leave you a few Diazepam, just in case. If I give you three days' worth, take one at bedtime, no more than that, and stop taking them after the three days."

"Thank you, doctor," she said, and then, moving like a faded ghost discovered unexpectedly by the pale dawn light, she crossed to the big sash window and threw it wide open to the darkness that shrouded the view of the ocean. Jonathan had seen this traditional part of the rituals of passing before. The unspoken concept was to allow the newly disincarnate soul a route to escape to the elements, and be free.

Jonathan knew, very well, how busy the Pascoe family would be for the next few days. Much of the ritual of dying is designed to occupy the living in those first raw few weeks, as the realities of the death sink in.

"If there is anything you need, Winnie," he said, "don't hesitate to call me."

CHAPTER NINE

Eleven days passed, and the funeral was arranged with full local ceremony. There could be no churchyard burial though, the little burying ground in the grounds of the parish church had been full to overflowing by the time Victoria ended her long reign, and the new cemetery, multidenominational, and pretty well characterless, was outside the village boundary. It was in a specially consecrated field where the dairy cattle had grazed until 1990 or so.

In one corner of the plot was an oak that had stood there as a shade tree for grazing stock long before the cemetery had been thought of. Nowadays, it provided the only natural element in a landscape of sterile rows of headstones. The site was kept meticulously neat by mowing between the graves every couple of weeks, but the strict, disciplined layout that allowed the regular mowing gave the impression of military order, rather than the Elysium fields.

In unconscious contrast, there was a faint, evocative scent of new-mown hay hanging in the air. The sun was bright and clear, and caught the austere black of the hearse and its following cars in wicked little spicules of light. Despite the bright sunlight, hardly anyone wore dark glasses to the funeral, the combination of shades and suits looking too much like a tribute to the Mafia. As a result, the figure of the vicar, despite his bright white cassock, was hardly more than a silhouette to most of those present, a shape seemingly cut out of darkness, against the bright background of the sky.

There was a good crowd at the graveside committal. Old Gerry had been well liked, and well respected. The vicar intoned the ritual, an essentially emollient form of words.

The man had a deep, rather pleasing voice that hung in the air like the tolling of a bell, seeming to echo after the actual words were done.

"For we bring nothing into this world," said the vicar, "and it is certain we take nothing out of it. As our good friend Gerry has passed from this life to the next, we commit his body to the earth. Earth to earth. Dust to dust. Ashes to ashes. In the certain hope of that glorious day of resurrection, when He shall raise our mortal bodies to be like his glorious body, and there will be no more death."

The undertaker's men offered each of those at the graveside a pinch of sandy brown soil to throw on the coffin as it lay, bright varnished wood against the raw, damp, newly excavated earth. Each tiny pinch of dust landed with a slight impact that marked the highly polished surface of the coffin. Finally, the mourners dispersed, leaving the empty burial ground to the sexton.

No one noticed the solitary figure in the shadow of the old oak. It was standing where the cattle had stood years before, taking advantage of the shade to escape the brilliance of the sunlight and the buzzing, pestering clouds of flies.

Presently, as the hearse drove away, and the cars of the cortege dispersed into the surrounding countryside, a bright yellow JCB trundled across the grass following a roughly laid track of scaffolding boards to the new grave and commenced filling the hole. A half hour later, it was done, and there was nothing to mark the spot other than a newly turned rectangle of earth, raw brown against the green of the unbroken turf around it. Once the digger was gone, the burial ground was left deserted. Even the dark figure was gone from under the old oak, though no one saw it go.

CHAPTER TEN

It was Monday morning surgery, and both partners were busy on the regular procession of those patients who had put off consulting the doctor over the weekend, hoping to recover by the start of the new week.

Tregadrew was no different to every other GP practice. The worried well outnumbered the really ill by a factor of three, though most of them genuinely needed a verbal pat on the head. In its way, reassurance was as valid as any other medical intervention. They needed that reassurance at least as much as the more obviously sick needed the antibiotics and steroids that made up the majority of the prescription load.

The morning trundled along uneventfully, and a succession of villagers passed through the consultation rooms. It was a textbook procession of the minor ills that afflict humanity.

There were a few oddities, as always, to keep things interesting. Jenny Tolhern was here for a Typhoid injection. It was not that she expected an outbreak in Cornwall, but she was due to holiday in West Africa, and was determined not to become a victim of the local bugs. Appointments were rather optimistically scheduled for ten-minute intervals, but Jenny had consulted 'Dr Internet' regarding health risks, and needed more than the average amount of reassurance. No, Lassa Fever and Ebola are not really a risk, and the last outbreak of Bubonic plague in West Africa was thirty years before.

Job done, and reassurance given, along with the usual tropical warnings: No sex with the locals – Jenny was old enough to know better, but it paid never to assume things – drink bottled water, mind the ice cubes.

By the time Jonathan was done, he was a good half hour down on time, and it was then that Janice Laity's daughter came in to try to plead her mother's case for a home visit, even though the old lady was notorious for being anti-medical. Jonathan drew the short straw that morning, and he was faced with an increasingly common dilemma.

Rose Laity was small, almost petite, and rosy cheeked and dark haired, like a Tolkien hobbit.

"She needs to see someone, doctor," Rose said as soon as the pleasantries were done with. "Her chest is something awful, these last two weeks now, and she'll take nothing for it, but ginger and comfrey and such."

"Well," said Jonathan, trying to be diplomatic, "the problem is, Rose, that if your mother really won't see one of the partners, it's hard to see how I can help. Do you have power of attorney by any chance?"

"No, Doctor. There's no chance of her agreeing to that. Trouble is with these old ones, by the time they are ready to agree to it, well, it's too late to sign the thing, isn't it? I've a friend in that same spot."

Jonathan thought for a second then said, "Well, I suppose I could visit, officially to see you, if you request it. Then, maybe we could arrange your mother's check-up along the way."

Jonathan was half nervous, even as he suggested it, thinking of what the ethics committee would make of that ad hoc arrangement. The words 'paternalism' and 'Patronising the elderly' clanged like a cracked bell in his head.

The Laity's house was a solid, stone built, four-square building on the outskirts of the village. It perched, seemingly precariously, on a steep rough slope that led downwards towards the cliff on the west side of the settlement. Jonathan guided the old Range Rover with some care down the few hundred yards of rough track that led to the yard.

Two dogs, both black and white Collies with odd, mismatched eyes, greeted him in the yard, jumping up, and barking a greeting.

Rose came out of the back door, alerted by the racket.

"Go down, you daft buggers," she said to the dogs, then rather less sharply, "Oh sorry, Doctor, I didn't mean to cuss, but 'tis the language that they understand."

"No problem, Rosie," said Jonathan, bending to ruffle the velvet ears of the nearest dog who quivered in appreciation.

"She's in bed, doctor," said Rose. "I've said nothing, and she's not really expecting you, but then not, not expecting you, if you see what I mean."

The sick room was a reflection of the old woman's life and approaching death, shabby and old fashioned, but spotlessly clean, with an Eiderdown on the old mahogany framed bed instead of a duvet. and heavy dark coloured curtains at the window.

Janice Laity was a stick thin remnant of a woman who had been solid in her youth, before age and infirmity had stripped away the fat and left her a skeleton clothed in loose flesh.

"I told her, Doctor. There's no need to trouble you," she said, by way of greeting. She lay on a bed with the sheets turned down, and the bulge that she made was hardly more than a gentle curve in the smooth expanse of the pristine white linen. Clearly, Rose had freshly changed her mother's bedding in honour of his visit.

Jonathan put on his best professional manner. It was something you learned as a medic, even if one look is enough to tell you all you need to know about a case.

He said, "Why don't you let me take look at you, Mrs Laity, while I'm here, you know? Rose tells me you are a bit under the weather."

Two minutes was all it took to confirm what that first look had told him. There was a large, stony hard, solid mass in the old woman's left abdomen, and her liver margin was grossly enlarged.

Jonathan said, "You're a bit swollen down here, Mrs Laity. I think maybe we really should get you a set of tests."

"What for, Doctor?"

Jonathan was taken by surprise, but he knew, full well, that if you mention the words 'tumour' or 'cancer', that is all the patient will hear, no matter how you qualify your advice.

He said, "Well…" but while he was trying to think of a less brutal form of words she beat him to it.

The old woman said, "Look, Doctor, I hear round the village that they think you are good at what you do. Well, I think that you are too good to mistake what's happening to me, boy. I know well enough that my time is near. I'm eighty-six after all. How long should I expect?"

'Never give up,' Jonathan thought. His old tutor used to say, "Don't stop till the patient is dead, and even then, keep on trying." Out loud, he said, "There are things we could do to help, to make things easier."

"Doctor Wilde," she said, "I'm dying, boy. Let's just leave it at that. I know you'd like to change it and bless you for your good wishes. Still, what is, can't be helped. But before I go, Lover, I've something to do. Something that you need to be involved with. This village is old, Doctor, very old indeed. Years ago, the villagers here did a thing, the echoes have come down through the years. It's coming to an end now, like a big old boil that's been left to get really bad. Soon it's all going to be done with. I know how you feel about the old ways, Doctor. Your way of healing is well and good, and it's done with a good heart, and that means more than anything. No matter what way of healing you choose, it's all the same. Your pills and potions, or the old herbs and chants, the way you take don't matter, the destination is what counts.

"There's a strange clarity comes to you, Doctor, when the time is near. For a little while you see past the veil. They'll come to you soon enough, those who love the old ways, all I'm saying is that you need to be ready to listen, don't turn away.

"Now, you've a part to play, Doctor, I'm sure of that, what it might be I'm not certain of, but you can't choose not to do what must be done. No matter what you believe at this moment, it's important to know this. If you go up against this thing with nothing but your pills and your science and all the fine ideas that live in sunlight, well, then, there's real danger for you, and that pretty maid you're married to.

"Science won't help you against it, Doctor. It was old when the first alchemists tried to turn everything to gold, and it watched them fail and knew that it could have the better of them if the need came. It's the old ways you'll need to use to best it. So, when it starts – and you'll know when that moment comes – remember that, over the years, that kind learn cunning, so tread carefully, Doctor, tread carefully."

Over the years Jonathan had seen enough cases of death bed psychosis to recognise the syndrome for what it was. Once outside the old lady's door and safely away from earshot, he took Rose aside for a moment.

"Well, Rose, I don't think it'll come as a surprise," he said, "but I have to tell you that your mother is seriously ill."

"Is it, cancer, Doctor?"

"Well, it could be something else," he said, and inwardly cursed himself as a prevaricator. "It's hard to be sure without tests, but honestly, yes, I think so."

"How long?"

It was the question everyone asked, but it was never going to be possible to give a straight answer. Besides, a straight answer, as often as not, simply blighted whatever time the patient had left.

He said, "Honestly, at this stage, we need to ask if it would be best for her to put her through very invasive treatments. Without that though, we would really be just letting nature take its course. But that has to be a decision for you two to make together."

"Thank you for being so honest, Doctor. So how long do you think she has?"

"Weeks, certainly, months if she's very lucky, less than a year in any case. I'm sorry I can't be more precise."

"It's alright, Doctor. It's not your fault."

Training took over again. In this situation the best way was to fall back on practicalities.

"Right. I'll leave a prescription for pain relief, just in case. It's an opioid. It's very effective, but you need to monitor the dose. Don't be too particular, help the pain as you need to, but no more than three tablets a day. If there is anything else we can do, you have the surgery number."

"Yes. Well, thank you again, Doctor, for your honesty."

"I just wish I had better news, Rose, but remember, if there is anything that we can do…"

CHAPTER ELEVEN

Outside the house, sitting in the astringently neat environment of the car, Jonathan called base on his mobile and outlined his diagnosis to Eric. It was a basic courtesy when a patient was diagnosed with a terminal illness. As senior partner, Eric was understanding.

"Not surprised, my boy," he said. "She has been abusing her body for years. Given her diet and weight, I'm surprised that her heart has kept up as long as it has. Actually, you did well to get her to talk to you at all. She's a practising pagan, you know? She doesn't really hate modern medicine, but she prefers to rely on nature. I was in her kitchen once. She has racks of herbs all along one wall, all in little glass jars labelled up, not just with the kind of plant, but with a note of where they were picked, and the phase of the moon. She really takes it all very seriously. Still, 'whatever bites your biscuit' as they say. I suppose if it helps her through it."

"I see," said Jonathan in a rather perplexed voice.

"Well, it goes on a lot down here. You'll meet quite a few of the local pagans as time goes on. Most of them accept modern medicine. They mainly base their ideas on Gerald Gardner's writings. You know the guy who wrote about the witch cult between the wars? Very nature worshipping and fertility god stuff. It's harmless, of course. Well, mainly harmless in any case. You prescribed the usual terminal regime for her?"

Ten minutes later, notes completed, Jonathan Wilde was on his way back to the surgery.

Sally was gradually growing rounder as her pregnancy progressed in its inexorable way towards birth. The change was subtle at first, a slight swelling above her pubis, a marginal fullness in her breasts and a darkening of her aureoles from girlish pink towards womanly pale fawn. At first, she suffered from morning sickness, not on a daily basis, but often enough to be an irritation rather than a debilitating grind. Jonathan prescribed for her, of course, another breach of the rules. Prescribing for friends and family was frowned upon, but, after the drug problems that had surfaced in the nineteen sixties, Sally, who knew enough from her husband's professional interest to be wary of drugs during pregnancy, wouldn't take the pills, unless she absolutely had to.

Not that she was completely without help. The younger women of the village regarded a new pregnancy as an entry ticket to their inner circle, and soon Sally was inundated with various folk remedies and suggestions to help her through those early months. Of them all, Jenny Horne, who was the local primary head teacher's wife, was most insistent on her natural cures.

"Ginger tea will help," she had said. "Just steep a couple of inches of the fresh root in hot water for ten minutes and swallow half a cupful. It worked for me every time."

Eventually, one morning when Jonathan was off on a conference at Exeter University on 'The problems of small practices in Rural Areas', Sally, miserable with her uneasy middle and queasy stomach, had tried it. Surprisingly, it worked. The nausea cleared like a rain cloud on a summer day and she felt ready to walk down to the village stores for supplies, if not ready to run a marathon.

She explained the effect to Jonathan on the following afternoon when he got back.

"I'm not saying that's it's a bad idea," he said, "but you do need to take care with so called natural medicines and treat them as you would any other drug. After all, strychnine is a natural product, and so, for that matter is cyanide."

Sally regarded her mug of ginger extract with resignation.

"It's just ginger root, Jon," she said. "I use it in your Friday night curry. How much damage can it do? And it works, for Christ's sake."

He suddenly felt that he was on dangerous ground. She sounded plaintive, almost on the verge of tears. He said, "If ginger helps, love, you use it, just go easy with the dose, 'cause it gives some people the runs."

Thy both knew that he had a more fundamental objection, that he saw herbal and alternative medicine as not simply ineffective but almost threatening to his whole practice. Still, the tension was broken.

Sally took a sip from her steaming mug. "Right, how was the conference?"

"Shit."

"That good?"

He sighed and said, "The guy leading it suggested that we designate a practice leader in 'Community Elder Affairs'. Christ! What fucking planet do these people live on?"

"I suppose he meant well."

He smiled and said, "Did anything come up while I was away?"

"Eric says to tell you that Janice Laity is doing better

than you thought she might. He says that, I think it was, the oxy is taking care of the pain, and she seems better all around."

"Good. At least she can enjoy whatever time is left to her."

Another day, another morning surgery. On that sunny, summer Thursday, the surgery was overwhelmed with the results of a low-grade virus that was making its slow inexorable way across the country. As always with such things, there was little that could be done, medically speaking, for those poor souls who suffered the sore chest, runny nose, high fever and persistent cough.

Jonathan found himself constantly repeating the same advice. "Drink plenty of fluids. Try to keep moving, keep warm, take a few paracetamol to cut the fever…" It was the routine business of general practice, vital, but hardly challenging. Every now and then, for a few minutes at a time, he found himself missing the old days of A&E.

Be careful what you wish for, the man said, some wishes come true.

CHAPTER TWELVE

Jonathan was driving back to the cottage, along one of those endless country roads that are a Cornish speciality. Every year, those lanes claim unwary tourists who are fooled into believing that those deceptively soft looking green hedges are no more substantial than a bush. Actually, they usually hide a wall of solid granite blocks.

Jonathan, well aware of the realities of the Cornish lanes, piloted the Rover gently around the blind corners, with one foot constantly ready to clamp down on the foot brake. As it happened, that morning he was absolutely right to be cautious.

The crash that blocked the lane completely was an unequal contest in the very extreme. Going in Jonathan's direction, a small, low slung silver sports car had come together with an armoured stone transporter from the local quarry. The sports car, built for style and speed, rather than strength, weighed a little under a thousand kilos. The stone truck, built for strength at the expense of everything else, weighed nine metric tonnes, empty. The car stood low to the road with the top of its bonnet less than a metre high, the truck was five metres tall, with a slab of a radiator that towered above the road in the front, and a huge, armoured steel bucket of a body, studded with armour plate on the back.

Jonathan's Rover came to a rapid, if undignified, tyre smoking stop, metres away from the edge of the wreck. Two people were on their feet in the road, a blondish girl in her thirties whose bleached and fashionably streaked hair hung in a blood clotted mess, and a man, who he took to be the truck driver, a big man with hands like shovels and a stubble of grey hair on his rather open, homely looking face. He was holding a mobile phone in his hand, and he was looking at the screen as if he had never seen one before. The third man, seated in the driver's seat of the car, was still, pale and unresponsive.

Jonathan climbed down, already in intervention mode. "I'm a doctor. Has anyone called three nines yet?"

The trucker said, in a flat, wandering voice, "I've tried, but there's no fucking signal, see?" He held the phone out as if they might not believe him.

Jonathan reached into his coat, and came up with his own phone.

He took a quick look at the screen. Two transmission bars, not good, but not bad. He handed the trucker his phone.

"Try this one," he said. "Tell them there's a doctor on scene, and tell them we need heavy rescue, and the air ambulance."

Without waiting to check that the truck driver was doing as he was told, Jonathan turned his attention to the casualties. The girl was bleeding an impressive amount, but the split in her scalp was visible, and obviously accounted for all the blood. The man, on the other hand, still behind the wheel, was silent, unmoving.

In training, it is an axiom that the quiet injured need checking first. Anyone whose airway is clear enough to scream, and with the energy to do that, is probably okay, at least for the moment. The quiet bleeders, the comatose ones who slip away while the medics are distracted elsewhere, are the ones who are saveable, in theory, but often not saved in practice.

The man at the wheel was too old for the car, in his sixties maybe, with white hair immaculately and expensively cut, and, even under these circumstances, he had an air of the well barbered and well-heeled about him. He had been thrown forwards by the impact and his head had met the old fashioned and trendy rigid wooden rim of the steering wheel.

Jonathan reached for the man's carotid notch and found nothing. First job then, clear his breathing. He rested one hand on the lower part of the man's face and went to tilt his head back to straighten the trachea and free his airway.

Even after so many patients, and so much hard-won experience, Jonathan inwardly winced at the crunching 'gravel in a balloon' feel of shattered bones as the man's skull moved in places where no movement should be. The man's head seemed somehow heavier than it should have been, as if the weight was unsupported. As his head came back beyond the balance point, it moved in a sick, boneless, unsupported way and fell sideways until his cheek rested on his right shoulder. Checking for a pulse was reflexive and completely futile. Routinely, Jonathan opened one eye of the corpse to check. The pupil was dilated, the iris taking up most of the white in a ring that gave the dead man a comical, surprised expression.

Jonathan rested him back gently.

The blonde girl, who was still standing there, spoke for the first time. "Is he dead? He is, isn't he?" She was shocked enough to allow her estuary accent to come through in full force.

Jonathan said, "Yes, I think he was killed on impact. He won't have suffered at least."

"God." She put one hand up to her ruined scalp and

said almost in a conversation tone of voice, "Will this leave a scar? I mean, I'm a model, so it matters."

"No, it should be fine," said Jonathan.

The truck driver was suddenly back on the scene, emerging from behind the crash. He said, "I had to go behind the truck to get a signal. I suppose it's all that metal."

"Did you get an ETA?" In the heat of the moment Jonathan reverted to professional speak, communicating in acronyms. "I mean, did they say how long that the ambulance would take?"

"They are on their way is all they said. I did my best, honest. He was going like a fucking bat out of hell around the corner back there. I was stopped when he hit me."

Jonathan said, "There's plenty of time to worry about what happened later. For now, we need to look after you two."

"You are sure it won't scar?" said the girl. "Only I need to look my best for the shoot."

The driver said, "Like a fucking bat out of fucking Hell. I couldn't miss him. Oh Christ."

In the distance, there was the warble of the two tones coming down the main road, heading for the junction that led to this lane.

Jonathan inwardly took a deep breath and waited.

Driving home afterwards, his route took him along an open stretch of road that skirted the coast. To one side was the broad open space of Tregadrew moor, a broad expanse of heather speckled at that time of the year with pinkish purple blossom and studded with multi-coloured wild flowers. To the other side, the land sloped gently away to the endless open, innocent blue of the Atlantic. Every now and then, a wave top caught the sunlight and reflected a bright point of white fire.

Jonathan was well aware that, all too often for him, the aftermath of unexpected emergency interventions was a migraine headache of vicious intensity. It was a simple response to stress and, as a doctor, he was well aware of that, but self-awareness hardly reduced the symptoms, and none of the usual drug remedies helped a lot.

With that in mind, he piloted the Rover into a rough layby on the seaward side of the road, and climbed down, intending to walk on the beach for a few minutes to let the sea air clear his head.

The sand was crisp and gritty under his feet, and there was a scurf line of drying seaweed that defined the high-water mark and added an olfactory undertone of clean, fresh fish to the breeze. Suddenly, as he stood looking out to sea, it was if something snapped into focus. The momentary change was as clearly defined as that, a neat cut off point in time, as sharp and uncompromising as a falling guillotine blade.

A moment before, the sea had been conventionally blue, the sky dusted with high cumulus, a perfect summer picture. Now, the tiny spots of broken water where a slight onshore breeze was ruffling the surface were sharply defined and a wheeling Herring Gull riding the up currents was delineated in pure white and dapper battleship grey. Its beak was a deep, dense shade of bright yellow, and the red fleck on the tip stood out in a splash of pure crimson. Each flower in the heather was a jewel, a tiny stud of perfection in a sea of grey green spikes of foliage. The day stood out clear, as if the world was new made, and the sweet, honey scent of the plants floated on a breeze that had a sight sharp ozone whiff of the sea about it.

Jonathan stood wonderingly, appreciating the tiny details that this new-found acuity had lent the everyday. For perhaps three minutes, the strange hyper-real state of being persisted, and then, as abruptly as it had begun, it was gone.

So was his incipient migraine.

The figure stood on the skyline where the soft line of the hill met the bowl of the sky. She was watching, cloaked in grey, almost part of the background. She seemed to fade in and out of view, as if she were no more substantial than a will o' the wisp, formed perhaps of nothing more than gas from the old tin mine up-cast shaft that was hidden in the heather beside the stark pointing finger of an old engine house.

Presently, as Jonathan Wilde was starting the Rover and pulling it back onto the road that led homewards, the figure flickered and went out.

CHAPTER THIRTEEN

Jonathan's summer went along the route of all summers in the South West, following a lazy, regular routine. Summer days in the far south are long, summer evenings are long and balmy. It is the time of drama shows in the open air, not just at the spectacular cliff side amphitheatre of Minack, but in a dozen other outdoor venues where people gather on summer nights to watch plays, while the moths gather in suicidal droves around the foot lights, and the little Pipistrelle bats flit in and out of the stage, taking in the unexpected bounty.

As the summer fades, edging slowly past midsummer day, and the local modern druids act out their greeting of the dying sun a little way to the north, the very first signs of the changing seasons come. At first there is a coolness in the late evening. The beaches are still washed in a golden glow during the day, but there is a subtle shift in evening light, a slight softening haze cuts the brilliant light of summer, and mist hangs in curtains out to sea, shrouding the outlying rocks of the bay with a gauze of golden haze.

In the mornings, in early autumn, the days start moist and cool. Dew hangs in rounded, diamond drops on the cobwebs that festoon the grass stems and curtain the hedges. It is not cold yet, not by any standards, and the frost that might come in three months as the day's edge shorter towards Christmas is still just a distant possibility.

Sally was obviously pregnant now, and her friends among the village ladies were speculating as to the sex of the child. Jenny Horne, in her capacity of local expert on the mysteries of motherhood, was in no doubt. "A girl, my dear," she said. "Carrying her that low, it has to be a girl."

Come the thirty-week scan and there was a chance, at last, to be sure. Jonathan was with her in the little bright lit cubicle with the humming ultrasound machine and the low examination couch. The duty midwife noted the baby's heart rate, checked the diameter of its developing head and found everything normal. Finally, she asked the now almost ritual question.

"Do you want to know the sex?" she said, and Jonathan surprised himself by saying, "No."

Sally smiled and acquiesced.

Later, in the car, on the way home, she asked, "Why didn't you want to know?"

"I don't know. Well, I'm a doctor. I'm embarrassed to say it, to be honest. It just seems presumptuous to ask. Like tempting fate somehow."

"God. Now I've heard it all," said Sally, "You, superstitious? What happened to rational man?"

"His wife got pregnant."

"Really? You know what? I love you, Doctor."

"That's good," he said. "Cause I love you too. Just tell me one thing. What colour are we going to paint its room?"

Later that night, in the quiet time as the sun warmed Earth drowsed around them, they made careful love, and it was very, very good for both of them.

Afterwards, in that warm peaceful hour after good sex, when the big king-sized bed was all that they needed in the whole world, she said, "We are lucky, you know? After all, what were the odds that we would meet?"

"Long, long odds," he said, "but we did meet. So, let's appreciate what we've got."

She snuggled closer, relaxing herself to fit against him in the semi dark. After a time, they slept, and neither one of them was aware that they were observed, from outside the house, where the grey clad figure stood under the old ash tree in the garden, seemingly one with the shadows around it.

Janice Laity had finally come to the edge of the borderlands where the land of the living meets whatever waits all self-aware creatures at the end. Increasingly, she found herself talking to, and seeing, people from her long-ago youth. Often it was Ted Hancock, the object of her adolescent passions from the post-war years, when the long summers of peace made it seem that the world would remain unchanging forever.

In her mind, it was once again that glorious spring night when all the village youth ran through the moonlit fields in the gloaming. Officially the girls were trying not to be caught, but most of them didn't try too hard.

Janice would remember for seventy-seven years, the feel of that cool summer night. She remembered, as if it had been yesterday, the delicious sharp cool of the night breeze on skin exposed to the air at last, and the quick cautious resistance that was no more than a token, before the delicious surrender that they both knew was coming.

Ted had been a gentle lover, even that first time. There had been a little discomfort at first, too little to be called pain, and then there was only magical sensation and the realisation that life was a thing of wonder. Now, as the concrete realities of that life faded at last, and as the little room expanded to become her whole world, Ted came to her again, and waited there beside her, an expectant lover, waiting only for her to cross the border.

Presently, on a quiet late night, when her daughter had finally succumbed to exhaustion and slept in the next room, the moment came. It was only then, in the very moment that she finally deserted the body that had carried her through the world for ninety-six years, that she finally saw the other, waiting beside Ted. It was a dark, tenuous figure that had shape but no real substance, a presence certainly, but the only presence there was of negativity, a structure built of nothingness.

Janice slipped past it at the border, joining Ted, turning her back on the other, crossing to whatever wonders were waiting, and leaving her body finally in the world of living things, for the other to do with as it would. It was, after all, no more than an empty husk now, of no more value than the empty chrysalis case is of value to the fully grown butterfly.

Alone at last in the little room, the other crossed over the borderland, took a few moments to savour its new existence, and then began work on the body that lay there on the bed.

As a doctor, Jonathan Wilde made a custom of sleeping with a phone beside the bed, but it rarely rang. On most nights, quiet was a guarantee, so much so that the local deputising service, whose radio equipped locums covered the territory extending from the Tamar to Truro, rarely billed the Tregadrew practice for cover services.

That night, struggling up from a rancid dream where he was pursued by an unseen assailant, Jonathan woke to find the phone's insistent repeated bleep running on, near his left ear. He fumbled for the phone, trying to silence it before Sally woke.

Finally, he picked it up.

"Dr Wilde," he said, and Sally, half-awake beside him by then, mumbled a sleepy protest.

"Dr Wilde," came the voice at the other end of the line. "It's Rose, Rose Laity. It's mother, Doctor. I think she's dead."

"I'm sorry to hear that, Rose," he said. "It's never easy, even when you expect it. You are sure?"

"Yes, Doctor. God, yes. I'm sure."

"Well, I'll come over first thing in the morning, and deal with the formalities with you. Right now, try to rest if you can. I'm afraid it will be a very hectic day tomorrow. If you like, you could take a couple of the Valium I prescribed for your mum last week. No more than two, mind you, just to help you get a few hours rest."

"It's not that, Doctor. It's... well... You'd best come tonight."

"Well, Rose, we don't usually attend at night. Especially if the death is expected. There's really nothing that needs to be done tonight."

"It's not that, Doctor. It's... I don't know how to explain. It's best you see for yourself."

Jonathan sighed inwardly, but from past experience he knew Rose was level-headed and sensible, not liable to sudden panics, so he said, "Well, if it's really important, Rose... Of course I'll come across."

"Thank you, Doctor. I'll see you soon, then."

"I'll be with you as soon as I can, Rose.'

He put the phone down, and Sally, most of the way awake now, said, "Old Janice? She's gone then? Do you really need to go over tonight? After all, you've got surgery in the morning."

"She's really upset, love. More than you'd expect, I mean. After all, her mother has been ailing for months. I'll be happier if I check on her."

"Can I make you a coffee before you go?"

"No, I'll do it. You try to go back to sleep."

"It would happen tonight."

CHAPTER FOURTEEN

The Laity house was lit up like a ship at sea. This was something that he'd seen often before. When a relative died, those who were left lit the house as if the lights would banish the presence of death. Yellow lights, shining out into the dark, cast bright rectangles from the windows against a dark shape of the building silhouetted against the sky.

Rose was waiting for him in the open doorway, standing in a bright triangle of light. She reached out towards him as if she were a drowning swimmer and he were a rock in a stormy sea.

She said, "Doctor, I'm so sorry to call you out at night but, well, you'll see why. It's this way."

The death room was as he remembered it, slightly old fashioned, a little shabby, a last reflection of the old woman's personality, but the resemblance of the room that night, to the room where he had last seen Janice, ended there.

There was a smell to start with, a fatty, greasy reek, like an overcooked cheap sausage. All around the walls of the room, at a height of five feet or so from the floor, was a perfectly horizontal mark of greasy orange with a stain that stretched up to the ceiling. It was as if some strange, dry flood had engulfed the room and then receded, leaving the mark of its passage as it went. Above the bed, a single clear glass light bulb hung on a twisted cotton covered cord. The conical shape of the shade was stripped bare to its skeletal wire cage. The plastic covering hung in tattered melted shreds. The glass teardrop of the bulb's surface was streaked with greasy orange trickles of staining that trailed down towards a single dark droplet at its lowest point. The stain lent the light a brownish orange cast that gave the whole room a strangely lit, otherworldly feel.

The body was on the bed, or at least what was left of it was. The bed stood as it always had, more or less untouched. The sheet was folded back, the blankets neatly tucked in, but where the old woman's body had been was only a roughly humanoid pile of greasy black ash. Where the legs would have ended were a pair of feet, with a length of leg that ended a little above the ankles. They were totally untouched, the soles still with the yellow callouses of old age on them. Also, at the end of the ashes that marked where the arms had been, were hands. On the left one, on the untouched fingers, were rings, a yellow gold wedding band and a platinum circle set with bright emeralds, that flashed green fire in the dubious light.

The head too was untouched, still perfectly recognisable and resting on the pillow as if it were still attached to the body that had vanished.

It was still possible to recognise Janice Laity, her face untouched, save for a small smudge of soot on her left cheek.

Jonathan Wilde stood in the doorway of the room, Rose beside him. He was dimly aware that she was twisting a bit of cloth between her hands. She was still wearing a homely plaid dressing gown over her nightdress.

He said, "You found her like this, Rose?"

"Yes. I couldn't hear anything at all when I got up to have a pee, and I thought… well, I don't know what I thought, but I opened the door, and there she was."

"When did you last see her alive?"

"Around midnight. I dropped in to say goodnight."

"Okay. Well, I think we both know that we shall need to involve the police, Rose."

"The police?"

"Well, under the circumstances I can't sign the death certificate and that means we need to involve the coroner's officer."

"It's awful, Doctor," she said, her voice disconnected. "I thought I was ready for her to go. After all, she was old and it was her time. But this…? It's like something off a horror film. Do you know what happened to her?"

Jonathan thought rapidly to himself, and said, "Honestly Rose, I have absolutely no idea how such a thing might happen. I don't understand it, nor, I suspect, will the coroner's man, but it's best we go by the book. In the end it's better for all of us."

"But doesn't that mean they'll think that I had something to do with it?"

"No. Not at all. Every time there is an unusual death, the coroner has to investigate. I'm afraid that, this time, there will probably need to be a formal inquest as well. I'm so very sorry, but there is nothing I can do to alter the progress of events now."

"What happens next, Doctor?"

"Well, we must leave everything in that room exactly as we found it. I'll ring the coroner's department. I think that you need to be prepared for the police to treat the room as a scene of crime. No," he said, noticing her expression, "it's not that they'll think that anything criminal has happened here. It's just that the law has to do things in one particular way."

With the calls made, the machinery took over. Presently the farmyard was peppered with flashing blue beacons, turning the first light of the new dawn into a flickering, strange collage of light and shadow. It seemed a final irony that there was, after all, no emergency here, just a mystery. Presently, with the forensic van parked in solitary glory, the men and women in white suits took over and began to work their own arcane, mysterious rituals of death. Jonathan Wilde meanwhile, with his part in the drama completed, went home.

"My old instructor used to say," he told Sally later that morning, at the end of a long explanation of events, "that you never assume that you've seen it all before. There will always be something new to surprise you, but this…?"

Sally was sympathetic, but she too, was finding it hard to understand the facts. "So, she was, cremated? In her own bed?"

"Effectively yes. But the heat that pretty-well totally destroyed her body left the room and the bed clothes effectively untouched. God only knows what they'll record as the cause of death."

Sally, as always, was practical, even under these admittedly strange circumstances. She said, "You should get a few hours rest. I'll tell Eric that you need cover for the morning surgery. You're in no state to work right now."

CHAPTER FIFTEEN

Hannah Wilson was not a frequent visitor to the surgery, mostly her regular appointments were for repeat prescriptions and attendant check-ups for the blood pressure increases that occasionally go with increasing age.

Hannah was forty-five, and taller than most of the locals, with dark hair that fell in a curtain across her shoulders. She had been married to George Wilson, a no nonsense, big shouldered, dairy farmer whose major interest in life was a herd of pedigree Jerseys. The market for high fat milk, dwindling to start with, finally collapsed with the closure of one of the local clotted cream producers and with the end of the small dairy unit George had lost the will to go on. She had tolerated his drinking for a while, before the couple finally separated, and he took himself off to live in the north. In due time Hannah found herself alone and living in a small cottage at the outer boundary of the village.

Hannah's family had been in the area for more generations than anyone could count, and she was a discretely practising pagan.

It was not that she made a big issue of her beliefs and practises but she certainly did nothing to conceal them. Her philosophy was gentle and almost pathologically easy going, reverencing life and the natural order of things. If anything roused her to direct confrontation, it was the ill treatment of living things.

She accepted the needs and methods of day-to-day farming, bull calves for instance, that inevitable by-product of a dairy herd, were routinely dispatched, without much regret, but in Hannah's mind that was the order of things. It was not gratuitous, not done to satisfy some primitive bloodlust, and so it was to be accepted.

She and a number of other like-minded villagers met at The Nine Maidens on the appointed days, four times a year. Marking the passage of the solar year, their meetings were decorous and peaceful, though they were usually 'sky clad', meaning naked to the elements, as the custom was, but the naked rites celebrated life. They were a thousand miles different in intent to the sadistic perversion of a Satanist orgy.

There are many similar believers in the far west and, like most of them, Hannah never proselytised, never tried to enforce her understanding of the world on others, believing as she did, that each small spark of life must find its own way towards an accommodation with the infinite.

All of that was, pretty much, common knowledge in the village. Hannah and her ways were as easily accepted as Jimmy Thomas who was the nearest thing the village had to an annoying zealot with his willingness to expound his extreme Salvation Army creed. Jimmy put his views forwards with a vigour that would have made even General Booth, that old evangelical soldier of God, cringe at his certainty. Jimmy was also possessed by a willingness to try to convert every living soul he met. Both extremes of religion, pagan and evangelical, were simply part of everyday country life.

Given all of that, when Hannah turned up in the 'spare' slot, that appointment that was tagged to the end of each surgery in case of some small emergency, Jonathan Wilde was mildly surprised, and a little interested.

"Mrs Wilson," said Jonathan. "What seems to be troubling you this afternoon?"

"This is going to be difficult, Doctor," she said, by way of opening.

Jonathan was well used to putting apprehensive patients at their ease. Often, the real problem was simple embarrassment over some routine but highly personal illness. He took refuge in the well-worn formula. "I promise you, Mrs Wilson, there is nothing that you can tell me that I haven't heard before, and, of course whatever is said within these four walls, stays here."

"Alright, Doctor, and call me Hannah, please. The whole village does, after all."

"Okay," said Jonathan, falling back on the routine business of gaining patient confidence, "Hannah it is. Now what's the problem?"

"The thing is, Doctor, it's your problem rather than mine, but I really need to talk to you about it. I believe… no, more than that, I know, that you are in danger."

In the years of dealing with the public, both the ill and the worried well, Jonathan had come across a good many patients with what most GPs thought of as a 'saviour complex'. They are the patients who commonly believe that their medical advisor is under threat, usually an existential one, that only they can help with. This is an annoying and time wasting, but hardly threatening, psychological quirk, that most doctors learn to deal with, with various degrees of success.

"Hannah, whatever you think is threatening me, I promise you I will take great care in the next few days. Will that satisfy you?

"We can't get anywhere with this, if you think I'm out of my tree, Doctor."

"I promise you I don't think any such thing, Hannah. I honestly believe that you think, for whatever reason, I might be at some risk from some external agency or other. But you must understand that, in the real world, these threats are mostly imaginary, even if they seem very real, at the time."

She took a deep breath as if setting her shoulder to a mighty wheel, and said, "Okay, Doctor, I'll go further. What do you understand of the other world?"

He sighed quietly and took a deep breath. "Hannah, before we take that any further, it's only fair to tell you that I am a convinced atheist. I have no belief in any kind of God."

"It doesn't matter, Doctor. What we believe or don't believe makes no difference to the reality. If you decide that you don't believe in gravity anymore, will that let you jump off the cliff at Hell's Mouth and float gently down to the beach?"

"It's hardly the same, Hannah. I believe in evidence and fact, not belief of itself."

"And old Janice? What happened to her the other night? Don't look so shocked, boy, this is a village and such a thing could hardly go un-noticed. After what happened, how does that fit with your evidence? After all's said and done, there was the evidence in front of you."

"You know I can't discuss that, Hannah. Apart from medical ethics, that is a coroner's case and I can't talk about it."

"Alright, Doctor. So I'll tell you what happened. Something, something outside of your 'science' reduced that old lady to ashes and left the rest of the room untouched. If there is nothing outside of your hard science, how can such a thing be?"

"Hannah, I told you I can't discuss that. Janice was a patient, and, even in death, that entitles her to absolute confidentiality."

"It'll all come out in open court in Truro, Doctor."

"And when it does, well, then we might talk about the evidence, but not until then. Now, how can I help you, Hannah?

She looked deflated and in a small voice said, "Doctor, if I leave this with you, will you make me a promise? Not as my doctor, but just as one human being to another?"

"That depends what it is, Hannah."

"Nothing you need fear, Doctor, just this. If you come to realise that you need help with what is coming, call on me."

Jonathan sighed inwardly. "Certainly, Hannah. If I have the slightest inkling that you can help out with the situation, you will be among the first to know. In the meanwhile, is there anything else I can do for you? Because otherwise, I do have a rather hectic round to cover this afternoon."

Eric, when Jonathan talked the case through with him at the afternoon meeting, was sympathetic.

"She's harmless, Jonathan. Though, I expect when you encounter her for the first time, it's a bit of a surprise. The thing is, she really does mean well. She's quite convinced that stirring up a few herbs and chanting a bit of gibberish to the full moon actually makes things better for the whole world, but she would no more harm another person than you would."

"She's borderline delusional then, wouldn't you say?"

"Yes, certainly, in the sense that she has a set of fixed ideas that don't fit with what we think of as normal belief patterns. But then again, within her own belief system, she is totally integrated and rational. If we brand her as crazy then we really need to brand every Catholic who asks favours from the Virgin Mary the same."

"Yes. Well, that's a distinction that I don't personally make. In any case, as long I don't have to discuss it with her too often, I can live with that. After all, we do have genuine medical patients to treat."

CHAPTER SIXTEEN

At the old meeting place in the little hollow in the heathland, in the open common land beyond the stone circle, Hannah Wilson stood naked under the full moon, and waited for the turn of time. This was a place that had been sacred to the old ways since time out of mind. When the only people who inhabited this land were simple hunter gatherers, in the time when the shallow seas to the west hardly divided the island from the land mass that would, in the fullness of time, as sea levels rose, become the continent of Europe, this outwardly nondescript-looking spot was special. Even then, before mankind thought of measuring time, this was a place where the membrane that divides the worlds was thin. At such places it is possible for those who have the will, and the knowledge, to reach across the dimensions of space and time, and touch other realities.

Hannah stood, sky clad, feeling the night air on her skin while she went through the complex preparations for what she must do next. If there had been anyone to notice, there would have been little to see. Much of what she did was internal, an unlocking of barriers that generations of people have built over the millennia to allow them to live exclusively in the dimensions of being that we call reality.

Gradually, as the moon rose further into a sky the colour of dark blue velvet, the boundaries between the worlds softened and dissolved. Hannah was no longer really inside her body, though she still stood alone in the little hollow… a plump-ish middle-aged woman standing naked in the moonlight, with the silver light washing her ample curves into the resemblance of a statue.

Presently, at the border of the hollow in the land, there was a shimmer in the clear air. The being that semi-materialised was not precisely of this world, and its presence was marked by nothing more than a violet stain on the air, yet it radiated strength and the kind of power that might create or destroy the fabric of reality.

Speaking inside her head, without a sound to disturb the quiet of the hollow, Hannah asked her questions and made her obeisance because this was, in a real sense, a Goddess, and, in the same quiet undisturbed fashion, she received her answers, and they were terrifying.

When it was done, Hannah fell to her knees in the open air, and there in the moonlight, she knelt and sobbed as if her heart would break.

CHAPTER SEVENTEEN

Billy Sherman was twelve years old. He was as skinny as a rail, and he was tanned enough to have passed as Asian. He was wandering the heathland around a mile from the village alone. He was one of those country children who embraced, rather than tolerated, his environment. Other kids at the local comprehensive to which they were bussed en-masse for eight miles or so each morning, loved the trappings of the city, far away from the open spaces and the sea. Many of them idolised rappers, adopting much of the mannerisms and vocabulary of a culture that they did not begin to understand.

Billy turned instead to the open fields and hedgerows, to the windswept rocky shorelines where the waves thundered against the rocks and the limpid pools of sea water, left isolated from the ocean by the receding tides, that held strange and enticing creatures in their depths.

Other kids thought Billy was strange, if they noticed him at all. They mainly regarded him as a little stupid, and occasionally they bullied him, as children will, but the truth was that he simply preferred his own company and the wild open heathland and coast, to the dubious companionship of his contemporaries, with their endless aping of mannerisms from other places, and their celebration of cities over what he thought of as the 'real' world.

That morning, with the sun already warm on his skin, and the scents of drying dew and wild thyme in his nostrils, he was headed for the cliff edge, to take a look at the colony of herring gulls that nested there.

As cliffs go, the cliffs near Tregadrew were not very impressive. They rose from a tumble of degraded rocks that stood against the sea, fifty-five feet or so, to a cliff edge that was fringed by the narrow, dusty path that was part of the South West coastal route that snakes right around the peninsula.

A little below that path, on a narrow ledge, the herring gulls had set up their house keeping. It was high enough to be clear of the breaking waves when the south westerly gales blew and exposed enough to the sea to allow the resident birds to fight off the attentions of thieving crows and other gulls. It was a noisy, screechy place, full of birds disputing a space to build, and robbing the small piles of nesting material that their neighbours had already formed into a rough circlet of vegetation that acted as a small barrier to protect their brood. On each ledge, there was a clutch of two or three large speckled greenish eggs, dotted with brown freckles. On some ledges, where the earliest arrivals had been the first to nest that season, the first indignant-looking fluffy chicks were already setting up a constant squeaking as they begged their parents for food.

Out at sea, gathered at the fringes of the gull colony, there was a wheeling cloud of corvids and gannets. The birds patrolled endlessly, mobbing the returning parent gulls and trying to force them to regurgitate a gutful of juicy fish offal.

It was a favourite spot of Billy Sherman's. He loved to lie, belly down, in the tussocks of cotton grass, with his head just over the edge of the drop, so that the gulls, and their nests, seemed close enough to touch. Billy himself, was never mobbed by the parent birds even though they must have been well aware that he was there, watching them from a few feet above.

It was a clear, bright afternoon, and out in the bay, he could clearly see Johnny Trevail's fishing boat as Johnny hauled in his nearer line of pots. The sound of the old Lister engine, puttering away as the boat kept station, came clearly across the sea. Looking down on the nearest of the nests below him, Billy saw a scrubby thatch of wild thrift, with purplish pink flowers thrusting up from a cushion of greenery. The plant had been sculpted by the elements to a perfectly rounded shape as if it had been topiarised.

There was a shift in the warm innocent afternoon. Details that had been inconsequential a second before were sharpened. Had Billy been more well versed in the folklore of his own community, he might even have been troubled but as it was he simply accepted the new acuity of his senses.

Presently, he became aware that a procession of ants was marching up and down the thrift stems, each one carrying a fat green bud as it went. Those buds were, he knew very well, the young caterpillars of the blue butterflies who deceived their way into the ants' nest and fed on their larvae – a strange example of one creature using the instinctive behaviour of another.

Suddenly the ants seemed very clear to Billy, standing out against the dusty olive-green foliage in extreme detail, even though he was a good twenty feet above them and by rights they should have been no more than moving reddish specks at that distance. He could, he realised, see each separate frond of the thrift plant. Each tiny spear of a leaf was covered in a bluish, waxy covering, and each flower stalk carried its own fuzzy coating of hairs. Fascinated, and not questioning this new ability, he leaned forwards to get a better look, noticing the tiny heap of dry earth that had gathered on the rocky ledge. It was that heap that the thrifts' roots were sunk into, an intertwined network of yellow white threads spread out in a complex mesh to catch every available drop of moisture.

He leaned further, edging out so that his shoulders were over the drop. The nearest gulls, only a few feet below him, shuffled their feathers and scolded him in raucous voices that sounded like an irritated barnyard rooster. On the edge of balance, Billy teetered, watching the ants, completely absorbed in the amazing acuity of vision that had come to him, unasked and unexpected.

He edged forward some more, another few inches. He could feel his body weight shift towards the drop as he reached the balance point, and the weight of his torso was nearly enough to begin the sliding seesaw movement that would end on the tumble of shattered reddish pink slate below.

At the last moment, just as it seemed that a fall was inevitable, something fluttered and screeched close behind him. It was so close that he could feel the air currents from its wings and smell the slightly carrion whiff that hung about it. The sparrow hawks that had long nested in the sea caves below had tolerated the intruder enough.

Billy, hearing the rasping in his chest, shoved back from the brink, breathing raggedly as if he had run a hundred yards sprint. He turned on his back, shuffling away from the drop, shocked by the near miss that had come out of a clear warm day.

It was then, for the first time, that he realised what was

standing there on the path behind him. He had time to scream, but there was no one to hear him, aside from the birds... and seabirds have no conscience.

Jonathan Wilde, back from sparse morning rounds, was surprised by the flurry of activity in the village square. In normal times, police presence in the village was confined to the odd visit from Joe Wetherbee, whose patch covered a broad scatter of settlements along the coast, and whose duties mainly consisted of firearms renewals and chasing up on missing road tax licences.

Now, along with Joe's police car, there were three other official vehicles in full police livery, and a plain white transit marked 'dog section'.

Jonathan parked in his designated slot and walked into the reception area. Julie Penhaligan was on duty, and all too obviously aching to pass on the news. Julie took her secondary role of passer on of village gossip very nearly as seriously as she took her duties as receptionist.

She said, "There's a boy gone missing, Doctor. Billy Sherman. They say he went out onto the cliff path first thing, and no one has seen him since. They've got the dogs out looking and everything." Julie's eyes were bright with the importance of the news.

Jonathan said, "Well, isn't that the lad who's always wandering around on the heath, looking at birds and bugs? He's probably just wandered off and lost track of the time."

"I hope so, Doctor. I'm sure we all hope so. But you hear such awful things about missing kids."

"I think if there was anyone in the village community who was a risk to the local children, Julie, we'd probably know. The lad is probably fine. Worst case is that he's hurt himself and having a job getting home. Give it a few hours more, and he'll be back."

Julie was not convinced. "They're talking about getting all the men to search the cliff top, Doctor. The coast guard search and rescue watch team is already out."

"Well, if it comes to it, Julie, let me know. I'll help any way I can."

A few hours passed, with no developments. The little clot of emergency vehicles was joined by a catering truck selling tea and coffee. A huge sign on the side of the van offered Cappuccino, Americano, Latte, and various kinds of Herbal Tea.

'Sign of the times,' thought Jonathan, catching a glimpse of the sign through the surgery window.

He was halfway through evening surgery, with the square outside the window still clotted with emergency service crews. The police cars had now been joined by the sleek, navy blue and yellow American style four by fours favoured by the coastguard rescue teams, and the search teams stood around, waiting in spruce, dark blue overalls, against the time when their expertise on the cliff face should be needed.

The last patient of the day was elderly Ted Jolly, a farmer who lived up to his name with a long series of jokes, most of them in dubious taste. Political correctness was not Ted's strong point.

Jonathan was well aware that, as the years had advanced, Ted had become increasingly aware of his approaching mortality and used his bluff 'hail fellow well met' exterior to cover a very real fear of the inevitable.

Ted said, "And then the barman says, 'I told you before about those sheep'!" providing the punchline to yet another joke.

Jonathan smiled politely and said, "The thing is, Mr Jolly, I think we should take just a bit more care of that blood pressure of yours. It's a bit higher than I would like."

"Don't buy any long-playing records, you mean, Doctor?"

"No. We're not at that stage, but these things are best controlled before things get really bad. I'm going to give you a drug called Lisinopril. You'll need to take one tablet a day to start with and I'd like you check in with the practice nurse in three weeks or so to check your response to the drug. There should be no side effects, but some people find that they get dizzy spells, so watch out for that. Normally those effects go away by themselves in a few weeks, but if not, come back and see me, and we'll try something different. Is there anything else I can do for you?"

Just at that moment, there was a flurry of activity in the square outside the surgery window. A few seconds afterwards, Julie knocked briefly, and came into the consulting room.

"I'm so sorry to interrupt, Doctor," she said, "but we need your help in reception. They've found the boy and he needs help."

Ted smiled. "Always happy to help," he said. "You go on, Doctor. I'll finish off putting my shirt on and I'll be off."

Jonathan smiled his appreciation, rattling the keys of the computer to print off a prescription. The printer buzzed in a business-like way and coughed up the green slip.

"Thank you for your understanding, Ted."

Billy Sherman was, outwardly, no different from the boy who had set out from home that morning. Jonathan introduced himself, noting that the boy made no response at all. He sat on the couch in examination room two, dangling his legs, his scabby knees and scratches bearing evidence of a long hard passage through the gorse. There was one difference though from the carefree kid from eight hours ago. His features were completely without expression. It was as if someone had turned off a secret internal relay and erased his personality.

Jonathan went through the routine of neuro-obs automatically, shining a light into each eye in turn, asking the boy to follow a finger side to side with his expressionless eyes. Billy went through the tests automatically, and silently, not resisting, not really complying, simply going through the motions.

Essentially, at first sight, there was nothing to see. Billy was, in all his vital details, normal, except that he was completely disconnected from reality. He sat on the examination table, as inert as a side of meat on the butcher's slab.

"What they used to call 'catatonic' in the less enlightened days of the last century," Jonathan said to Sally a few hours later, as they were sitting up in bed, discussing the day's events. "I've seen this sort of thing with very severe shock but there was nothing physically to account for it."

Sally nodded her head in sympathetic understanding. Sometimes he thought that these late-night discussions were tending on unethical, but doctor's partners have long been recipients of confidences, and neither of them found anything strange in them.

"That's a cruel term to apply to a young boy, surely," she said.

"Yes," he said. "Cruel, but apt. A few years ago, when I was training, they used to put severely brain damaged patients in what was unofficially called the 'C&T' ward."

She thought a moment, and finally said, "No, I don't see the acronym."

"Cabbages and Turnips," he said, then, noticing her wince, added, "The thing is, if you have to live with these things day to day, you can't start taking an emotional interest. You'd go bloody mad yourself, if you did. So you just do what you can. Forced exercise, to improve what's left of their muscle tone. Turning them every few hours to ward off bedsores, and then you wait, above everything else, you wait."

"For what? Are you waiting for them to die? What is the point?"

"Sometimes, not often, but every now and then, you get a miracle. Every now and then, one comes back."

"And are they the same as before?"

"No. Not usually, especially if it has been a prolonged episode. They are not really the same. The personality that was there to start with seems to retreat somehow into a different state. Often, they are disinhibited, talk about their sex fantasies in public, that sort of thing. But they do come back. The thing is when they do, sometimes they remember what was said around them, even when they seemed inert."

"Christ."

"'Locked in syndrome' they call it. Aware but not able to even move a muscle to communicate. Of all the tragic nightmares that happen, I think that must be the worst of all."

"And Billy what's-his-face? What are his chances?"

"Impossible to say. Still, he's young and he has that on his side. He's fit, there's no obvious head injury. He's got everything going for him."

"So, what did that to him, Jon?"

"Now that's the sixty thousand dollar question."

"Well, something must have happened to him."

"Well, it wasn't a physical injury. Of course, sometimes a really profound emotional shock can do this."

"Jon, I have to ask. Was he raped?"

"No, almost certainly not. That sort of forced sex leaves signs, tears, maybe bleeding, bruising, at the very least. I checked that right off. Of course, the forensic examiner will have to confirm, just in case, but I'm sure he'll find nothing."

"Poor little bugger."

"Ineptly put, dear. But I concur completely. Poor little bugger, indeed."

CHAPTER EIGHTEEN

David Esterbrook was a fourth generation fisherman who had operated a lobster boat all of his life. His first fishing trip was as a boy of eight years old or so. At fifty-six years old, it was a way of life that he would not have changed even if he could. His boat, the 'Sea Bird', was a trim eighteen-footer clinker built out of solid English timber and painted bright white with red trim. Most of the 'Sea Bird' was open to the sea and the air, the only shelter on this small, inshore vessel a cubby built in the bows like an afterthought. She was powered by an ancient Lister Petter diesel that had puttered across the bay thousands of times over the years, never missing a beat of its ancient, low tech motor.

The morning after, while the village was still digesting the shock of the sad and strange case of Billy Sherman, a situation that was only made worse by the fact that no one had any real idea of what had happened to the lad, David was hauling pots, as always. Thanks to the efforts of the lobster hatchery up the coast at Padstow, numbers of the creatures on the reef and the long subsea bar of rock that ran parallel to the shore near the harbour had gradually increased.

In the bad old days of the eighties, when lobsters had been pretty well fished out, the local boats had dropped out of the fishery, one by one, as age and infirmity had overtaken their skippers, and as the young men had found less dangerous, and more lucrative, work elsewhere. Eventually, only David was left.

Now, with the young lobster stock growing up to the

regulation size to take, there was a good, if precarious, living to be made laying trap lines and harvesting the crustaceans for the local restaurant trade. The fact was that a lobster that was taken out of the sea changed hands on the quayside for five quid, and ended up costing ten times that much on the plate. Even so, there was enough of a living at the sharp end of the business to keep the boat, and the cottage, going. It helped that David lived alone, his wife of eighteen years standing, having decamped for the bright lights of 'up country' three years before.

It was a peaceful morning, the sort of day that fishermen regard with a degree of suspicion when they come that late in the season, when bright innocent-looking skies might revert to a violent south westerly gale in a matter of a few hours.

The location buoys for the trap lines were simple orange plastic balls, each one trailing a long length of white two-centimetre nylon line that trailed off into the blue green shadows where the surface daylight barely penetrated. At the end of each line, there was a set of traps, each one a series of half-moon shaped hoops of iron fixed at both ends to a wooden baseboard to form a rough tunnel. The traps were fixed in a long row, like beads on a string. The hoops were covered with nylon mesh forming a cage, and the whole trap was weighted with a lump of tramp iron to sink it. Each trap had a single opening, a funnel shaped structure whose narrower end opened into the body of the trap. A lobster, attracted by a bait of putrid fish guts, would climb easily into the funnel and then find it impossible to climb back out again.

David hauled on the line, taking the weight of the traps on the end of it and automatically shifting position to compensate for the boat's list as the weight came into play. The first pot of the string of eight swam into view, at the limits of vision, where the light barely penetrated. He shifted the weight of the trap as it broke surface, to rest it on the gunwale of the little boat, noting the three good sized lobsters that were the night's catch.

He was disentangling the last lobster from the mesh of the trap, where it had somehow managed to snag itself, when he noticed that something had happened to the day. There was a shag cruising the surface close to the boat. There was nothing unusual in that. The birds were a constant presence in the shallow waters of the bay, swimming alongside passing traffic, and ducking neatly below the surface in search of fish. They left hardly a ripple to mark their passing from the air to the water.

This particular bird was nothing special, its blue/black feathers iridescent like the breast feathers of a starling, and its beady eyes – and David could have sworn that the bird was watching him – a deep lustrous sapphire blue that seemed to reflect the day, picking up the colour of the bowl of the sky.

David had often seen shag before, met them actually, on most days when he went fishing. Often enough, when he was feeling good with the day's work – which was most days, because he was a cheerful sort of man – David would throw the birds a piece of discarded fish, either spare bait, or odd creatures that were caught in the traps. Feeding the birds made him feel comfortable with his day.

This bird's sapphire blue eye caught his attention with its unblinking stare. After a few seconds of that fixed stare, David felt a strange floating sensation, as if he was suffering an episode of low blood pressure. The world swam in and out of focus, finally settling into a hyperreal sharp focus vision of a perfect seascape.

Like most human beings on the planet, David had a secret fear that he rarely shared with others. He felt that, as a fisherman, it was almost shameful. For some, that fear is snakes, for others rats or spiders. Often the phobia is irrational, involving something that is actually harmless, but the perception of danger is not the real cause of the fear. It is simply that some things are intolerable, and their presence is not to be borne. They are the hidden terror in room 101, simply the worst thing in the world.

David was well used to most of the strange, even grotesque creatures that inhabit the sea. Sharks, huge though they sometimes were, were monstrous and fearsome, but the odd mako that swam past, cruising the limpid surface waters with lazy sweeps of its tail, held no terror for him. Once, twenty years ago, in an especially warm season, the bay was invaded by sunfish. Huge disc-shaped creatures had lazed across the surface of the water. For a few memorable days, they were everywhere, before, obeying some hidden collective impulse, they were gone. There was a single occasion when a venus girdle, a huge primitive deep-sea life-form like a living curtain of iridescent light, had drifted past, undulating its way through the gin clear waters. None of these marine oddities troubled David, but there was a single creature in the deep that frightened him. Occasionally, not often, but often enough to trouble him, a pot would come up with an octopus lying like a living blob of jelly on the floor of the trap.

Most fishermen, faced with an octopus, saw nothing more than a chance of a bonus. The local seafood restaurant was prepared to buy them at a premium rate. David, faced with the creatures, saw only elemental horror. Those eyes, with their vertical pupils, seemed to gaze at him with a real intelligence, and it seemed to him, with violent rage at their predicament and malevolent intent.

Octopi were David's nemesis. They were the one thing that was intolerable, the living equivalent of the rats in Orwell's room 101.

The shape that swam into view at the very limit of his vision was no more than a shadow at first, a long shadow, tapering towards one end with the extended cone in front and a set of elongated fins at the other end.

As David watched, it grew larger, swimming up from the depths, where an old volcanic sink hole on the ocean floor dropped away three hundred feet into the gloom where the wreck of the old liner Dusseldorf rested in perpetual darkness. The shape was completely silent as it rose slowly towards the light and David would, one might have thought, have had time to fire up the Lister and make a run for the safety of the harbour basin.

But the eyes stopped him. The eyes were each one a foot across with vertical pupils that divided them, and they fixed on David and locked their gaze on his, just as the shag had done a few minutes before.

As David watched in growing horror, the squid, sixty feet long from the tips of its tentacles to the membrane fan of its tail, rose to the surface. Architeuthis dux, a true deep-sea monster, the stuff of the old sailor's nightmare tales, and, thankfully, a rarity in the shallow waters on the continental shelf.

And now it was David's nightmare, as the long tentacles, grey brown and tipped with an elongated, flat paddle, two feet long and studded with suckers that were ringed with thorny spikes, rose out of the water and reached for him.

David, a perfect victim, simply stood there passively in his boat and waited for them to grab him. After a few endless moments, they did. His last thought, before the darkness took him, was that he should have listened to his father's advice against going to sea.

Presently the surface settled again and the empty boat floated on an ocean that was so still that it seemed as reflective as oil. The only sign of the event was a tang of ammonia in the air, the olfactory signature of a monster. Three hours afterwards, a passing yacht, crewed by two weekend sailors from the local yacht club, came across the empty boat and took her in tow, but, even though the lifeboat searched the empty ocean, and the coast watch teams checked the long line of coves to either side of the harbour, David Esterbrook had vanished as if he had never been.

CHAPTER NINETEEN

Jonathan Wilde, at the end of that evening surgery, was troubled at the thought of the next day. Inquests were hardly unknown territory to a GP but Janice Laity's inquest with its bizarre circumstances promised to be anything but routine. Eric was, as always, bluff and matter of fact.

"It's not as if anyone can possibly call your professional competence into question," he said. "Your treatment regime was exemplary. Whatever killed that old lady was absolutely nothing to do with your treatment and we can hardly be held responsible for patients who apparently auto-cremate."

"No," said Jonathan, "but it will be a bloody circus. After all, imagine what the local press are going to say, never mind the bloody nationals."

The coroner's court was like most such places of justice. The room was modern and clean, all white walls and blonde wood. There was a smell of furniture polish and freshly hoovered carpets. Quite clearly, great efforts had been made to make the place look as little like a formal courtroom as possible. The jury, eight men and two women, were seated in upright modern chairs with small writing surfaces attached to the arms so that they could take notes. Each chair was provided with a pad of yellow legal paper and a blue HB pencil. There was no dock, just three separate tables for legal representatives and witnesses.

They came into court one by one, each one introduced by the court usher and sworn to honesty and frank and complete disclosure. First came the medical examiner who was, of course, unable to suggest a cause of death. That formality done, it was Jonathan's turn to answer questions.

The coroner was a venerable old man who had the look of a biblical patriarch, with longer than fashionable white hair that curled to his shoulders, and a heavy hooked nose and full fleshy features.

After formal identification, Jonathan was ready for questioning.

The coroner said, "Dr Wilde. You were the first medically qualified witness on the scene, were you not?"

"I was, Sir, yes."

"Very well, Doctor, could you describe the room as you found it?"

Jonathan took a deep breath, gathering his thoughts, then he said, "The body, or what was left of it, was lying on its back on the bed, at least as far as I could tell. There was extensive tissue loss, most of the body was simply ash."

"And the bed that the body was lying on, Doctor?"

"There was virtually no damage to the bed as far as I could see. The sheets were white, aside from the area in actual contact with the body. In fact, they were clean, as if they had been freshly laundered."

The coroner was scribbling notes in black biro on a yellow legal pad. Pausing, he said, "And did you move the remains at all, Doctor?"

"No. There was no doubt that the lady was dead, and the circumstances were so strange that I immediately decided to refer the case to your officer as a suspicious death."

"Quite so, Doctor. Was there anything else that you noticed about the scene that you think might help us here?"

"The walls and ceiling were stained from a height of five feet or so from the floor. Even the light bulb was coated with a yellowish deposit. The line that it created on the walls was absolutely straight, as if it had been painted on. Below that line everything seemed normal and untouched."

"Did you form any opinion as to the nature of that staining, Doctor?"

"Well, it would be at best a conjecture but..."

"On that basis, please feel free to speculate, Doctor."

"I believe," said Jonathan, hesitantly, "that the material was condensed fat, evaporated from the body. Though, of course that would have to be subject to analysis, to be certain."

"Thank you, Doctor. That was a most informative and concise description. I refer the jury to photographs of the scene of death. They are in your exhibits folder, numbered AC one, through seventeen."

The jury members turned the plastic covered pages, each one goggling at the eight by ten glossy photos of the scene, with suitable expressions of horror and disbelief. One of the jurors, a middle-aged man with the red face and solid build of a man who works in the open air, turned pale and shut the folder with a small shudder.

"Is there anything, Doctor..." said the coroner from his raised dais, "that you could contribute to this, admittedly rather unusual, scenario? I am not expecting a professional assessment, but was there anything that you noticed at the scene that you believe might help us to reach a conclusion?"

"No, Sir." Jonathan shook his head in unconscious reinforcement of his negation. "There was nothing else."

"Was there an open fire in the room, Doctor? Or a heater of some kind? Some simple source of ignition?"

"Not that I saw, Sir."

"Just one more thing, Doctor. This lady was your patient, I assume?"

"Yes, Sir. She was a patient."

"And did she smoke, Doctor?"

"According to our records, Sir, the lady had never been a smoker."

"I see. Thank you, Doctor. You may sit down."

The witnesses followed each other in a steady stream. Coroner's officer, Rose Laity, the fire investigator, a sergeant from the local police. One by one they gave their evidence, and at the end of it, it seemed that nothing substantive was added.

Eventually, the inquest reached its inevitable, and essentially meaningless, conclusion. The cause of death remained unknown, and the court recorded an open verdict.

Jonathan got back to the village in the twilight that evening just in time to see the blue lights flashing on the quay. The search for David, whose empty boat had been discovered floating in the sea, a half mile from his home port, was winding down. It was a common tragedy in seafaring communities where men worked small boats, single handed. No one noticed that high on the headland overlooking the quay, a solitary figure was watching intently.

CHAPTER TWENTY

Morgan Richards was the third of his line to carry that name and he was, of all the villagers, the man who everyone regarded with steady dislike.

All small communities are a pyramid of numbers. At the top were the doctor and the well-to-do farmers. Once, when religion counted for more, there would have been a priest too, but nowadays, the local vicar served eight scattered churches and rushed around his parish on feast days trying to hold services one after the other. He ministered to a series of congregations that were aging and dwindling as the years passed. Below them in the village pecking order were the skilled workers, the local builder, and Mervyn Knowles the handyman, who was far overqualified for the work that he did, but who was prepared to accept the loss of status to allow him to live in the country on his own terms. They were the people who kept the wheels of daily life turning.

On a similar level of respectability were the small businesspeople. They were the solid middle-class citizens who ran the post office, the village store and the local garage.

Then there were the casual labourers who survived by picking up work from other people. Once, when the demand for labourers on the land had been higher, they had been day laborers on the farms, moving around, following the cycle of planting and harvest. Today they carried out deliveries at minimum wage, or spent their days driving creaking old farm machinery, breathing diesel fumes and dust, or working in a cloud of stink from the reeking muck spreader that they towed.

Sometimes, one of these casual workers crewed on a passing fishing boat for a few weeks, klondyke-ing the fish for the few months that the season lasted. They were the bottom of the social pyramid, always one payday away from absolute financial disaster, relying on an increasingly fragile benefits system to keep going.

Morgan Richards and his family were the bottom layer of this stratum. The family tree of the Richards was hopelessly tangled and inbred, mostly staying just this side of legal. There were five Richards children born to Jenny, a woman so downtrodden that she seemed to have dust gathered in the creases of her face. At some point in the past, she had suffered a brain bleed of some kind and the left side of her mouth was drawn down in a perpetual sneer. Three of their children were no longer living in their wreck of a cottage, north of the village. It stood there alone, as if it had been cast out of respectable society. Of those three children, one was presently resident in Exeter Prison, and two were permanent residents of psychiatric care, suffering from inhcrited damage so profound that not even care in the community could offer them a place.

So much could be said of more than a few families, out in the more rural areas, but for the Richards, their nemesis was the rumour mill. It was held, among the regular group that gathered in the village shop, that not only had Morgan and his ill-used partner engaged in sexual congress with various of their daughters, but that they had encouraged the boys of the clan to join in.

Social services swooped one early morning and the whole brood was taken into care. The rumour was helped by the members of the family who had suffered massive genetic damage over the years, but for once, the clan held together and raised a wall of silence, and in the end, the remaining children were returned, through lack of solid evidence of any wrongdoing.

Nothing was ever proved, but the constant warning signs lived on, and in the village, the Richards family were regarded with disdain. Credit at the village shop, even credit on the basis of the usual, 'Drop it in the next time you're by, my bird', kind was cut off. Morgan found that the work situation dwindled and dried up. No one was willing to employ him, even on a day-by-day basis.

He took to drinking rough Alembic, a fiery spirit illicitly imported across the water from Brittany, by passing Breton crabbers. Days slipped by him in a stupor of drunken unconsciousness. He missed the fortnightly signing on appointments, and benefits, the family's one sure source of income, dried up. One day there was not even food enough to make a meal, and the power had long since been disconnected. That night, the only light that showed was the yellow glow of the old paraffin lamps. Somehow there was still enough cash to pay for drink. Finally, there came a day when there was nothing left in the house, no food, no money for the meters, no heat, no light. Two kids and two adults were trapped in the dingy little Cornish unit local authority home on the bare plot in the outskirts.

All human beings, from the strong, affluent, and well positioned, to the bottom of the social heap, have a breaking point.

Morgan Richards's old grandfather, a scabrous old wreck of a man whose vocabulary was so limited and repetitious that he was known in the village as 'fucking Morgan', had brought the gun back from his time in the army. His military service had been as disreputable as everything else in his life, ending in a dishonourable discharge and a spell in the Aldershot military prison.

How he smuggled the old .445 Webley in, from a posting in the disputed territory of Palestine during the chaotic days of the aftermath of the Balfour declaration, was a mystery. And how, having achieved that, he had contrived to transport both the gun and the five cardboard boxes of ammunition home to the South West, was a secret that he never vouchsafed to anyone, even in his cups. However he had achieved it, the gun had lurked in the cubby under the stairs among the dust and the spiders ever since.

There was no premeditation in the elder Morgan owning the gun. It was just that, as he saw matters, the world had treated him badly, and he wanted to be sure that, if he ever needed to hit back, he would be ready. As it happened, there was never an occasion to use it, but the old man had left the weapon in its hiding place. A few years later, as the lung cancer that ended his miserable existence crept onwards, and the pain began to gnaw away at him with its sharp, ratty little teeth, he had completely forgotten that the Webley existed.

His eldest son, and the current Morgan Richards's father, had never even known of the revolver lurking there in the cupboard, but his son, exploring as boys will, had found it there, even before his father had taken a long sea voyage, crewing on a tanker out of Falmouth, and somehow forgotten the way home to his wife and six children.

As he grew to manhood, Morgan Richards the third, became every bit as scabrous as his grand-daddy and considerably more ill-tempered than his wandering father.

Secretly, during the early morning hours when the world slept, he had considered, many times, how that secret, illicit revolver might come in useful. He had thought of robbery, but common sense suggested that that was more likely to lead to a long sentence rather than a life of luxury.

That last night, as he listened sleeplessly to the old house creaking around him, smelling the smell of bitter poverty in the stuffy air, and watching the first sliver of the moon rising out of the sea outside the window, it came to him what the gun was really for. It was as if the path ahead of him was suddenly illuminated, as if it had always been there, just waiting for this moment of realisation.

His ill-used and ill-favoured woman lay beside him, either sleeping, or else too afraid to move in case she drew his attention. Her breathing was slow and regular. For a moment, he considered that it might be nice to rape her one last time before he did what he had to do. He had often raped her before.

The night closed in round him like dark crystal, shimmering and strangely transparent. Finally, ignoring the sleeping woman, he went downstairs, not taking any real care to move quietly. The under stairs cupboard was pitch dark but he knew exactly where to go.

The Webley was heavy in his hand but it was clean and shiny as if he had oiled it just yesterday, even though, as far as he knew, the gun had not been touched for thirty years and more. He released the catch, and the gun obediently fell open, exposing the empty cylinder. Almost without thought, because, by then, the time for thought was past, he opened the dull brown square cardboard box of ammunition. It was stamped on the top in faded smeary green lettering, '.445 ball pistol'.

He shook out the shells into the palm of his hand, heavy, greasy, lead slugs with dull brass casings. He loaded them, one by one, until two were left in his palm, and he dropped them to the floor indifferently. Six would be enough. He closed the gun, relishing the heavy snap of the locating spring. Just to be sure, he thumbed the hammer back and made sure that it locked cleanly at the full cock position.

Finally with preparations done, he mounted the stairs one by one towards his sleeping family.

CHAPTER TWENTY-ONE

In Cornwall, as in many such rural areas, emergency health response services are faced with an essential problem. A scattered population, together with an infrastructure that is pretty well stuck in the late nineteenth century, means that ambulance response times are a constant headache. Simply put, the distances are too great, the road system too narrow and convoluted, and the lone helicopter that is available for ambulance response is too often unavailable.

To an extent, a partial solution is to disperse response vehicles, and the sight of an ambulance or a first response estate car parked in a lay-by in some out of the way rural spot is a common sight in Cornwall. Even then, there are areas with well-spaced villages and many isolated farms, where emergency cover is difficult, and patchy. The answer is an expansion of the first responder scheme.

Originally, it was designed to allow trained members of the public to get quickly to an accident scene, so that they might stabilise casualties until the emergency team arrived. Among the volunteers, a few GP practices had taken up the baton of emergency care, standing ready to cover their area and provide care until more conventional cover arrived. It sounds far more onerous a duty than it is in practice. The number of serious incidents in a given area was very small, so Jonathan Wilde had no especial problems in carrying a pager, but, that early morning when it started its regular high-pitched bleeping at three thirty, and the tiny green LED flashed away in time to the bleep, it was unwelcome.

Sally, heavy with her late pregnancy, was finally asleep.

Her growing bulge was accompanied by a rise in body temperature, so much so that simply lying under the lightest of covers was enough to make her uncomfortably hot. Most of the bedding, duvet, sheets and all, was shoved across to Jonathan's side of the bed. He slipped out from under the heap, trying to disturb Sally as little as possible. The night air was cool against his skin in contrast. She grumbled sleepily and he caught her scent, warm and musky and somehow comforting. He pressed the button to silence the pager, thus acknowledging the call out and calling up the incident address on the three-inch screen. Eight, Trelawney Villas – the Richards's house.

It was less than a half mile away. Jonathan, fully awake now, slipped out of the room and picked up his phone from the bedside table as he went. Outside on the landing, and far enough away from Sally to avoid waking her, he thumbed the phone open and dialled the Response Centre number.

"Doctor Wilde," he said as the receptionist responded. "I have a call out to Trelawney Villas in Tregadrew." He listened for a moment then said, "Oh I see, okay, I'm on my way. Log the ETA as five minutes. The police are responding as well, of course? Yes, thanks for that."

The bag was sitting in its accustomed place beside the front door. It was bright green with reflective straps that glittered in the light. Jonathan picked it up along with the ignition keys, on the way out.

Ten minutes later, he was first on the scene, first, that is, of the official response. There was one other person waiting in the early dawn light, an older man dressed in a heavy rather shabby fawn Mac over his nightclothes. At the open neck of the coat, grey hairs stuck out in a tuft.

Jamie Tregenna, sometime farm labourer and local builder's mate, whose skinny, white, blue veined shanks stuck out of his raincoat like the support of a scarecrow, stood there.

"Dr Wilde," said Jamie. "Good to see you, boy. I'm sorry to drag you out. I called 999, so I expected an ambulance."

"They'll be along soon, but I'm nearer. What's the problem, Jamie? Not Doreen, I hope?"

"No, Doctor. She's still asleep, bless her. Slept through it all she did. It's next door. Old Morgan's place. I heard things in the night."

"Things?" queried Jonathan.

"Gunshots, Doctor. Maybe I'm wrong, but I know a gun when I hear it."

Jamie was a notorious local poacher, so Jonathan let that go as an accepted truth.

"So, that's all it was, Jamie?" he said. "Shots in the night? You are sure someone wasn't out lamping in the back field?"

"It was no fucking shotgun, that, Doctor. Pardon my language, but the fact is, it was a rifle, or maybe a pistol round, sounds different like."

"Okay. Have you actually seen anything, Jamie?"

"No. Not really. Thought I'd better wait. At least I did after I looked through the letterbox, like…"

"And?"

"Blood, Doctor. There's a fucking great pool of blood."

Jonathan Wilde took a rapid glance through the letterbox slot, and, looking at the pool of blood in the hallway, it seemed just as big as Jamie had suggested it might be. Jonathan was well aware that someone had to be carrying a really serious injury. No one loses that much of their blood volume without serious damage, but Jamie had mentioned multiple gunshots and going blindly into what might well be a very dangerous situation would help no one.

Jonathan lowered his head to the letterbox again and shouted through it. He felt a fool like a bit part player in a bad TV drama.

"It's the doctor, Morgan," he shouted, as if that professional reassurance, and a wooden door, might fend off the bullets. "What's going on, mate? There's no need to be afraid. I'm here to help."

There was no reply. Nothing, just silence. The house was as quiet as the grave.

Out on the doorstep, the dawn was starting to give a cold, feeble bluish light as the new day started. There was still no sound of approaching two tones, no flicker of blue lights.

Jonathan tried again, shouting through the letterbox, still feeling a fool.

"Morgan," he shouted. "Please, if you can hear me, shout back if you can. Otherwise, I'll come in. Is that okay? Please, Morgan, try to tell me what's going on."

More silence. It was smooth, and eloquent in its way.

Jonathan turned to Jamie, and said, "Have you got anything we could use to break in, Jamie? A spade maybe, or a screwdriver even. I don't know, anything…"

Jamie opened the lid of an ancient concrete coal bunker that stood beside the front door and rooted through the dusty webs inside. He came up with an ancient axe. It was rusty and pitted and the haft was silvery with age and worn silky smooth with years of use.

"Will this do, Doctor?" he asked.

"I reckon. Stand back, Jamie. Let me get a good swing."

The door was old and riddled with patches of dry rot under the peeling cream and brown paint. One blow did the job, as the woodwork parted company from the hinges and the door lay in the hallway like a fallen warrior.

Jonathan, reluctant even then to cross the threshold, tried calling again. He shouted, "Morgan, are you there? It's the doctor. Can you hear me? Anyone there? Just make a noise so that I can find you."

Nothing, just a bloodstained house, that smelled like a butcher's shop on a hot summer day. With the first sunlight starting to flood through the windows, golden light penetrated to illuminate the night's carnage.

There was no way to avoid the blood, but Jonathan tiptoed through it as if that might help matters. He realised suddenly that he was holding his breath, half expecting a shot from cover. Nothing came. He pushed gently against the door to his right, the door that led, he thought, into the front downstairs room.

Morgan was sitting in the chair to the left of the fireplace, the Webley still in his mouth like an iron lollypop. Most of the back of his head was sprayed over the dirty beige paintwork of the wall behind him in a splatter of blood, brains and shards of shattered bone. Jonathan didn't bother to check that Morgan was dead. There really wasn't any point, but somewhere in his racing thoughts was relief that he had located and neutralised the gun as a risk. The chance of a second weapon never even occurred to him.

Leaving Morgan's body, Jonathan climbed the creaking old stairs, stopping twice to call out, to see if anyone was still alive, though even then, he was pretty sure that it was a waste of time.

Jenny Morgan lay in the bed she had shared with her husband. There was a single blackened scorch mark in the very centre of her forehead, placed there, as if by some fastidious draftsman with symmetry in mind. The pillow under her head was clotted and thick with blood.

The kids were in the other bedroom, a boy and a girl, still in their nightclothes. The boy was lying under the window, and Jonathan's relentless analytical brain insisted that he could envisage exactly how it had happened. The girl killed while she was either still asleep or cowering in bed, the boy killed trying to make a last desperate bid for the outside. He had been shot twice, once in the centre of the back, high up between the shoulder blades, and the second round the killer fired had been into the top of his head.

The girl had died of a single gun-shot. Five rounds fired, Jonathan's relentless interior analyst told him. He saved the last one for himself.

Outside in the distance, the first faint echoes of two tones wafted on the breeze. They were coming closer. Outside the sun was hauling itself out of the east, climbing into the sky as if nothing was different. It was going to be another lovely day.

Jonathan Wilde, processed like any other witness, gave his statement and signed at the top and bottom of each sheet of laboriously handwritten text.

From the start it seemed that the police had formed conclusions as to the circumstances. Morgan was a drunk and a wife beater, with a long train of petty violence behind him. Where he had come by the weapon was a minor mystery, but to be realistic, it was only one of dozens of obsolete, but still lethal, bits of war debris that litter the country, even seventy odd years after the event.

It was just another small tragedy of isolated rural life.

CHAPTER TWENTY-TWO

Hannah Wilson, the village witch, whose slant on matters was rather different to that of most of the villagers, saw things rather differently. Her belief system, eccentric though others found it, led her to a constant search for patterns in the run of events. To Hannah, the random shifts of circumstance were evidence of the workings of other forces that turned the great wheels of universal existence. A run of tragic events in the small geographical area was a case in point. Her problem was that to convince other people of the dangers that she saw in the sequence, was going to be difficult.

That young doctor for instance, a nice enough young man. He was clever, no doubt, but he really believed that the world of solid objects, and simple causes, was all that there was. He even thought that you could capture time in a pretty little dial and carry it on your wrist like a captive in chains. Hannah, with one foot in the other world whose existence most of the village might have suspected, even if they did not openly accept it, thought very differently. Knowing what she did was one thing, but convincing the young doctor, even though that was vital, was something else. Villagers who were faced with adverse circumstances would comfort each other by saying that the events were, 'not the end of the world', the problem now was that Hannah was not really even sure of the truth of that.

Hannah had been a pagan since her very first encounter with the belief system when her old grandmother Betty had initiated her into the ways of the craft at the age of fourteen, but she was already very much a child of nature long before that.

Hannah had a reverence for life that was almost obsessive. If one of her three cats brought home a mouse, and the fields at the back of her cottage teemed with them, Hannah would carefully rescue the furry scrap, gently recovering it from where it hung in the cat's jaws.

That done, she would warm it on a hot water bottle wrapped in a towel, and then she would nurse the creature back to health before freeing it again into the cool of the evening. Even when the mice invaded her home, she would take no direct action against them. Instead of laying traps, she burned a pungent mixture of herbs that filled the little rooms with a strange smelling vapour that drove the creatures to seek less inhospitable accommodation elsewhere.

Thus far Hannah Wilson was no different to hundreds of others in the South West, most of them people who held a sort of wistful nostalgia for a mythical past when things were simpler and people lived in harmony with the world rather than trying to dominate it. But the fact was that Hannah, for all her twenty-first century exterior, was the inheritrix of a very long tradition that reached back, probably to the time when the people of the peninsula wore little clothing, aside from body paint. Those same people had developed a reputation so violent that even the Romans, that notable group of proto-fascists, never really extended their conquests so far south, preferring instead to trade.

Hannah certainly had the 'sight' as she referred to it. She had the ability, simply by force of will, to tear the veil of time and space and look into the infinitely malleable future to consider the possible versions of events that might yet come about.

She also, as a matter of fact, had a globe of rock crystal on her table, in pride of place in her cottage. It was a mighty, heavy, lump with a surface polished to a mirror finish, but in truth, it was no more than a symbol. Her real gift, the real ability of foresight, was an interior thing. It was not dependant on physical props to support it.

That late summer afternoon, Hannah was troubled. Lately, she had felt it coming, the shadow of an event that presaged her own ending. Her unease was far deeper than that. Hannah had no fear of her coming death, though she had no great wish to cross the divide, but what was coming was far more profound than that.

That night, as the villagers sat inside their houses, behind doors that were securely locked, many of them locked for the first time in decades, the village came to terms with old Morgan's massacre of his family.

Hannah sat at her table, by the light of a dark blue candle whose wick burned with a clear lilac flame. In front of her, there was a thurible, a small brass cauldron on three sturdy feet that prevented the contents scorching the surface under it. It was a family heirloom, and its surface was embossed with an intaglio of strange designs. It contained a pellet of charcoal, a compressed tablet originally intended for use in church incense burners. That was the nature of the craft, always changing, using those modern adaptations, as they arose, but always closely following the spirit of the ancient ways,

She took a pinch of dried leaves, crushed to a greyish-looking powder, in her hand. They were a mixture of herbs. Vervain, legend-haunted Mandrake, Bryony and

Foxglove root, all of them herbs associated with the sight. There was also just a touch, no more than a little, like the seasoning of a fine recipe for a classic dish, of Datura seeds. The Angel's Trumpet is a plant that is a rarity in the north, that grows well in Cornwall. Datura was the one plant whose effects outsiders might well understand. Datura, with its powerful hallucinogenic properties, is, in itself, a way to tear the veil.

Hannah used her left hand to pour the mixture onto the glowing charcoal and the smoke rose, bluish in the candlelight. Breathing deeply of the incense of seeing, Hannah felt her head swimming from the purely physical effects of the fumes. Presently, her head cleared, and at that moment, the sight was on her.

Hours later, when she woke, in her chair, with the candle guttering out, and a crick in her neck, she knew what it was that she had to do. In the cold fireplace a mouse was scurrying. It favoured her with a glance from its beady little eyes. Presently, it found a crevice in the skirting and vanished. Hannah's older cat, jet black Mystic, watched the creature with his wise, sea green eyes, ears pointed towards it, but he made no move to catch it. Outside, the new day was breaking.

CHAPTER TWENTY-THREE

Sally, who was temporarily alone while Jonathan attended to the business of morning surgery, was enjoying the morning. The disruption of the village life by tragedy, impinged on her life, but it impinged at the fringes, like an event from far away. The horrors of that summer were like a famine in a faraway land, cruel, and dreadful in themselves, but somehow lacking in reality, and emotional tone. Besides, her pregnancy had reached the third trimester stage where she felt relaxed and easy with herself, looking forward to her new status as a mother, as well as Jonathan's wife.

She was sitting in the big leather upholstered chair in the front room, reading. The tome balanced on her bulge was a Winston Graham, one of the Poldark series, a gentle escapist piece of beautifully crafted fiction. It also had the advantage of weaving into the storyline the background of the land and sea all round her. Sally supposed that she was in that stage of pregnancy when intellectual effort was growing less important, and for a time at least, she was content with that.

Presently, there was a knock at the front door. Sally climbed to her feet, a little unsteadily, as the unaccustomed weight of the bulge had shifted her point of balance a little.

Outside the front door, Sally could see a vague shape through the stained-glass panels. She opened it, expecting nothing more challenging than a salesman trying to interest her in some useless product or other.

Hannah stood there, an ageing hippy in a kaftan with

a plethora of beads and amulets about her. Her arms were skinny, and the silver bangles on her deeply tanned forearms clinked slightly as she moved.

She said, "Sally Wilde? I'm Hannah Wilson, I expect that you've heard of me around the village, most people have."

"Surely," said Sally. "I've seen you around the village. What can I do for you, Hannah?"

"Well," said Hannah. "Maybe we could talk inside. It's all right, I'm not dangerous, no matter what they might tell you about me turning people into wildlife."

Sally could only laugh. This woman was one of those people who she felt instinctively that she could trust. She said, "I'll bear that in mind. And I promise to be very kind to any toad I happen to meet about the place."

And right away, just like that, they were friends.

CHAPTER TWENTY-FOUR

They were sitting in the Wilde's living room, drinking coffee. Sally had restricted her intake to three cups a day during her pregnancy, but she was willing, on this occasion, to make an exception.

Hannah took a decorous sip from her coffee. "I expect you were wondering why I have come to see you."

"Well, you are welcome, of course," said Sally, "but I must admit I was wondering."

"Right. Well, first things first. I'd best get this out of the way before we start. You do know that I am a witch?"

"I hear what they say. I don't take village gossip seriously in any case, but, to be honest, Hannah, your religious beliefs don't trouble me. It's between you and your own mind. I've always found that people who attack other people on grounds of religion are usually pretty crazy themselves. You know the type… 'My God is bigger than your God', my father used to say."

Hannah smiled to herself. She said, "That makes it a bit easier. But in any case, ladies like you… well on in pregnancy… well, you all have a touch of the sight in you."

"I suppose," said Sally, not sure where all this was going.

"You know that the baby is a girl, don't you?" said Hannah.

"We haven't asked. I could have at the thirty-week scan but we didn't."

"Sorry to spoil the surprise, but it's clear as day that that's a little maid that you're carrying, dear. She'll do great things, will that child of yours, great things."

"Thank you," said Sally. "At least, I think so."

"This is harder than I thought it might be, dear," said Hannah. "But there's something that might convince you. After you find out the truth, come back to me and we'll think what's best to do."

"All this is very interesting, Hannah," said Sally. "But honestly…"

"I know. You don't believe a single word of it."

"Well," said Sally. "I believe that you mean well, Hannah, I really do."

"If I ask you to do something, will you give it a try?"

"That depends."

"It's nothing frightening, my dear. I just want you to take a look at your family history for me. Your aunty lived here her whole life, didn't she?"

"Aunty June? She was my mother's sister. Mother used to say that the family have been here in Cornwall since God knows when."

"Look back to where you came from, Maid. That's all I ask of you. After that… well, if you don't want to talk to me, all well and good. Will you do that for me, at least a bit?"

"Why, Hannah? What do you know that I need to find?"

"Maybe nothing, dear. And if there's nothing to find, then I'm wrong, and you can put this down to a visit from a daft old hippy lady. But I feel I'm in the way of knowing that it's important to all of us that you find out the truth. Well, I'll leave you to your afternoon. Blessed be, dear."

"Thank you."

Three days after her visit to Sally, Hannah was sitting alone in her cluttered little living room in the cottage. Mystic the cat, home from his night's hunting, was asleep on an old bean bag that conformed perfectly to his body. Aside from her cats, Hannah lived alone, and apart from the odd visits from villagers who came almost furtively to her door to ask her advice on some small problem or other, Hannah was usually alone from dusk to early morning.

As it happened that suited her very well. Her ex-husband George had always regarded her eccentric cultural practices as something to be tolerated with a sort of amused interest even when they were together. He loved Hannah dearly then, and before the collapse of the dairy farm wrecked the easy pace of his life, he always felt that, if burning a few herbs and reading the cards made her happy, he was quite willing to go along with it.

In fact, George would have been the first to admit that every now and then her abilities came in handy. That time he had mislaid the keys to a forage harvester and Hannah had gone right to them, where they lay on the barn floor, for instance. What Hannah was planning might have given him cause for thought though. Casual observance of the old ways, and a little use of second sight was one thing, ritual magic was something else.

Hannah actually had little use for the great ceremonial rituals. She found the classic works on ceremonial magic sedative rather than majestic. The great key of Solomon the Wise, the lesser key, the Lemegeton, with its constant ranking of supposed 'daemons' into aristocratic subdivisions, as if the other world was ordered by the protocol of the British House of Lords, they were all familiar ground. Hannah had read them all, but all too often, she found that they confused the craft with Satanism and many of their 'arcane rituals' were nothing more, at heart, than simply sticking two fingers up to the rituals of the established Catholic church.

To Hannah, who was interested only in the real powers that drove the universe, such adolescent crudities were less objects of fear than objects of complete ridicule. Magicians of the Crowley school of thought, to Hannah's way of thinking, were about as powerful as a twelve-year-old who deliberately farts during a quiet prayer in a cathedral.

All that said, there were rituals that she was familiar with, though they were rarely used. They were the ceremonies that had real power, not its hollow appearance. Such things were not to be set in motion casually, but there were times when they had a place. Methodically, checking each step of her preparations like a chef following a complex recipe, she began her preparations.

The circle was old, the stones that formed its perimeter had stood on that site for three thousand years. They had been set upright with a terrible cost in human labour, when the shamans of the bronze age tribe that had lived on the site, had first realised that this place, the small, nearly circular patch of nondescript ground, was sacred, and always had been.

Hannah stood, naked to the late summer evening air, intoning the old words under her breath. She had no real fear of being interrupted standing there, naked in open air. Before she began, she had used her craft to prepare a zone of repulsion around the stones. Anyone passing by, from wandering amorous couples, to adventurous hikers, whoever approached that night, would suddenly find that they had good reason to turn aside, and leave the circle to itself.

Within the flat clearing, among the stones, Hannah placed her offerings at the cardinal points. Small cones of incense smoked and produced coils of blue vapour that rose straight into the still air.

Facing the rising moon, Hannah began the summoning. Once, long ago that would have been the point of blood sacrifice, but Hannah knew that such symbolic cruelty was not needed to achieve the call. All that was really needed, was to understand the nature of the being that was called.

Outside her circle, but still within the outer perimeter of the stones, was a small equilateral triangle marked out in the earth. This was the triangle of manifestation, where whatever answered the call would be confined.

Without its secure boundary, the results of the calling might well prove dangerous. As Hannah watched and the moon rose higher into the sky, a misty nebulous form came into being inside the triangle. At the same moment, the circle in which she stood, reacting to the threat that was so close, began to take on a violet flicker of spectral light that glowed round its perimeter.

Speaking, apparently to nothingness, Hannah said, in a level calm voice, as if she were addressing an acquaintance, "Show yourself. You are summoned by the ancient rites. You cannot disobey the call."

There was no reply, at least not in words, but the misty form in the triangle began to take on more solidity, which, in its way, was answer enough.

"Why are you troubling the village?" said Hannah in

that same conversational tone. "Why, old one? You have no place interfering in the ways of men. Why have you torn the veil of the boundary?"

Nothing, no concrete reply. Just a shadow of a form and the suggestion of an infinitely old face looking back at her from incredibly old eyes.

Hannah tried again. "You are bound," she said, "bound by the laws that govern all things and all beings. You have no place on this plane of existence."

Around the perimeter of the protective circle, the violet flicker of light shimmered, pulsing as if it were being tested against a force that was almost, but not quite, its equal.

Hannah was, for the first time, afraid. Until that point, she had faith in the barrier that the circle represented. She made a great inner effort. To lose concentration now would be a disaster.

She said, "You cannot cross the barrier, old one. You cannot."

But there was just a shadow of doubt in her voice as she said it, and, in such matters, the shadow of a doubt is more than enough.

Desperate now, Hannah fell back on the ancient rituals of defence. She said in a loud, very clear voice, "I conjure you, old one. I am a servant of the white. You cannot cross the barrier. Go back to the plane where you belong."

The lilac light on the circle boundary was flickering now, guttering like a candle, and the shape crossed from the triangle, breaking its boundary as if it was no more solid than a spider web. Suddenly, it stood on the very edge of the protective circle. Hannah, seeing that, knew that she was in desperate mortal danger. Not for her spirit… this creature, whatever it was, was not of the order of beings that could threaten that. But it was from the outer circle, and in its own brutish way, powerful.

It was her body, that frail mantle of flesh that carried her through the world, that was threatened. And, as she allowed that smidgeon of doubt to grow inside her, the defences that had seemed so secure, hallowed as they were by thousands of years of use, came down and failed like a weak old dam in a torrential river.

She had time for one thought before the dark one took her across the boundary.

'May the woman be strong enough to take you, monster,' she thought. 'If the Dumb Supper holds.'

Afterwards, a few hours later, as the late summer dawn lit up the circle, there was nothing much to see, just four scorched cones of herbs that sat among the trampled grass. Of Hannah, there was no sign except for her clothes lying neatly folded outside the circle.

CHAPTER TWENTY-FIVE

Sally Wilde went into spontaneous labour on the eighteenth of August, on a day when summer was starting to show its age in golden light and a light chill in the air, during the gradually encroaching hours of darkness. As always in the South West, the payoff for the lengthening days of late spring that seem to come earlier in Cornwall than in the rest of the UK, is that in the autumn, the nights rapidly draw down, as the long days of summer begin to erode towards the gales of winter.

She was exactly three days beyond her due date, not so far over that they needed to be considering induction yet. Also, as Jonathan Wilde was in the mildly annoying habit of pointing out, it wasn't an exact science, especially when the start point of the whole process was not precise.

For three days and more, she had felt an obscure restless sensation, as if some inner clock had decided that it was time that something happened. She wandered the house from room to room, vacuuming carpets that needed no more cleaning, and batting away dust that was hardly there to start with.

Sally had heard of this restless pre-delivery mood that comes to women in the few days before the actual process of labour starts. But now that it was actually on her, she appreciated how all-pervading the process was.

For weeks now she had woken in the small hours plagued by Braxton Hicks contractions that threatened always to develop into the real thing before subsiding again to the background cramping dull ache. At first, Sally thought that this was yet another episode of the same, but presently, as she was sitting rather awkwardly, in the kitchen on a tall stool, she was aware of a trickle of liquid. For a few moments, she simply sat there, appreciating the enormity of it all, then finally she picked up the phone.

"Angie," she said to the duty receptionist who picked up the surgery phone. "It's Sally Wilde. I've started. Could you tell Jonathan as soon as you get a break in proceedings. I think I'd better get down to the unit."

The midwife-led maternity unit was one of those amiable hangovers of rural life that survived amid the far-flung edges of the monolithic NHS. It was a small, twin ward facility, with only two separate delivery rooms, and it was staffed, almost exclusively, by local midwives who ran all the essential services.

Sally, who was more aware of all of the shortcomings than most of such a system, was still determined to give birth on the unit. It was a long way from the clinical sterile excellence of the big hospital unit at Truro, but it had something less tangible, and more satisfying, about it. The midwife unit was not run like a production line and it was simply nearer to home.

Jonathan Wilde was at the delivery. In a way, as a doctor, he was in a false position, but in the end, he accepted the role of first-time father and simply supported Sally where he could, while the midwives did their necessary and rather undignified work.

Presently, after seven hours or so of sweaty, arduous labour, he was presented with a red-faced bundle of miniature humanity. She was wrapped in a white towel that was streaked with blood and fluids, and covered in white meconium. She was bawling at the abrupt awakening from her long nine-month dream of being, into a world of air and light and sounds and strange, antiseptic smells.

Jonathan held his new daughter. She was, as Hannah had promised, a perfect infant girl, and, holding her, he wondered, as always, at the events that bookend a human life.

Sally, tired and spent, submitted to the stitching and horrors of the pudendal block, gratefully drank a cup of awful hospital tea, and cuddled her new daughter. By the time she was finally put gently to bed in a hospital cot that had the look of a plastic fish tank, Sally was able to achieve a fitful doze. The baby was wrapped in a close-fitting blanket to simulate the close confinement that she had so recently left. Both mother and baby rested, the one in a deep sleep, the other in a sort of restless half drowse that follows labour.

Thus, it was that Siran Wilde, first of her family to be Cornish-born for fifty years and more, made her debut into the world. Jonathan and Sally were delighted by their ever more demanding new addition, and for the first three months of her life, as the nights drew in and the weather edged towards late autumn, everything was peaceful in Tregadrew.

The letter that changed all of that came in the first week of October on a warm village morning, when it seemed that the sun had decided to stay on for the winter rather than going south. Sally had been nursing Siran, a process that she found uniquely satisfying. At the start there had been some pain, and, in any case, her feminist beliefs, carefully tended for the formative years of her singleton existence, had always led her to a belief that women were far more than mothers, and child bearers. Breast feeding seemed to go against a good deal of all she had believed for so long. In the face of those things there was a simple overwhelming, instinctive need. There were a few difficult moments at the start, but, thankfully, for all of them, Sally made the gentle transition into motherhood with good grace and not a small degree of satisfaction.

It was a strange rather unexpected transition for Sally, yet in many ways it was the most normal of changes.

In her youth she had embraced the tenets of feminism and regarded the bearing of children with a degree of suspicion, if not actually as an instrument of the global patriarchy.

With Siran in her arms, with the warm reality of a helpless infant depending on her completely, Sally was overwhelmed by the sheer emotion of it all. She had expected that she would bond with her newborn, what she had not expected was the almost primal reaction to the whole process.

As a new mother Sally had a hitherto unexpected route into the magic circle of village mothers. As Siran grew into a healthy, happy infant who was just beginning to make articulated sounds that might be possibly words, or perhaps just an example of doting parental wish-fulfilment, Sally found herself sharing her experience with the other young mothers of the group and liking it. Most of all, with the birth of Siran, Sally felt that she and Jonathan had finally become a real part of the community, integrated into the great stream of time that reached backwards into the past and forwards, like a mighty river, into the unknowable future. They were, from then on, rooted in the place, in the most intimate way.

It was a fundamental thing, this sense of belonging to

a place that was so strong that it seemed nothing could disturb that bond. And then, one morning, the letter came and everything changed.

CHAPTER TWENTY-SIX

The letter was in a long white envelope. It was the sort of thing that, as often as not, contained a flyer from the local estate agent. The property market in rural Cornwall had rocketed yet again, and it had spawned a long succession of chancers trying to generate a sale. Sally opened it, expecting to chuck the contents straight into the recycling bin. Inside, instead of an estate agent's flyer, there was a hand written missive on blue paper.

The paper itself was thick and heavily finished, and that, with the script in dark blue fountain pen ink, gave the whole letter a rather stately, old-fashioned appearance. Sally quickly realised as she skimmed through to the signature at the bottom of the last page it was from Hannah Wilson.

Hannah's abrupt vanishing had been a nine-day wonder earlier in the year, but there were those in the village who claimed that George had never been much of a husband to the free spirited and kaftan sporting Hannah. They said that there were matters to be taken care of before she grew too old. Some of the gossip at the Post Office counter had placed her in a relationship with a fine young student bar worker from Polkerris way, a tall lad with roofbeam shoulders and, they whispered rather more quietly, an unusual level of endowment hidden in those faded, tight fitting, jeans of his.

Others said that Hannah had just taken herself off to find herself some space. The truth of Hannah's strange disappearance had never been considered. Even the clothes she left behind had been shredded by small animals for bedding, and carried away for nesting materials, long before they were noticed.

Now, from wherever she was, here was Hannah, communicating with the village that she had left behind.

'Dear Sally,' the letter began, *'First off I need to congratulate you, maid, on having your new one safely. It's the gift of the goddess to women to give birth to new life, and I salute you for it.*

When we last talked, I sort of hinted that sometime in the future I might need to call you to help with something that you might find strange and a little scary. I know your feller don't believe in such things, and that's well and good. We all find our own way to the truth, but it's you I have to ask, maid, no one else.

Things might settle down yet, and, if they do, this letter will never be sent, but I'm in the way of knowing that there are things here in Tregadrew that won't rest, left to themselves.

I can almost hear you saying, tis as clear as if I was standing there by you, "The old fool has finally lost it," you're thinking. "All that magic rots your brains." Well, you must believe as you will, maid, but I need to prove what I'm saying before we go any further.

This village to start with, well, it goes back a long, long way, maid, and over the years things have got no better. Something in this village needs cruel happenings, like we need water to drink. You don't believe that, not yet anyway, so what I want you to do is to look back at the history of the place and see if there is a pattern there. I can't point you at the happenings, dear, but a bright girl like you will surely see what's right in front of your face.

So, here's where to start. Look at what happened here in 1647, lover. And again in 1775 and then in 1823 and onwards.

If you see the pattern then you'll understand why you need to act, for yourself, for your man and for your little maid. There is a way, even now, that I can help you through it, but you'll need to use the

Dumb Supper. It means nothing? Of course it don't, why would it? But later, I reckon you'll understand what's needed. If you call me, maid, I'll come in honest love.

Your friend
Blessed be, lover.
Hannah Wilson.'

It was three days afterwards that Hannah's body was found, floating in the cove just outside the surf line. Again, it was a nine-day wonder, accepted as things are always accepted, perhaps more so because Hannah had transgressed the boundaries of normal village life.

The sea has always taken life as well as giving it, and the villagers were more willing to ascribe sad natural causes to Hannah's death than they might have done for a more conformist member of the community.

Sally was of course still incredibly busy, in the way that first time mothers are always busy. For the first few weeks while they established a routine of feeding, changing and sleeping, Sally had time for nothing but her baby. Hannah's last letter, even though it had arrived only a few days before her body was found, hardly rippled the surface.

In less hectic times, Sally might have thought that it should really be sent on to the investigating authorities but with Hannah dead, and nothing in the letter to suggest that it might cast a new light on her demise, Sally was not keen to involve yet another time-consuming complication in her life.

She thought that, in any case, the letter reflected strangely on Hannah's state of mind, and she had no wish to cloud the reputation of the dead woman. Besides, Sally was in that rather detached state that follows a birth, when external events seem distant, almost irrelevant. Because of all those things, it was late in the old year before she finally had a few idle moments to fill and took a chance to go through accumulated emails and posts on her laptop.

In a way, in the serendipitous way of things, it was the laptop that made the whole thing possible. Hannah's final letter, no matter how deluded she might have been at the end, had suggested that there was a mysterious historical pattern of events to be found. Sally, like most human beings on the planet, could not resist investigating a mystery. It was the same basic drive that keeps people reading to the end, no matter how outre the plot. It was the need to discover what really happened.

CHAPTER TWENTY-SEVEN

Fifty years ago, searching though the records would have involved endless time-consuming trips to the county record offices in Truro and searching through acres of dusty files in poorly lit reference libraries. Now, thanks to an EU cultural grant, the records were all computerised, fully searchable, and available to anyone who was willing to invest the five pounds registration fee.

Sally was unusually idle that afternoon. And, as it happened, Hannah Wilson's final communication was at the top of the pile of flyers for local businesses, and unanswered communications. Siran, from the very start, was a peaceful baby, able, by the fourth week of her life, to sleep through the night, with only a brief interlude for a quick feed. That afternoon, she was sleeping peacefully in a carry cot while her mother rattled away on the keyboard beside her.

Almost casually, and not expecting any great revelations, Sally typed 'Tregadrew + Cornwall + 1647', and was rewarded with a long list of documents ranging from parish records of births and deaths, to bills of mortality for those long-ago days. The EU grant had not stretched to transposing the old documents and the images that came up were photographic, grainy and black and white. There were pages covered in spidery text that were blotched with ancient stains.

At the end of the list, one document set stood out: the trial record of one Patience 'Goody' Penrose, for 'consorting with the devil, Witchcraft and Necromancy'. Trial held before the magistrate and justice Simon de

Montford. The trial listed witnesses, such as they were, and the verdict 'Guilty as charged' and the sentence 'To perish by flames in the village square and afterwards her mortal remains to be scattered at the shoreline'. The record ended with the words: 'Sentence was carried out on the following day'. Master William Hawkins, blacksmith, was to be paid three shillings for carrying out his duties as executioner, the fee to be a burden on parish funds.

The bald record, the simple statement of fact, reached out across the years in a series of single phrases. 'Guilty as charged, sentenced to perish by flames'. It was as if she could see the whole tragic, pointless scene in her mind's eye. One other detail stood out, the name of the justice who had overseen the trial, de Montford. It sounded Norman French. It also sounded familiar, her aunt June was a Mountford, descended from a long line of families in Tregadrew. There was family legend that they were distantly related to local aristocracy who had once lived in the manor house that stood outside the village boundary. The old place was long derelict now, the last tenant had left in the nineteen twenties and no one else had lived there since. Nowadays the building was nothing more than three grey stone walls with tracery of windows, empty of glass, that had once looked into the ballroom. The local kids, of course, claimed it was haunted.

Sally shook her head wonderingly. If the old family tradition was true then her distant ancestor had tried an old woman on a charge that made no sense, and then witnessed her execution. Thus far, Hannah Wilson's cryptic note was mirrored in reality.

Not really expecting anything, mildly interested as we all might be at discovering a dark episode in her long-gone family history, Sally typed in the second set of search parameters, 'Tregadrew + records + 1776', expecting nothing, intending only to pass a few minutes before making a fresh pot of coffee and waking Siran for her feed. What came up next started her looking into the historical events in earnest.

In 1776, Cornwall stood on the brink of a mining boom that would last for nearly two hundred years, only really coming to an end with the collapse of tin prices and the mass migrations of the 'Cousin Jacks', who gave Cornish mining technology, and Cornish engine houses, to hard rock mines all over the world.

Before the new Boulton and Watt engine, pumping water in Cornish mines was a hit and miss affair. Pumps were driven by huge waterwheels on the surface, and smaller wheels in manmade caverns below ground. In Cornwall, the water was the miners' enemy. Mines in Cornwall were ever wet.

In the North of the UK where coal, not metal, was the target, mines all too frequently filled with deadly gases, and accidental explosions were the major risk. Down in the West Country, hard rock bodies of ore produced no methane. Instead, huge volumes of water trapped in the pores of the rocks formed underground lakes and rivers that were a constant threat if they were breached, and a steady source of seepage into all the workings that effectively limited the depth of the tunnels. Water was the bane of Cornish mining, nowhere more so than at Wheal Jenny, the small single shaft working outside Tregadrew. The workings led down two hundred fathoms towards the great west lode where the rock was seamed through with rivers of ore that carried jewel-like green deposits of copper, black tin, arsenic, and even a low level of silver.

The pump was a steady regular beating heart to the mine. It was fed by a simple Cornish boiler and produced just about enough steam to keep the beam rocking and the long lengths of wooden rod that hauled water from the dark in steady motion. It needed a team of three enginemen to run it, endlessly shovelling coal into the furnace to keep the monster fed. Even starting the thing from rest was an exercise in ducking through levers and valves, edging the pressure up, cooling the condenser and observing the beam, that huge iron girder that had been cast not thirty miles from the mine at Harvey's iron works in Hayle. Finally, with that monster caught on the very edge of stasis, it reached the tipping point and edged itself into movement, the tonnes of dead weight hauling on the pump rod, straining against the weight of water down below until, finally, the weight was enough and the rods started to move. From there on, it was a regular routine, opening and closing valves, cooling the condenser, and injecting a fresh charge of steam, a regular mind-numbing routine, that went on hour after hour, in that near silence that seemed almost unearthly, given the size of the engine.

Down below, in the pitch dark of the ninety-fathom level, the only light was from the tallow candles on the miners' helmets, held in place by a dab of clay. The pump's steady breath, the wheeze and suck of the rods as they moved over the sleepers, greased with tallow that edged the rods past crooked places in the shaft, was a constant reassurance that all was well with the world. Even so, the air was foul. Not with the deadly fire damp but with the more homely smells of old sweat and human waste, and high humidity. At the working face, where the vein of ore ran counter to the adit and sloped steeply downwards, six miners were slamming away at the face with rock drills and sledgehammers. They worked, in teams of two hammer men and, between each pair, a young boy, maybe eight years old, was kneeling, turning the drill a half turn between blows of the hammers. That way the drill gradually hollowed out a circular cavity in the rock. It was a routine that would go on well into the nineteenth century, before the pneumatic rock drill was invented. Even then, the dust created was so toxic that the drilling crews called their drills the 'widow makers'. As for the boy, officially an apprentice, his job was more dangerous than it looked. Most drilling crews were practically deaf from the constant ring of hammer on steel and to communicate with the crew the lad had to indicate that the drill was no longer cutting cleanly by flicking his thumb across the striking face of the drill to tell them to stop hammering, so that the drill might be withdrawn and replaced. The used steels could be returned to the smithy above ground for sharpening, tempering, and re-use.

More than once a boy misjudged the rhythm, and his thumb would be crushed between the ten-pound hammer and the polished and splayed steel end of the drill.

Those were the sounds of the mine. The steady hammering of the drilling crews, the wheeze and thump of the pumps, the thud of a ventilation door as it was opened and closed in the dark to keep the airflow around the workings going. Then there was the blasting.

When the holes were made in the face, the powder team would come down, lugging a fifty-pound, copper bound barrel of black powder. In charge, was Richard Penhaligon, a veteran of the King's navy, and a master gunner, well used to the ways of powder. Routinely, he checked each barrel as it arrived from Kennal Vale mills where the stuff was made. Powder making was still as much an art as a science and the quality of the final product was variable.

The copper banding on the barrel was to avoid sparks. Black powder was at best volatile, unstable, crudely compounded, and none too reliable. The holes that the drill had made were carefully dried, filled one by one with powder and stemmed with a clay plug that would direct the force of the explosion into the rock. For each hole, there was a straw filled with loose powder sticking through the clay. Come the time, the lower workings of the mine were supposed to be cleared, then the powder man would take his candle and touch it to the end of the straw.

The powder burned fitfully, until finally it reached the main charge, then there was a week's hand work done in an instant. True, it filled the gallery with a foul-smelling sulphurous fume of grey smoke and they had to wait an hour or more until it cleared, to go in to clear the broken fragments.

It was that rough fusing that caused the problems. Most powdermen damped the powder in the fuses just a little so that it would smoulder down the length of the straw, rather than rushing the flame through to the charge as soon as the fuse was lit.

It was on the thirteenth of July 1776 that the system failed. There had been a fresh delivery of powder from the mills. Strictly, it was bad practice to take more powder down below than was needed for the day's work, but Richard was answerable to no one, except the mine owner, and he was an absentee landlord who only had an eye for the profit. The adit was driving through a hard area of rock, and blasting supplies were more ample than usual.

That morning there were three barrels of fifty pounds weight each, of fresh Kennel Vale corned powder stored at the deep level. The stack was covered with a rough brown tarpaulin and should really have been safe enough from stray sparks. After the men had returned to the level above, safe from the blast, Richard lit the straws and made a hasty retreat to a curve in the tunnel where he would be protected from the pressure wave.

There was first the roar of the explosions and then the rattle of displaced rock, then, as the thirty or so gathered miners who were underground that morning, relaxed, there was the usual small round of jokes that released the tension after a blast was done.

A spark floated in the dark after the blast. That spark was no more than a tiny clot of unburned powder, in the last stages of manufacture, when ripened powder cake was pressed and ground, small lumps of coarse powder often remaining in the finished product. Lumps were slow to burn and floating sparks were common after the blast was done. It was just a speck of baleful red fire glowing in the dark, until, wafted by a stray air current, it found the loose plug on one of the barrels and settled in a tiny smear of spilled powder that lay next to the bung.

The propagated blast that resulted from that spark caused such a massive over pressure in the confined volume of the mine that everyone underground stood no chance. Afterwards, there were few survivors at the mine. They were mainly surface workers, boys and bal maidens, whose work involved smashing up raw ore into smaller pieces for the crushers. They had mainly been above ground at the time and, when they had recovered themselves enough to investigate, they finally went below.

There was little warning of what awaited them. The only outward sign of the devastation below had been a huge blue smoke ring that puffed out of the shaft as if a Cornish giant was enjoying a pipe down there.

It was a hard climb down the ladder way to the deep level. Many of the iron cleats that bound the ladders to the wall of the shaft had been loosened by the blast and the shafts-men had to tighten each of them before the others could go below. Most of the underground workers were on the third level, eighty fathoms below surface. They lay where they had fallen in untidy postures of collapse. Men and boys were together in death, as they had been in life. Without exception, every inch of exposed flesh was a dark purplish black colour, and the whites of their eyes were speckled with bright red flecks of blood.

Years later this strange effect would become recognised by naval surgeons as 'Wind of Ball'. Later wars would refer to it as 'blast', but that Thursday morning it seemed almost evilly magical, a strange disturbing mass death that had invaded the mine and killed where it would. The remaining miners recovered the bodies, sweating their way up the crooked ladder way in the dark, edging towards the pale rectangle of light, bringing the dead to grass for the very last time.

Afterwards, the shaft was judged too damaged to continue mining and the landlords could find no one to take over the lease of the lode. Mine owner and landlord alike were destroyed financially, the villagers on the other hand were simply destroyed.

Few families remained untouched, and the graveyard had to be extended to accommodate the dead. The mine, 'Wheal Jenny', named for the owner's daughter with such hope of great returns ten years before, was sollared over, the shaft covered with thick granite slabs, and it was quietly forgotten. In time, it became yet another failed venture in the history of Cornish Mining. Presently it was even forgotten by the villagers.

Sally, looking at the old accounts, saw nothing more than a simple tragedy of the early industrial revolution, but she felt, as if she had been there, the nightmare that those early miners lived and died through all those years ago. As she reached the end of the file, Siran began to finally stir from her afternoon nap.

Sally shut the laptop down, and shook her head, clearing her mind's eye of the images of those long-ago miners dying in the dark, far below ground. Always able to empathise with others, she was helpless to avoid the intrusive thoughts of how it must have been for them, in the dark, and breathing the last of the air, air that was full of sulphur and choking smoke. They had died, seeing nothing, trapped in the damp clammy space underground.

Siran, sensing her mother's distress, began to grizzle, and Sally picked her up to comfort her. Presently with the baby latched on and feeding, Sally's strange fey mood lifted. It was, after all, just a historic event. Even though it had happened nearby in space, it was far distant in time.

By the time Jonathan came in from morning surgery, Sally was nearly herself again. They went about preparing food, exchanging notes about the morning until finally

Sally felt confident enough to raise the topic of Hannah's letter.

"It didn't come 'til a few days after she was found," Sally said. "I thought at first that maybe I should pass it on to someone but there was nothing in the note that might have explained how she died. The thing is, she thought that something scary is going on in the village, maybe something really disturbing, but I didn't think passing the note over to whoever is looking into her death would help. After all, it was an accident as far as anyone knows."

"It's a bit odd," agreed Jonathan over a mug of coffee, after reading Hannah's last missive. "But, honestly, that note is just so, well so, Hannah. She thought she was a witch, you know?"

"Well," said Sally, "perhaps she was. After all, it's just a belief system. If she thought she was a witch then I guess she really was."

"Maybe, but there's nothing in that note that suggests she knew anything that anyone couldn't find with a bit of research. After all, you got all the gen on that mine disaster, with a few minutes work on a laptop."

Sally, in the rational part of her mind, was sure he was right, but still there was, something. She said, "I know, love, but…"

"But?" he said questioningly.

"Well, lately things have been weird around here. In six months, there were all those odd happenings."

Jonathan, aware of the vagaries of post-partum women and seeing everything through the logical prism of training, simply said, gently, "Yes, but they aren't connected, are they? It's just a nasty run of coincidence."

"I wonder."

"Well, aside from a single case of a body that seems to have auto-cremated, all the rest were natural accidents. Besides, if you take a long enough time scale, very nearly every community will have a few skeletons in the cupboard."

"But there's so many of them and, just recently…" she said.

"True. But things really do run in series – you know that really. Look, three years ago there was a run of air crashes. Four, one after the other in four days. But there wasn't a connection, at least not one that we could pin down – like a mechanical fault, say. It's just the universe playing silly buggers, and our human tendency to see patterns, even when the pattern isn't there at all. It's the same effect as seeing a figure lurking among a heap of bedding in a half-lit bedroom. We expect patterns, so we see patterns. As for Hannah, you know, and I know, she was not the most stable character in the village. It'll be an open verdict, but if I was going to lay bets, I reckon it was really suicide. As far as the burned body goes… well, I've done a bit of research of my own. The whole thing is just misinterpretation of a perfectly natural event."

"Natural where? Would that be Transylvania?"

"No, but there are recorded cases that go back to Victorian times. Nowadays, we reckon that what happens is that, when someone, for whatever reason, is dead or unconscious, that could be a CVA or maybe a cardiac event, or maybe it was even a simple case of being dead drunk. Whatever, you have someone effectively unconscious. Then something catches the victim's clothing on fire. That could be anything, a match, a candle, a cigarette end.

Instead of burning, the clothes start to smoulder, and then… Hell, do you want to hear this? It's pretty nasty."

"Yes. If you can explain it, go ahead. I'm a big girl now."

"Okay. Well, the smouldering clothing melts subcutaneous fat out of the body from just under the skin. That soaks the cloth that's already smouldering, and the smouldering goes on, slowly soaking up the fat and cooking the muscle so that it softens and burns in turn, until the body is reduced to ash. Most times, not all the fat burns, and that gives you that yellow/orange deposit in the room on the walls, wherever it's cool enough to condense. The parts of the body that aren't covered by clothing, like the hands, the feet, and the head are left more or less untouched, because the heat is confined to the smouldering clothing. It's called the 'wick effect'. If you don't know what happened, and come in at the end of the process, it's really disturbing, but it's nothing supernatural. It's just physics."

"Hannah thought that there was something behind it all," said Sally thoughtfully.

"Yeah. Well, God rest her, she was not too stable, wasn't our Hannah. She was just seeing patterns, as I said. It's just us being human, but Hannah thought it was magic at work, because Hannah saw everything through the lens of magical thinking."

Siran, full of milk and warmth, snuggled into the crook of Sally's arms.

Sally said, "Well, I'd better change her and put her down. It's a big responsibility, isn't it? Another human life."

"Where did that come from?"

"Oh, nowhere really. It's just that I thought this place

was so idyllic, a perfect place for a child to grow up, but recently it's been one nasty thing after another."

"It's just a run of coincidence, love. Things will settle down and the village is the same village as it's always been."

Sally looked pensive. "I really hope so, Jon," she said, "I really do."

Later, when Sally had a moment to herself again, she googled '1823 + Tregadrew + Cornwall'. What she found was beyond, well beyond, her expectations.

CHAPTER TWENTY-EIGHT

In 1823, the village was quiet. Mining was undergoing a boom and the men were employed either underground or on the land. Life was running along a steady, almost predetermined course. There were births, weddings and funerals, sowing and reaping, and occasionally, there was the bounty of the sea.

Salvage was a well-established activity in the West Country. Thanks to the rocky coastline and the uncertain weather, the winter months took a regular, steady, toll on passing ships.

The numbers were, to modern ears, astounding. In the single year of 1840, no fewer than two hundred merchantmen were lost on the West Country coast, and that was no means an unusual year. Eventually, the toll of callous owners and badly equipped ships would become a national scandal and the practice of over-insuring 'coffin ships' and sending them to sea to sink along with their crews, was finally ended. Until then wrecking, not actually causing wrecks, but simply stripping the wreckage of anything valuable was an accepted part of life that went on until the early nineteen hundreds.

On the peninsula, the miners of St Keverne had an especially fierce reputation as violent and determined strippers of anything that washed ashore. There were dark rumours of still worse activities. The laws of salvage allowed anyone to save loose and valuable materials from wrecks and take custody of them – unless there were survivors from the ship. That law was a clear incentive to commit murder. As long as any living thing from a wreck remained alive, right down to the ship's dog, the salvors had no legal rights. The ship owners still owned every stick and spar.

In the cold, starving month of December, the great Christmas gale blew up out of the south west. For four days, the seas rose, gradually growing worse as the winds struggled upwards towards hurricane force.

In the cove, the few fishing boats that had been left drawn out on the sandy bottom of the small granite harbour, were first lifted to the limits of their moorings, and then, finally, torn loose and smashed against the granite groin that protected the tiny harbour basin from the worst of the weather.

On the end of that granite wharf, there was a small stone structure, built originally as a hewer's hut for a lookout man to spot the sea signs of passing shoals of fish. The old hut had stood a hundred years and more, braving out the worst that the sea could do, but that night, the twenty seventh of December, a single wave swept it bodily off its foundations and reduced the end of the quay to a pile of scattered stone blocks and crushed lime mortar.

Far out at sea, the 'Southern Endeavour', a three masted sailing vessel in the immigrant trade to Australia, was running before the weather. She had been caught in the great storm by pure bad luck. Without accurate means of forecasting the weather, the only warning had been a catastrophic drop in the barometer reading as the ship sailed into the western approaches to the English Channel. By the time she was clear of the ever-present menace of the Wolf Rock reef, the situation was already becoming desperate.

In those days of sail, the major risk was becoming embayed, trapped within the enfolding arms of the land, without the sea room to tack out to sea. It was a cruel situation, because everyone involved was well aware of what was going to inevitably happen. Once embayed, there was no chance of escape. The ship could only end up in the shallows while the sea beat her to matchwood.

For the crew and passengers there was little hope. A strong swimmer, given a huge amount of luck, might make it ashore, but for the majority, the choice was to stay with the false security of the ship as she was gradually destroyed around them, or to strike out through the savage undertows and cross currents, towards the beach.

On the night that the Southern Endeavour wrecked in the cove, the watchers on land knew what must happen as soon as they saw her, less than a mile offshore. She was visible for a few moments, then lost in the flying scud before reappearing, always closer to the breakers. With the running tide and the gale driving her in, it was only a matter of time. Most of the menfolk were gathered on the beach, taking good care not to get thrown off their feet by the breaking surf. Cordage in hand, they waited.

The ship was thrown onto her port side in the first breaking line of surf. It was so close to the beach, the onlookers could see figures clambering into the rigging to try to find a space. They could hear the screams too, and the rattling, tearing sound of the ship's timbers breaking up. No one spoke much. There was no elation at the sight of the wreck, even though she represented an opportunity to make more money in a few hours than they could earn by their labour in a month.

Presently, the first bits of flotsam came ashore. It was

barrels mainly, those ubiquitous containers for everything in transit, from fresh water to fine brandy, from whale oil to bitumen. Mostly they were ignored by the waiting onlookers… there was the hope of items of far greater value still to come.

After a time, the main collapse of the wreck began. By then, the Endeavour was smashed open like a massive egg in the shallows, and the sea was littered with the signature of the wreck. There were floating spars, cordage in great snarls of hemp spiderweb, oars from the boats that were never launched, and presently, the bodies. Most sailors at that time wore heavy gold earrings, mainly to pay for a Christian burial if they washed up, dead on a foreign shore. The gold, even then, was worth a month's pay for a labourer and it was easy enough to tear loose and pocket. But there were other, richer, pickings that night. There were gold chains and rings, and then there was that one corpse that wore a huge green stone in a heavy golden ring.

The story of that ring was a saga in itself, not that anyone on the beach that night recognised it. Originally it had been worn by the first officer of the Spanish capitana, the 'San Pedro'. Many years before, it was part of the loot taken during the great Spanish pillage of the new world. The stone once graced the stylishly oiled body of an Inca official in far away, fabled Cusco. The man who took it, along with the finger the official wore it on, was a simple mercenary who had once worked for Cortez himself. Over the years, that ring changed hands many times. Once, it was given as a gift for the favours of a mullato whore in Port Royal. Twice it was wagered, and lost, in a card game.

Finally the ring was sold, as a last resort, by a man who had found himself in the colonies, desperate for money. The ring was his last possession, and he had sold it for a handful of coinage to a British emigrant, who had been transported to the colony at Botany Bay and done his time. That man, Jeremy Harrison by name, worked his way up to a minor position in administration and finally, Mother England having forgiven his chequered past, he was on his way home on the Endeavour. It was not his most inspired choice of transport.

When that lost soul washed up on the beach, he was already nearly dead, smashed about by the sea, bleeding from contact with the barnacles on the reef on the port side of the bay. His clothes were sodden and heavy with sea water but he thought, as he dragged himself through the limits of the surf, that, finally, he was home. Two figures appeared out of the drizzle and flying scud and stood over him.

"Help me," he croaked, "I'm English, please."

English he might have been, but, neither of the wreckers cared much for that. As long as a single member of a ship's passengers or crew remained alive, there were no rights of salvage. One of the figures reached out his hand, but not to offer help… there was a solid heavy iron wood belaying pin in it. One blow was all it took.

They looked down at the corpse with its sprawled limbs and its cooling brain splattered on the wet sand. Presently, one of them noticed the ring on the man's hand. The sea green stone was washed by the ocean and glittered in the light as if from some inner energy. It was stuck fast, reluctant to leave the hand that was calloused by years of hard labour, but there were ways to remove it. It was just another minor horror in a night of horrors. By the time a grey dawn crawled out of the sea, the beach was littered with wreckage, human and materiel, but there was little of value left on the sand.

James Edward Laverty was a proud member of the nascent police force in Helston. The town only ran to two paid constables who roamed the streets of a small market town, arresting the odd drunk and generally being rather more officious than their limited authority supported. At least there was a police force in Helston – in theory. True, the chief of police was notoriously a target for drunken miners, who made a sort of pastime out of half throttling the man in a gesture of contempt, but the Laverty brothers were another matter entirely. The family believed in law and order, almost as an article of faith. They were unusual, in that they chose policing as a career, at a time when membership of the local militia was more lucrative, and the law, at least in the minds of most Cornishmen, was seen as something that was created to supress the working man.

Laverty's young cousin, also called James, was to gain notoriety in Falmouth in 1884 when his absolute insistence on a trial for murder led to the crew of the yacht Mignonette standing trial for cannibalism and murder after the cabin boy, a dying youth called Richard Parker, was killed and eaten to sustain the rest of the crew after many days adrift in an open boat.

The rescued crew, what was left of them, had reported the event to the local officers in the honest belief that they had done no wrong, and the populace of Falmouth, supporting the sailors to a man, were content to let things stand, but Laverty, almost single handed, forced the issue and pressured the local magistrates to take the case to the high court.

It was just another example of the Laverty family's unbending application of the law without fear or favour, or for that matter much compassion. They were contemptuous of the miners, sailors and agricultural workers in Cornwall who the Lavertys saw as a pit of vice and iniquity. James Senior's mother had been a puritanical Methodist of the most unbending stripe. By the time he came to the village that Friday to investigate reports of looting and worse around the wreck of the immigrant ship Endeavour, he had already made up his mind.

Backed by three customs riding officers, technically responsible for the enforcement of import regulations along that section of the coast, he came to the main square of the village, top hatted, blue uniformed, and sporting a brace of pistols in his broad leather belt. He was a small man with a red face, bristling mutton chop whiskers, and deep set, little, bright blue eyes that glared out, like those of a small unpleasant animal, always ready to bite. Laverty went through life treating everyone he encountered to a constant threat of confrontation.

Laverty carried a leather pouch at his waist and within it was a proclamation signed by the local magistrates that required all persons who had salvaged wreckage from the Endeavour to bring it forward to the square within three hours from the time of the proclamation being announced so that the owners of the wreck might be properly compensated for their losses. He read the paper out in a cracked voice, declaiming to the few villagers who could be bothered to listen.

That formality done, the paper copy of the proclamation

was tied to the market cross. Three hours later, during which time – as was required by law – no official was watching the place, Laverty returned to find a large, sickeningly fragrant dog turd left on the ground under the notice. Other than that, there was nothing.

Now, on most such occasions, any other official would have bowed to the inevitable and would have folded their tents and left.

The bodies from the beach were already buried in the churchyard in a common grave. The wreck was reduced to spars and shattered wood on the beach. None of them were worth the trouble of removal. The wreck had long since been picked clean.

Laverty was not most officials. With the customs men backing him up, he went from house to house in the village, hammering on doors, roughly searching the poor interiors for evidence, shouting at those who he thought would offer no resistance, interrogating the ones who looked as if they might be cowed enough to respond to threats. Some of the villagers looked ready to respond to his threats with threats of their own, and those he left alone, and in the end, after a full two hours of bluster he found… well not much, a few bits of cordage, that might, or might not have come from the wreck, a few bits of damp timber, a pewter plate, some items of damp clothing, but otherwise, nothing, at least nothing until he reached the cottage of George Martin.

George lived in the end cottage near the cove with his wife Mary. She was a downtrodden woman of thirty who looked seventy-five, and dressed in dowdy brown clothes that covered her neck to ankle like a new England puritan. The search of that cottage would have been the same as all the others except for the flash of green fire that caught Laverty's piggy little eye.

"Where did you get that, woman?" he asked, addressing Mary directly.

"I give it her," said George before she could answer for herself. He had given his wife the ring to mind, intending that no one would think of searching her person for anything of value.

"No one was asking you," said Laverty.

"A man can give his wife a pretty token now and then."

"He may. If he can afford it. Where does a labourer find money for jewels?"

"Family treasure. Been in my family for years."

"You, Master Martin, are a lying bastard, damn your eyes. You are under arrest. Cuff him up."

"What?" The prospect of restraint was enough to rouse George Martin to resistance. He said, "A man has rights in England, even against a jumped-up bastard like you."

"Bastard, am I?" said Laverty, rising to the insult. "Well, we shall see soon enough. Take him."

The riding officers put the cuffs on and, tugging George by his tethered wrists, led him into the sunlight outside. They made a sad little procession through the main street. The villagers formed a silent, watching crowd as they passed. One or two men spat in the dust. The tension was so great that everyone watching that morning knew that it had to break.

Jimmy Hewlet, a village lad who was thought generally to be an idiot, was the first to pick up the mood of the crowd. Lacking the inhibition that a more nuanced mind might have had, he picked up a stone, a rough, angular, egg sized lump of quartz, and he threw it.

Jimmy had long passed his summers in the apple orchards, throwing stones at the birds who pecked at the swelling crop, for a handful of pennies each day. His aim was perfect.

The stone caught Laverty above his left eye and the blood flowed instantly. It was like a signal, the three representatives of the law vanished almost instantly in a scrum of bodies, kicking, biting, punching, using whatever came to hand as a weapon. In five minutes – and it seemed a very long five minutes to the victims – there were three dusty bundles left in the square, surrounded by a spreading pool of blood. Someone had torn Laverty's breeches off in a gesture of contempt, and his pale buttocks bulged upwards like twin half-moons, white against the brown dust.

Such contempt for the law could not go unpunished. Official reaction came to the village three days later, in the shape of a detachment of militia. No policemen this time, not even the stiff-necked guardians of the law of Laverty's stripe, but men in bright red uniforms with white cross belts and cold bright steel muskets tipped with glittering bayonets. They were led by an officer on a brown horse, that looked as if it had been polished that morning, and the men were commanded by a sergeant at arms, a bristling little man with a voice that could reach from one end of a parade ground to another.

The officer spoke without dismounting from his vantage point on his horse. The people listened silently, expecting trouble.

"The villagers," he said, "have been responsible for a riot, and, as a result of their illegal assemblage and actions, officers of the law have been killed." An example would be made. The villagers' actions had put them beyond the civilian rules. Either the village would give up those responsible for the deaths, or ten men would be chosen at random, tried by a military drum-head court martial, and executed by firing squad under martial law.

The villagers could not believe it, but a sort of dumb acceptance set in and three hours later, at eleven in the morning, the chosen ten were standing against the smithy wall while twelve muskets were levelled at them. Even then, at the last moment, the feeling was that they couldn't go through with the executions. The chosen men were those who, the soldiers thought, would not fight back, when the time came.

On the command, the muskets crashed a single ragged note, gaping wounds appeared on the victim's bodies as if by magic, and they crumpled to the floor. Of the ten, eight died instantly, but two writhed and twitched in their own blood, so that the sergeant had to finish them with pistol shots. The 'Tregadrew Massacre' was a novelty for a while. Even in lawless times, it was a popular cause with rabble rousers of the Chartist stripe. But as public memory faded, it was lost amid worse and crueller events further north.

Everyone forgot it, only the village remembered. Sally, rediscovering another facet of the village's dark past, closed the website down with an inner shudder.

CHAPTER TWENTY-NINE

As every parent of a new-born quickly learns, restful sleep is very much a movable feast. Siran, quiet and easy going as she was, still reduced her parents' available sleep time, and that led, in time, to a sort of constant state of mild fatigue. It was as if nothing that Sally or Jonathan did really satisfied their need for sleep. As a result, Sally developed the habit of napping for an hour or so after lunch, when a full stomach and a full baby gave her a fairly regular chance of a break.

She was asleep on the squashy old sofa with the autumn light stealing through the big old fashioned sash windows, when the dream came.

Sally had always had vivid dreams and, at first, this was no different. In her dream, she was in a field of wildflowers, everywhere corn marigolds, ox-eye daisies and yellow rattle studded the rough tussocks of grass with jewel-like colour. In the dream, the weather was warm and comfortable, even though there was no direct sight of the sun, just that bright daylight that threw everything into high relief.

For a time, dreaming Sally was content simply to admire the countryside, wondering at the scuttling of a tiny, rather fluffy harvest-mouse that climbed a grass stem and regarded her with beady black eyes before returning to a perfectly round nest of plaited vegetation, as if it had things to do, and no time to concern itself with this human intruder.

She became aware that she was not alone in the dream. A rather dumpy figure, dressed in a kaftan, that was tie dyed in bright primary colours stood among the grasses. The legs that jutted from under the hem were rather lumpy and pale, threaded with swollen varicose veins and ending in feet that were the white of a fish's belly and vaguely soft looking. The features of this apparition were not in the least ghostly, they were middle aged and slightly heavy, the features of a woman entering her early fifties, and accepting her age with some grace, neither aping her youth, nor giving free reign to a dowdy middle age.

As Sally watched, with no great apprehension, the figure came closer, coming effortlessly through the tussocks of cotton grass as if it moved without touching the surface. Presently, it was close enough to see the features clearly. Three metres or so away from Sally, the figure stopped.

"Hello, maid," said Hannah.

"Hannah," Sally said, or maybe she only thought she said it. She had the strange feeling that she was speaking inside her own head. "Hannah. But you're dead."

The heavy features broke into a small gentle smile.

"I am that, dearie, but no one really dies here. Not in the way you think of it. This is a place outside of space and time. Death is nothing here, nor life either. Here, thinking beings think, and thought, conscious thought, is immortal. This place is not a place that most people can ever visit, at least not before they cross the divide. You are privileged, maid."

"But, why, Hannah?"

"Because the things that have happened in our little village are an affront to the order of things. There is a balance to be held between the forces that create and those that destroy. There is no better way for you to understand it, not while you stand on your side of the divide. But you have become meshed in a battle that can never be lost, or won for that matter, nor should it be, because the reality of that battle is eternity, and the only real success, is a balance."

Sally said in that strange inner voice, "But Hannah, I can't do this. All I want to do is live my own life and raise my child. I don't understand what you want of me."

"I want nothing from you, maid. Besides, my wants are nothing to the point. You have free will, you can choose to ignore all of this. The world will still go on. But the disturbance in the balance of things will go on too, and, at your level of existence, matters will go on in ways that you will find harder and harder to understand, or live with. That's your choice, child. I can no sooner tell you what to do than I could move the moon unaided. I am the messenger, not the message."

"But I don't know what you want me to do."

"Use the Book of Shadows. It will tell you what to do. Some of it will seem nonsense to you at first, but all I can tell you is this. You must follow the book exactly, or things might happen that will cross the line between nightmare and daily life, in your reality."

"But why?"

"Because that error in the pattern must be corrected. There are more things at play here than you can even imagine. Years ago, as you understand time, an old woman was murdered by this village, and that killing started a chain of incidents that have echoed ever since. Most of the time, the results have been small ripples in the tide of history but, recently the pattern has become unstable. It is vital that balance is restored."

"I can't do this, Hannah. It's too big for me."

"You can child, and you must," said Hannah, and abruptly, as is the way of dreams, the scene changed. In front of Sally there was suddenly a yawning pit. It might have been one of the hundreds of old shafts that pockmark the central belt of Cornwall, but there was no friendly ring of rubble stone and wire around this one. Instead, there was just a shallow saucer-shaped depression in the land that ended in a cavity that led down into the dark. It was as if the world's biggest Antlion had made a burrow there.

There was the sound of distant, running water, and a scent of damp air wafting up from deep below. What was different about this shaft was the almost palpable air of terror that hung about it. It was like the fear that some phobics feel when faced with a great unfenced drop, a deadly, perverse draw, that was trying to force her near to the edge of the saucer in the ground, drawing her ever nearer to the chasm, drawing her closer and closer to the drop into the dark.

It took real effort to break the spell, and, when Sally woke, she was soaked in the sweat of nervous tension, apocrine sweat, greasy and sharp smelling, and her heart was racing as if as if she had barely escaped some deadly peril. The dream was so real, so all pervading, that she took at least ten minutes to reorient herself to the familiar room with its tall sash windows and the early afternoon sun washing the homely furnishings with pale gold. Finally gathering herself, she stood up. Siran was sleeping quietly in the cot beside her. As Sally watched, Siran stirred and stretched, like a cat waking from a long sleep.

It was only then that Sally saw a book lying on the sofa where she had been sleeping. It had certainly not been there half an hour before when she settled down for a rest.

There was nothing of the ephemeral about it. The book was as solid as any other object in the room, as prosaic as a fireplace or a table. It was around twelve inches by nine and bound in a thoroughly normal pale leather. A high-end binding to be sure, but not a particularly unusual one. The margin was stained slightly, as if by long handling by greasy fingers. On the outer cover, in black gothic type which might have suited a book of Victorian ghost stories, was the title. It said: 'The Book of Shadows'.

Sally looked at it as if it were a rat that had suddenly appeared in the living room. She was suddenly and irrationally determined to hide the thing, to place it where it and the still sleeping baby were not in proximity, as if it might somehow carry a contagion of some kind. The cover, when she picked it up, was slightly slippery in texture, as if the leather had only recently been flayed from some beast or other, and not properly tanned. It felt… well, strange.

Almost against her will, Sally opened the cover. The title was repeated in the same gothic text on the fly leaf inside and the paper of the pages was creamy and expensive looking, and still it had an air of great age as if it was really printed on old parchment.

Within, the first page was a drawing of sorts. It was rendered in black ink, a complex drawing of a wheel-shaped structure. At the four corners of the page, the cardinal compass points were marked, and at the north, there were a few words written in perfectly normal pencil. They said in a cramped, tiny, hand, 'Not Valerian, try Mandrake at the north gate'.

Sally flipped through the pages, coming upon more and more of that cramped, tiny writing. There were lists of materials, each annotated with a time and place, some with the stages of the lunar cycle carefully written in.

Finally, towards the back of the book, she found a title in that same gothic font, printed, or maybe carefully inked in by someone who was a master of calligraphy. It was on a page all by itself, the page otherwise blank, as if the writer had wanted to emphasise the importance of this particular entry. It said, in that same ominous text: 'The Dumb Supper'.

She was about to turn the page when Siran, who had been quiet until then, first stirred and then whimpered to herself as she awoke. Sally shoved the book under a cushion as if it were something shameful and best out of sight, and went to tend to her daughter.

CHAPTER THIRTY

Jonathan Wilde woke with the distinct feeling that all was not well in his world. One of the few disadvantages of living with someone who you believe is truly your soulmate is that disagreements tend to be felt deeply and to carry on from the day into the small hours of the night, when the mind has no distractions to blot out the concerns of the previous day.

Sally had raised the matter of the book, and its weird provenance that evening, when Jonathan, who was tired after a long day in the surgery, was finally able to relax.

There really was very little common ground in the discussion that followed. Jonathan Wilde had spent a lifetime learning the virtues of evidence-based scientific medicine. Sally, whose upbringing and education was courtesy of the Catholic school system, had been conditioned from an early age to accept the possibility of the occult as part of daily life.

Certainly, her conditioning had involved miracles rather than spells, but what was the mass, if not a prolonged ritualistic spell?

But accepting the set of beliefs, even if over the years she had more or less rejected the trappings of the church, really meant that one had to accept at least the possibility of magic.

Jonathan saw the arcane mumbo jumbo of witchcraft as no more than early attempts to answer the big questions that every human being faces. While practitioners of the magic arts said the cure for the ills of human beings was belief, spells and ritual, he believed passionately that the real cures were antibiotics, psycho-active compounds and surgery, assisted, maybe, by the placebo effect.

The two viewpoints were of course totally incompatible. Sally, prepared to at least accept the possibility of the occult, stood on one side of the argument. Jonathan Wilde, the arch rationalist, was on the other.

By the time they finally went to bed, there was an atmosphere of sullen irritation between them. Sleep was a long time coming, and, when it came, it was thin and disturbed.

Jonathan finally woke at four thirty in the morning. A few months ago, before Siran was sleeping through the night, this was a commonplace experience, but for the last couple of months, her sleep pattern, and as result, their own sleep, was usually uninterrupted. For a few minutes he lay, rigidly awake, before he eventually decided that by staying there in the marital bed he would only disturb Sally and achieve nothing of use. Finally, he decided to get up and brew a coffee.

Jonathan's idiosyncratic response to caffeine was a source of mild amusement between them. Most human beings, including all their friends, found coffee a stimulant, an aid to concentration.

Jonathan found it quite the opposite. A couple of cups of coffee and his sleep was more or less guaranteed. Relying on this metabolic freak, he brewed a mug of a powerful high caffeine roast, and took a brief, visceral pleasure in the strong semi bitter taste.

He was half-way down the mug, when the window seemed to lighten with a reddish glow from outside.

A few weeks before, prior to the ancient and hallowed British ritual of the clocks going back to GMT that red light in the eastern sky might have been no more than the signal of a new fresh dawn. Now, it was far too early for sunrise.

At first Jonathan told himself that he was still asleep and dreaming. That much rational thought remained, but, if this was a dream, it was the most incredibly detailed dream that he had ever experienced. He found himself standing at the window. The curtains were drawn back and it was slightly cool now that he was out of the warm confines of the bed. There was nothing ephemeral about the landscape he saw outside… it had the solidity of a concrete block. Suddenly, he was very afraid of whatever lay outside that window, of whatever star it was that was casting that awful dead light. He took real effort to take a grip of himself, telling himself, almost as if he had spoken aloud, that beyond that window pane, bathed in that dreadful light, was nothing more fearsome than the same old view of fields and tussock grass dropping away to the endless moonlit ocean in the distance. If the night was clear, there would be the loom of the Wolf Rock light, sweeping its endless eight second cycle to warn shipping of the Wolf Rock reef.

Outside the window, that light revealed a scene from a madman's nightmare. Last night there had been a rather untidy vista, washed by a silver white moon. Now there was a landscape of black sand that extended as far as the eye could see in endless undulating dunes. The moon was gone. Instead, there was a sullen red sun glowering down on this desolate land. There was a constant low-level sound endlessly playing in the background, discordant and profoundly unpleasant, not so much the music of the spheres as the cacophony of Hell's own gateway.

In the distance, a small blot of darkness materialised as he watched. It flickered like a mirage on a hot day, one second as insubstantial as a heat haze shimmering above hot tarmac on a summer afternoon, the next solid, and as real as a brick.

As it came towards him, the object resolved itself into a figure, wrapped in a cloak that fluttered in the hot wind that blew through this place. Jonathan could not see if the apparition was human or not, but there was a sense of vile inhuman hatred of all that lives, that flowed from it in a foetid, viscous flood. It was as tangible as if it had been a physical thing.

He stepped back from the window, afraid in a way that he had never experienced before. All his rational arguments, all his certainty that there was only the material world, shook to its foundations. This was genuine evil incarnate, real elemental evil. This was the force of nature that he had always denied the existence of.

As the thing reached the threshold, separated from him only by a pane of glass, Jonathan stepped back again, and finally regained the power of vocalisation. It was not speech, he was too frightened to articulate speech. The fear he felt was for his very soul. Speech was for everyday dangers. This was more fundamental by far.

Finally, his throat unlocked, and he screamed. Inside him, it was a great yell of sound that he could never have associated with himself, but all that came out of that cry of fear was a whimper. Finally, as the apparition reached the outside of the window, and rested hands that were little more than grey skin over bone against the glass, the spell broke, and Jonathan Wilde, rationalist, doctor and convinced atheist, faced by the reality of the other world, felt the world swimming away, as he collapsed to the floor in a faint.

He came to himself with a crick in his neck from lying on the hard floor, and for a few moments he was unable to re-orient himself. At first, he was unable to account for being on the living room floor, and not in bed with Sally warm and soft beside him. He shook his head to try to clear it.

His first waking reaction, and his innate rationalism, said the night before had been no more than an episode of sleep walking, and a particularly nasty dream, occasioned by his strange conversation with Sally the night before.

But then memory came back like the fall of a guillotine blade, hard and sharp and uncompromising. Forgetful of his aches and pains and ignoring the chill kiss of the early morning air against his skin, Jonathan came to his feet at a rush. The landscape outside was just as it always was, the morning light casting a rosy glow over the tussocky grassland and lighting the sea in shades of coral and fuchsia.

The dawn was washing the surface of the window, with golden light picking out each particle of dust in a scattering of glowing spicules.

As he looked, something began to form a pattern in the dust outside. What at first he took to be two simple smudges in the film that all windowpanes develop within a few hours of being polished, in houses so close to the sea, gradually took on form. It was like one of those 3D pictures that look like random patterns of dots, until they suddenly spring into life. There was something about those two smudges. Finally, as he watched, the light caught them at an acute angle. Jonathan Wilde realised that the smudges were two handprints, that realisation informing the next, the palmprints were outlined in dark coloured dust. It was nothing like the salt staining around them. Two hours before, a nightmare figure had rested its skeletal palms against the glass, while its hideous face had leered at him through the glass, and now it had left its calling card.

CHAPTER THIRTY-ONE

Jonathan was still sitting at the table, when Sally came down. With her, the small disagreements of the night before never carried over to the next day.

"Jon, how long have you been up?"

"A while. I couldn't sleep and I didn't want to wake you, so I came down. I must have gone to sleep in the chair."

"Look, about last night. Life's too short to waste on crap like that, Jon. I know how you feel about things and I'm happy to respect it. Let's just agree to differ, and let it go. After all, it's not our job to sort out the problems of the world. The world has lasted this long without our help. I'm sure it will last a few years more without our getting involved." She broke off, seeing his expression. "What? What did I say? Jon, for Christ's sake, tell me."

"It's like this," he said, in a dead uninflected voice that was quite unlike him, "last night, after we went to bed, I couldn't sleep… so I came down to make a drink."

After ten minutes, it was all out. The strange light, the arid nightmare landscape, the figure that had first threatened him, and then left traces outside the glass as a token of its reality.

Sally was shocked, but not surprised. Some part of her, the old Celtic ancestry that spoke across the centuries, was quite accepting of this nightmare.

She said, "Look, love, if it happened, it happened. We can't pretend anymore, that's all. Something in this place really is very, very wrong. I would far rather ignore the whole thing and let it lie, but it seems we can't. We didn't choose this, love. It has chosen us. What we have to do now is to decide what best to do."

"What can we do? That thing, whatever it was, is beyond anything we can deal with."

"No, actually it's not. If we accept that what you saw last night is real, then I suppose we have to accept that the book is real as well, and according to that vision or whatever it was, when Hannah brought it to me, the book has the answer. She said to 'use the Dumb Supper' whatever that might be. I know nothing about these things, but I do know that there is a chapter in the book with that title."

"So," said Jonathan, "what are you saying?"

"Let's look in the book, read the section on the Dumb Supper, and then maybe, do whatever it suggests."

"But…"

"Hush. I know what a big leap it is for you to go this route but it's a case of fighting fire with fire, isn't it? I didn't want to accept the reality of the other world, whatever it might be. Believe me, I wanted to ignore it, just as much as you do, but pretending that it didn't happen, is like a little kid who doesn't want to eat his greens pretending that his mouth is glued shut. It's there, it happened. Now we have to deal with it."

"Christ, how am I going to go to morning surgery with all this running around inside my head?"

"The way you always do, love. Nothing of that has changed. Your skills are still your skills. You're a bloody fine doctor and always will be. This other problem is outside all of that. Now. How about breakfast? Can you face a full English?"

"If my patients find this out, my credibility is buggered."

"Because of suddenly believing in witchcraft?"

He grinned, and it was like the sun coming out from behind a cloud. "No," he said, "because I ate a full English."

"I love you, Doctor Wilde, you know that?"

"And I love you too. Now how about that fry up?"

CHAPTER THIRTY-TWO

A fundamental problem with the practice of ceremonial magic, as the Wildes very quickly realised, is that there are no simple signposts or manuals to follow. The attempts of the notorious bad boys of the nineteen hundreds to codify magic were mostly a bad joke. Mainly concerned with their own sexual preferences, hymns to spanking and sodomy, most of their writings as insightful as those of an immature twelve-year-old boy discovering the realities of sex, and desperate to show off his new found knowledge.

There are many routes to the truth, but, in the end, each practitioner has to find their own way, and the problem that the Wildes immediately faced was that they had limited time to do whatever they had to do, and very little instruction to help them along. There was, of course, just one major advantage on their side, the mysterious and enigmatic Book of Shadows, that lay accusingly on the table in the living room.

It took Sally just a ten-minute session on Google to discover what the book was, or rather what it purported to be. Each witch, said the article, had to maintain a record of every attempt at a magical operation, giving all the details of times, places and the various impedimenta used. That record, peculiar to each person, was the Book of Shadows.

This, then, was Hannah's legacy, a set of instructions and a signpost on the route to dealing with whatever it was that threatened them. Sally read the instructions for performing the Dumb Supper with an increasing certainty that the practice calling on the dead to help the living was more, much more than a simple comfort blanket for the bereaved.

To call the spirit of a dead Celtic Witch to attend a symbolic meal, and then to question them for information that might defend them against an occult attack, suddenly seemed not just logical but inevitable. The problem for the Wildes, granted that Hannah's magic might actually work, was time, or rather the lack of it.

They were not free to suddenly drop the whole structure of their day to day lives and give their whole attention to the issue. There was still a small child to care for, and patients to be seen and tended. Life, normal, everyday life, had to go on.

Still, Hannah had left a major signpost for them to follow. Sally took the Book of Shadows in her hands and began to search for references to the Dumb Supper.

It was then that she found a single loose sheet of paper interleaved into Hannah's old book. It was folded so that it was held tightly within the sheaved pages. It was covered in tightly written script in Hannah's rather cramped but legible hand. By then, so many strange things had happened that Sally was not even very surprised to see that her name was scrawled across the top.

It said:

Sally, if you are reading this then you have already come well along the way, and I reckon that you know a good part of what you have to do.

I will be truthful as far as I can, but there are laws that govern the whole of existence, and I cannot transgress them. I have already visited you once in a dream, Sally, and dreaming true is more of a rare privilege than you can ever understand.

Well, maid, I'll help, as far as I can. There are forces at play here that you cannot fully understand, nor should you wish to, if you and yours would stay sane.

There is a balance to be held, not between good and evil as you understand it, but between the forces that maintain the whole structure of existence. What happened in the village at the very start of this was different, the balance itself was threatened, and whatever happens now, it is vital that the structure is restored. For a little time, the basic pattern of existence can sustain the faults in the fabric of time and space, though, as long as that fault exists, it allows things that would be better confined in their appointed place, to wander, more or less at will.

For centuries, there was no great risk in the situation, but matters are coming to a point where the damage cannot be tolerated any further.

You have a chance of calling back the shades of those who can reverse the wrong that was done so very long ago, but, if you are to succeed it must be done soon. Three weeks off, Sally, is the old festival of Samhain, that you call All Hallows' Eve. It is a time when the tides of existence run slowly and the veil between the worlds is thin. That will make what you have to do easier, but it will still be hard, and dangerous, maybe. I cannot lie to you, even if I would. You still have free will and the pattern requires the truth. You can simply ignore this message, ignore the dreams, and throw away the book.

There is even a chance that, if you do that, sometime in the future there may be another opportunity, but this much I can tell you: if you two choose to reject this path and leave the righting of the wrong for the future, it will follow your bloodline, Sally, and, by refusing, you will pass on a legacy to that little maid of yours that you would not wish for her.

Time is short, maid, very short, twenty-one days to All Hallows'. It is not long to prepare for the Dumb Supper, but you cannot change the stream of time, we can only work within the flow. If you choose to make the attempt, you will find much that you will need in the book.

As for the rest, if you look in my old cottage, there is a workroom. Look behind the dresser in the kitchen and you will find a door that leads to the cellar. Few people, even those in the village, know that it is there below. They say that, many years ago, it was a smugglers' cache, certainly it is well hidden. Over the years, it has served me well. Read the book, go to my cottage, take what you need, with my love. The guardian will respect you, though you must tell it, in my name, that it has no business with you. If you are brave, nothing else that you find there can hurt you. By rights, you should prepare the things you will need for yourself, but time is short, and I give you my blessing to use whatever of mine that you need.

Call the spirit of Goody Penrose back. She will tell you what to do next. Pay heed to her. Hers is the original pain. You must help her discharge it and close the gate forever.

Remember, this burden is yours, not because of anything that you have done, but, if you look back at your bloodline, you will maybe understand why it is you, and you alone, who can do this thing.

May the Gods walk with you, child.
Blessed be,
Hannah

For a few minutes, Sally sat, pensive, looking at the folded piece of paper. It looked ironed and flattened, much as an old love letter looks, when it is discovered between the pages of a book many years after that first glorious flush of young love has become a distant memory. It was as if it had been pressed between the pages of the old book for many years, yet Hannah was less than six months in her grave.

Presently, Sally turned again to the section on the Dumb Supper and began to read. As a ritual, she found it a curious mixture of the arcane and the prosaic. With at least a good outline of what was involved in the ritual fixed in her mind, she took a little time to follow up Hannah's dark hints of her family history in the village. In many ways, it was a relief to turn from the obscure processes of magic to a simple record search.

Family history had never been one of Sally's interests. She accepted, as part of apocryphal family history, that Aunty June, last of the Cornish family line, had descended from a long line of West Country people, but beyond that, and the usual vague family legends that everyone creates, tales of lost fortunes and colourful black sheep, she had no really solid information.

Even so, Hannah's suggestion that current events followed Sally's bloodline as if it were a familial curse, piqued her interest. Besides, there was always the possibility of discovering something that might help in a situation where any wisp of information was worth grasping at.

Once again, the digital parish records came to her rescue. The most difficult part of the search was making sense of the somewhat eccentric spelling and spidery calligraphy of long-gone parish clerks and curates. But finally, she came across a learned article by a local antiquarian.

This gentleman had been a Victorian clergyman of sorts, who had taken up investigating the history of the parish as others might take up country dancing, or the study of folklore. This man, who went by the euphonious name of the reverend Montague Tresilver, took an interest in the local aristocracy, partly because he instinctively believed that the 'old days', when everyone knew his place, were a golden time of peace and harmony. The Montfords, according to Tresilver, who had spent a lifetime searching through those very records that Sally had been so relieved to avoid, were descended from a family who originally were Breton French. Various scions of the family had been settled in Tregadrew for many years, and the line stretched back, through liaisons with dozens of Bal maidens, mine captains and agricultural workers.

There was even a breathless description of the doings of a yeoman farmer who had been chiefly noted for his all too fruitful association with no less than eight of his female workers, and at least two of their men folk, by way of a little variety.

This line led, via a spiderweb of relationships, to the Norman French local aristocracy, and, finally, to a man called Simon de Montfort. He had been the last of the line to use the aristocratic prefix 'de' and he had styled himself simply 'Simon Montford' during the time of the commonwealth when aristocratic roots were not something to be advertised.

Fascinated in spite of herself, Sally searched the scant information on her long-ago ancestor. He had been a local magistrate, landlord of the local estate, and by all accounts a good, if rather rigid, administrator.

Finally, she found, almost as a footnote, among the long accounts of civil war strife and parliamentarian rule, the nugget that gave the whole thing shape and substance. Simon de Montfort was her direct ancestor, and as far as she knew, though – given the family's habit of 'irregular copulation' as the records put it so delicately – it was hard to be sure, she was the probably the very last adult living representative of the De Montford line. He, in turn, had been the very last magistrate in the West Country to hold a formal trial for witchcraft, and to condemn a woman to death by burning in the village square.

Suddenly, more of Hannah's cryptic communication made sense. Turning away from the records with a new understanding, Sally finally had an inkling of what it was she had to do.

Hannah's old cottage was still empty, at least of human inhabitants. The last living relative, a cousin who lived far to the north in Dundee, was really only interested in the old place for what it might bring on the febrile Cornish property market. Hannah's old possessions, the overstuffed chair, ratty old sofas and old mock Jacobean furniture, stood, gathering dust, along with a flat screen TV. It stood alone in its modernity, the only concession that Hannah had ever made to the twenty-first century. The estate agent had taken one cursory look, done a quick inventory of the contents, and suggested a low asking price. Even in Cornwall, a low ask was needed, allowing whoever was brave enough, or foolhardy enough, to take on a three-hundred-year-old building in a mining area, to do whatever they would in the way of house clearance and development.

With the old place standing empty, and nothing left to steal, it was easy enough to get a set of keys from the selling agent in Truro on the spurious pretext of a possible sale. Later that day, Jonathan and Sally found themselves outside the peeling, green painted door that was flanked by tiers of flowering bushes, that cascaded down in floods of blood red blossoms on either side.

"It still doesn't seem right," said Jonathan, as he stood there.

"Hannah wouldn't mind," said Sally. "Besides, it's the best way to find out what the hell is going on."

He made one last try at rational argument. "Even so," he said, "what are we expecting to find?"

"Whatever it is, we'll know it when we find it."

With an inner sigh, Jonathan slipped the perfectly un-witchly Yale key into a slightly sticky keyway and turned the lock. The door opened on hinges that moved effortlessly. There was no theatrical creaking, and no draft of cold air, just a smell of damp, and long disuse, and a pile of junk mail that had to be pushed back against the wall to allow the door to open.

"Okay," he said, "now what?"

"The kitchen. Hannah's letter said to go to the kitchen."

"What are we going to do? Make ourselves a coffee?"

"Just let's look, shall we?"

"Sorry," he said, but he didn't sound as if he meant it.

The kitchen was a perfectly normal kitchen, a little dingy perhaps, with a small, rather grimy, window that looked out over the square of garden outside. While Hannah was alive, the glass had sparkled... now, with months of neglect, it was flecked with dried salt spray.

There was a deal table, a big one, maybe eight feet long, with a white scrubbed top, and six mismatched chairs scattered round it. There was a stainless-steel sink with a double drainer, a conical yellow plastic shade over a pendant light bulb, and terracotta tiles in worn squares on the floor.

There was also a Welsh dresser against the wall opposite the window. It had four shelves above a two-door cupboard, and it carried a fine display of blue and white, transfer-printed china.

Sally pointed to it. "Hannah said to look behind the dresser."

"What?" said Jonathan, looking at the huge piece of furniture. "It'd take a JCB to shift that thing."

Sally, ignoring his doubts, pulled tentatively at the right-hand margin of the dresser. Jonathan stepped back, expecting the inevitable crash of smashing china, as the top-heavy looking thing overbalanced, but instead, the whole dresser swung smoothly away from the wall on rubber castors exposing a door set flush into the plasterwork.

CHAPTER THIRTY-THREE

"Well," said Sally.

Jonathan shook his head in wonderment. "Christ," he said. "I don't think Hannah would appreciate that reference. Still, now we've come so far."

The door itself swung open at a touch, exposing a set of rather splintery-looking wooden stairs, leading down into the dark. Beside the door was a light switch. Either by some oversight, or possibly because Hannah's direct debit was still live, unlike its originator, the power was still on. At a touch, the whole place was flooded with bright light.

Hannah's old workroom was a masterpiece of practical design, albeit given to a rather unusual purpose. There was a solid-looking workbench on one side of the room, its top littered with various bits of thin, delicate-looking glassware. It looked like a school laboratory bench, even down to the two canister gas burners whose bright blue gas tanks gave an incongruously modern look to the whole thing. On two walls were rows of neat shelves containing dozens of small glass jars of the kind that are sold to contain culinary herbs in the supermarket. Each was neatly labelled in Hannah's small, neat script.

They were roughly organised in groups, and the shelves themselves were labelled. 'Incense ingredients' one said, and another 'Goddess charms'.

Yet another read 'Love potions' and at the very end of the last row, in a small group of canisters isolated from the rest, was a collection of dried plant materiel labelled 'Necromancy'.

Beside the workbench were shelves of books, some modern paper-bound copies of classics on the occult that you might find in any bibliophile's collection. 'Mastering Witchcraft' said the spine of one, 'The Secret Lore of Magic' another. There were two copies of Crowley's cranky old tome on 'Magick in Theory and Practice'.

But besides these modern curiosities were other books, most not so easily classified. Some were bound in leather, some merely stacks of crudely sewn heavy paper as if they had been roughly bound by an unskilled hand. One was stained on the spine with something that looked like ancient blood.

Jonathan idly picked up a long bladed, black hafted knife from the workbench. Its silvery blade was intricately engraved with an intaglio of images... female nudes twined with animal forms, that defied the eye, as he looked at it.

Sally, meanwhile, was involved in examining the shelves of herbs that lined the other wall. Somehow, she had expected that, having come this far, it would be obvious which of this massive collection of botanicals they might need. As it was, the array was simply overwhelming. As she was engrossed in the labels, one particularly caught her eye for its quaint overtones. It said 'Haitian John The Conqueror Root'. She was so engrossed that she failed to realise that the quality of the light in the room seemed to be changing. Suddenly, everything seemed sharply defined, each tiny detail standing out. At the same time, the bright, prosaic, naked, overhead bulbs were dimming to a soft glow.

She saw that, at the end of the row of jars, there was a small, desiccated heap of insect bodies where some enterprising spider had set up his residence in a crevice. She noticed that one of the jars contained a roughly ground powder marked 'Mandrake' and beside it there was a curious dried root that had either grown or been carved in the semblance of a male human figure with a hyperbolic erection.

It was about then that they both realised that something was about to happen. The temperature in the room, until then a steady, pleasant coolness, dropped violently.

Jonathan realised that he could see his breath, condensing into a fine mist in the air, and that the light summer shirt he had put on that morning, anticipating another warm day, was suddenly far too little protection against the frigid air.

He said, "What the hell?"

"It's alright," said Sally. "Hannah's note mentioned a guardian. She said it would recognise us and do us no harm."

"To hell with that,' he said. "There's something happening over there in the corner," and, for the first time, Jonathan Wilde sounded truly afraid.

At one corner of the room – it was at the east side, had they but known it – there was a neatly marked, white triangle, on the floor, that seemed to be either painted or actually inlaid into the surface in strips of some blonde-coloured wood. Inside the boundary of the triangle, it seemed that the very air of the room was changing. There seemed to be an infinitely long vista confined within it, as if the space above the marking on the floor gave onto some profound inner void that reached away into the distance.

In the space revealed there, a misty presence made itself known. It coalesced as a figure made of wisps of diaphanous rags that swirled as it moved, one second allowing the light to shine through it, the next taking on something like solidity. The apparition drifted like smoke but had an all too tangible air of deadly menace about it. It was vaguely human, but where the face should have been there was only blankness, an absence, combined with the sense of something watching and fearsomely aware, and totally evil.

It raised arms that were little more than mist, and advanced towards them, moving along the space within the triangle as if it was approaching from a vast distance. It seemed to come on increasingly rapidly, moving with a creepy gliding motion. Jonathan was too shocked to do more than watch, fixed like a rabbit in the headlights of an approaching car. But he had sufficient awareness to realise that this seemed to be a classical figure of justice, sprung to some kind of life, right down to the blindfold that crossed the emptiness where its eyes should be. It reached for them as blindly as a deep-sea anemone reaches for passing prey, blind, and random, and deadly. There was something terribly threatening in that groping, as if the creature, whatever it was, was feeling for them, like some nightmare children's game of blind man's bluff. It spread those empty arms as if to take a grip on some unseen prey, and shifted towards them.

It was then that Sally spoke.

"No," she said in a firm voice. "Hannah called us here. You have no business with us. Go now, and leave us to do what we came to do."

The figure visibly checked. It hesitated as if in indecision. Its forward movement stopped. Then, it reversed its progress into the room, and with the same other worldly gliding motion, it receded back into the distant space from where it had come. Finally, no more than a point of shadow without definition, it diminished to nothing.

"Christ," said Jonathan in an awed voice, "what the hell was that?"

"That, I think, was Hannah's guardian," said Sally. "It's just a sort of watchdog, I think. It's there to scare off the curious."

"It's certainly succeeded there. How do you know this, anyhow?"

"She told me, in the letter, or at least hinted at that. Don't worry, she said it wouldn't harm us."

"Looking like that, it doesn't need to. What was it anyhow?"

"Who knows? Now. Now that we've found Hannah's stores, we need to go home and consult the book. There are lists of stuff that set out exactly what we need to take from here. We need to go back soon in any case. Siran will need feeding, and I know Julie will give her a bottle but I don't like to impose. Anyhow, somewhere among all this stuff is everything we need."

"You really want to go through with it?"

"It's not really a matter of choice, is it? After all, if we just let things slide, we might well have to deal with that thing, or maybe something even worse. Maybe even your visitor from the other night. For now, let's just gather what's needed."

That afternoon, in that quiet time in the day that all parents of young children savour, they sat with Hannah's book on the table in front of them.

Sally broke the rather awkward silence. "Well, whatever else that might have achieved, I think we have to follow Hannah's directions now, don't you?"

"Much as I hate to admit it," said Jonathan. "I've always believed in the absolute truth of science but, I also believe that you don't ignore evidence in favour of fixed beliefs. As Galileo said, after the inquisition tried him for his teachings, 'The Earth still moves'. Mind you, he spent the rest of his life under house arrest for saying it."

"So, you'll go along with actually doing the ritual?" she suggested, a little hesitantly.

"It looks as if there isn't really a choice, is there? It seems I must accept the existence of magic, no matter how much I dislike the whole concept. After all, what happened, happened. It was real. We both saw the thing. Okay, a really good special effects team might be able to fake it, but Hannah was a dotty old bat with no tech savvy. I doubt she could even open an email. Suggesting that she had the knowhow to fake it somehow is preposterous. No, I might hate the idea of magic but it's real, alright."

Sally had a pensive look about her as if she had a great and serious message to pass on. Finally, after a pause that seemed longer than it really was, she said, "Jon. Look, I have to say this. We both agree that that thing this morning was real, solid, proof that the other world exists. Everything else, up until now, could be passed off as one person's folly."

She shook her head in unconscious emphasis. It was as if she was trying the idea for size, then she said, "That thing was different. We both saw it, there's no point in denial. That's shocking in itself, and we need to deal with it. The thing is, we can't have doubts. I'm certain of that.

A lot of this depends on belief. It's like any religion. I think if we go on with this, we can't half-believe. If we go into this with the idea that, maybe, this old ritual will work, and maybe something might happen, I really think it could turn nasty. It's not some Victorian séance sitting round a table in the dark while some fat old faker produces cheesecloth from her mouth and says that it's ectoplasm. That thing, this morning, it couldn't harm us, but only because Hannah said it couldn't and we were certain of that. I really think that the defence worked because we believed that would work. All I'm saying is that taking this on like a parlour game might be really dangerous."

"I understand that," he said almost defiantly. "Christ Almighty, after this morning, how could I not?"

Sally took a deep breath. "Well, I've read a bit of Hannah's Book of Shadows. It's really a set of instructions, combined with a work diary. What we have to do is to follow her instructions all the way, and that means some preparation in advance. It's a practical thing really. Oh yes, and I don't think that Siran should be in the house while we do this, so Julie Penhaligon will need to baby sit. It's no big deal, Siran is going through the night, every night now, so really all Julie needs to do is to be there. But I really don't want Siran in the house while we do this."

"Agreed," he said, privately thinking that any force that could rupture the boundaries of time itself was going to be no respecter of a few hundred yards distance. "Christ, I can't believe we're really going to do this."

"Believe it, Jon," said Sally grimly. "For everyone's sake, believe it."

CHAPTER THIRTY-FOUR

Twenty-one days to Hallowmass Night, Hannah had said. Twenty-one days to prepare. Three weeks that took on the character of a nightmare that ran on and on, always present, alongside the normal activities of daily life.

Jonathan Wilde saw his patients, wrote prescriptions, referred people on to the hospital clinics, did his house calls, stood his turn on the air call roster to cover night-time emergencies, lived to all, intents and purposes, as any GP should. But, beneath the calm routine, there was an undercurrent of frantic activity.

Sally, following Hannah's precise instructions, set aside the small sitting room at the back of the house. In that room she began by reducing the furnishing to the absolute basics, a table, bare of any ornaments, covered with a pristine white linen cloth, and set with three chairs.

Again, following Hannah's instructions, she took care to see that a single chair, set apart from the rest, was placed at the east side of the room. According to the Book of Shadows, the east was the compass point associated with the dawn and rebirth.

She made several visits to Hannah's old house, and rumours spread in the village that the doctor and his wife were planning to join the throng of locals who operated holiday lets, but they said, Hannah's old place was so old fashioned and tatty, it would need a huge investment to prepare it for letting.

In reality, Sally used those visits to collect the impedimenta that she needed, including the black hafted knife, that the book called an 'Athame', whose handle was strangely twisted and carved. She collected two jars of powdered plant materiel, a small brass crucible-shaped dish, with squat legs that raised it slightly above the table surface, a packet of charcoal pellets, compressed and shiny-looking, and candles, of course, seemingly endless candles. Some were white, the traditional colour of mourning, two were deep black, and various others were of rainbow colours that gave the whole room a sort of nineteen sixties hippy ambience.

The theory, such as it was, called for a close link to the person to be called back from the grave, and as the old woman had been burned to ashes four hundred years before, Sally expected that to prove impossible, but a single jar stored by itself on Hannah's shelves was labelled in ancient brown spidery script that looked as old as God. The jar contained a greyish powdery substance and the label said 'Ashes from the last burning'.

The ritual called for a relic closely associated with the spirit to be summoned. Hannah's scrawled note suggested a photograph but as that was not a possibility, ashes from the old woman's body were surely a connection.

As the autumn nights gradually drew in, Halloween approached with a series of sea mists, interspersed with sudden gales that blew in and out again in a few days, never lingering, but always there to whip the sea into an angry grey mass that battered the land, in spiteful thumps and crashes.

By the time of the gales, the little back room had been transformed. The table was set with place settings, and, at the east corner of the room, an equilateral triangle was neatly taped on the floor in white masking tape.

The apexes of the triangle were set with blue candles in small round, beaten silver holders.

The week before Halloween came. Pumpkins were carved and set in village windows like fallen orange moons, and the local pagan groups prepared for their great annual festival of the dead.

At St Nectan's Glen, reputedly the most haunted site in the South West, there was a brief rise in offerings, in the form of precariously stacked piles of stone, and fresh clooties of cloth were tied to the branches of the old wishing tree.

A few days before the night of Halloween, Sally was satisfied that the preparation was as far advanced as they could be. The room was locked, the words of the ritual had been transcribed, using a brand new pen, onto a vellum paper especially chosen for the purpose. Sally made a point of writing the incantation in large print so that it would be easily legible in dim light.

The night before the big night drew in like any other. There was a slight burning smell in the air as if, all over the peninsula, people were raking and burning the fallen autumn leaves.

The trees stood bare branched, against a bone white moon that washed the world in pale silver as they went into the little room. Jonathan Wilde was struck by the incongruity of it all, a ceremony that seemed older than time itself, a call to a long dead witch, who had been executed less than three hundred yards from this very spot.

Outside, the everyday quiet life of the twenty-first century went on unperturbed. Yellow light shone from windows, wood smoke wafted from chimneys, and the occasional car trundled home from a job at one of the outlying farms, all of the villagers going about their business just like any other night, while, in this prosaic little room, an ancient ritual began.

Sally had her carefully transcribed notes, and she began by igniting the candles and carefully positioning the phial of blackish dust in the triangle on the floor. With all the preparations complete, and feeling self-conscious, as if there was an audience, other than her own husband to see it, she said, in a clear voice, as if addressing the empty air, "Goody Penrose, you are conjured to approach the gate of the east by the flames of Banal, by the mysteries of the East, Berald, Beorald, by the ancient rites of Hecate, mother of the night, by the name of Habondia, immortal lady of the wild woods, by the power of Cernunnos the lord of misrule and creation, I summon you. Come, Goody Penrose, and answer truthfully to my just demands of you."

Sally took a pinch of incense and poured it through her hand onto the glowing block of charcoal in the burner. Blue smoke rose, smelling like a bonfire on an autumn afternoon. The smoke formed a cloud, a discrete layer in the still air. It lay in a raft of bluish vapor in the candlelight.

Jonathan watched wordlessly. He had held, far down inside where the real person lived, an inner belief that this was ultimately nonsense. Not even the encounter with Hannah's guardian had really convinced him otherwise. The smoke of the incense was slightly narcotic, he knew, containing wormwood and artemisia. Both of them were mild hallucinogens, and both had a tendency to make the head swim, if the vapour was inhaled. He was still comforting himself with that thought, when the smoke cloud shimmered like a mirage over hot tarmac in summer, and the figure of the old woman materialised.

She stood there in the flesh. There was nothing ethereal about Goody Penrose. She was old, incredibly ancient, as if she had passed the centuries year by year and experienced every moment of them. Her voice was old and soft, and her West Country accent was so thick that it was hard to follow, but nonetheless, it was absolutely intelligible.

"You called me here," said the soft old, voice. "What is it that you want of me?"

Sally, glancing at her carefully transcribed sheet, said, "You are Goody Penrose? In all truth, you are the shade of the one who was so called?"

"I am, Goody Penrose, Wise Woman. Witch if you will. I was, in life, someone to frighten children with, and yet you have dared to call me. Why do you disturb the infinite?"

"To give you peace. To release you from this village forever. To put an end to the long chain of deaths."

"You believe, child, that it was I who caused all those murders over the centuries?" There was a hint of amusement in the old voice. "For someone who claims to wield the power of Hecate, you have small understanding of the truth, child. Have a care, or the forces that you are meddling with will swallow you, as they once nearly swallowed me. Is that what you want? To spend all eternity in the nothingness between worlds?"

"I want to free this place from your meddling. You have no place in human affairs, Goody, not anymore. What happened to you was a dreadful wrong, cruel even, but it is long done, and those who did it have long ago gone to their rest."

"I have done nothing to claim my revenge, child. Is that what you imagine these events are about?"

"What else?"

The shade stirred, seemed to fold in on itself, before finally settling into visibility again.

"When they... burned me," she said, and here the ancient face twisted, as if in the memory of old pain. "When they did that, they not only took my life, but they did it in the worst way that they could imagine, and they enjoyed doing it, they relished my pain, they revelled in it, and it was that enjoyment that is the root of all your woes, child.

"When people enjoy the forces of destruction, when they agree to link hands with the forces that would unmake the world, they sometimes open a portal, a way through to another dimension of being. The realities beyond that barrier are not something that mortals can survive. What is there is not evil, it is just a negative, the absolute opposite of everything that makes humans more than the beasts.

"Most times, nothing dreadful results from such things reaching through the veil. Nothing more happens than a few bitter little acts of petty spite. They are incapable of affecting the great flow of events so they exaggerate cruelty and bitter discord, often they use the faults that they find in a human being and twist them into something monstrous.

"A man goes home and rapes his partner, a young girl puts glass splinters into the cakes that she bakes for her mistress, the priest devises a cruel penance to inflict on his penitents. Nearly always, the results are just the small nastiness of people hating and hurting. It does its petty vileness, and then it is gone. The force released dissipates and spreads like a ripple, always growing weaker, until, at the outer edge of it, there is nothing there that matters.

"But, every now and again, something more happens. On the other planes of existence there are beings that hate mankind, your Christian bible was right about that at least. The forces of evil hate people and seek their destruction. Why? Well. Simply, because they are. These beings are no more than haters, they do things simply because they can, and you and they cannot share the same plane of existence in harmony. Some call such things 'demons', and that is as good a word as any, though the word itself simply means 'wise one' and these entities are as far from wisdom as the dark is from the light. When they burned me, my death, my pain, opened a gateway. The people of this village enjoyed that burning, not because they hated me, but because they knew me, and they enjoyed seeing the pain inflicted on one of their own. Their enjoyment opened the gate more and still more widely, and a thing came through that would have been better confined on another plane. That thing has been in this village ever since, feeding on the pain and deaths that have haunted this place forever. It loves pain, and revels in death and sorrow.

"Its strength is in human weakness. Centuries ago, the church called such events 'demonic possession' and it's true that the watcher can reach into a human being and twist their actions. It can do little of itself, not really, even that much creativity is beyond it. But it can take the seed of destruction in a human mind and feed it, and make it grow into something huge and terrible. When a child goes missing, used and then discarded by some half-witted stranger, the watcher is the real cause, and afterwards the poor idiot who actually does the deed is left unable to explain why. A man beats his wife to a pulp. The watcher is there, feeding on the pain. An old woman burns, it is the flame, and feeds on her pain. It is neither male nor female though it can take the attributes of either sex at need. A man dies at sea. The watcher feels and enjoys that last desperate struggle for air as the man sinks and fights to breathe. Its meat and drink are suffering and pain. For endless years this thing has troubled the village and now the time finally comes for that to end.

"In the end, child, this monster is yours to dismiss, yours and your man's. He has a part to play though, whether he will or no. Not yet maybe, not for a little time, but you will know when the time is right. I'm constrained by laws that you do not even suspect, but I can tell you that you have a little time to prepare. Once, long ago, your ancestor did a thing, now the debt follows your bloodline. For your very soul, child, prepare as best you can, and then, when the time comes, do what must be done.

"There are ways to dismiss these creatures, to send them back to the chaos where they belong.

"You must find the way for yourself. That I cannot do for you. You have Hannah's books to point the way. That will start you on the path, but in the end, child, you must find your own way, as all seekers after truth must. I can only tell you that the path exists, I cannot put your feet on it."

The shade was growing misty now, losing solidity, slipping away, the voice seeming to come from far away, echoing, and attenuated by distance.

Sally, sensing that time was short now, said, "Wait, please, I don't know where to start."

"Use Hannah's book, child. You must call this monster as you called me – but not by using the Dumb Supper. In the end, the Dumb Supper is to be used for knowledge, not as a weapon, no matter how good the cause might seem. You must dismiss this monster, send it back to the plane that it came from, and then, with that done, you must close the portal. You need power to do that, child. You might not suspect its existence, but your ancestors knew the way. This nightmare and its kind were well known to them. The stone circle is a lens of power. It is your only chance to win this battle. I am called back now, and I cannot refuse the call."

The shade was pale by then, tenuous and transparent like smoke in the wind, dissolving in tatters as they watched. The figure of the old woman shivered and faded, the candle flames flickered, and, quite suddenly, a draft blew through the room, and the candles whiffed out, leaving them in darkness.

"Bloody hell," said Jonathan. "What the fuck was that about?"

"That," said Sally, "was the 'essence' I suppose you could call it, of a seventeenth century witch, who my ancestors burned to death, not a hundred yards from where we are now."

"Well," said Jonathan Wilde, "I suppose that, at the very least, we finally have proof of life after death."

"I suppose we do, but considering what she said, I'm not sure I wouldn't rather have done without that, for now."

"Well, what do we do now?" asked Jonathan.

"What indeed? I feel as if I'm at school again and facing some exam that I know nothing about, you know that dream? The one we all used to get? That feeling of absolute hopelessness even though you think that really you should be able to deal with it?"

"Yeah, but this is a bit more serious than failing a paper in GCSE maths."

Sally said, "Do you really want to go ahead and try to do this? To get rid of that thing, like the old woman said."

"I get the feeling," said Jonathan, "that if we don't look for it, sooner or later, it will come looking for us."

Sally looked at him, her expression unreadable. Then she said, "You know what, Doctor? You are something else."

"In what way?"

"Well, I thought that you'd be dead against doing anything more about this."

"Because I hated the idea to start with?

"Because you didn't believe in any of it. The whole supernatural thing, I mean. You're always the rationalist."

"Denying the evidence of your own eyes isn't rational. It's cant."

"But it's a big leap to ask of you."

"Look, whatever I believed before tonight, the reality is that the old woman came back to us, across time. How that can be I have no idea, but I have to accept that as evidence of a reality that I previously never suspected. Given that the occult exists, and it obviously does, we'll get nowhere by denying the fact of that existence. So, we are left with what to do now."

CHAPTER THIRTY-FIVE

Morning came ushered in by a blood red sunrise. Sally occupied herself by clearing the remains of the ritual from the night before. The materials that they had gathered so carefully were simply ashes and pooled burned-out candle wax now, without any further significance. In the cottage living room, with the everyday furnishings around them, the whole episode seemed like an evil dream that they had shared.

Sally finished off cleaning up the remains of the ritual with an almost obsessive thoroughness, as if the act of cleaning up itself finally put an end point to the night before. It was almost a ritual in itself.

"The big question is…" she said, busying herself stowing the last of the cleaning materials away. "According to what she told us, what we really should do is to finish what my ancestor started, all those years ago. The thing is, I'm not even sure where we start to do that. Where the hell can you find out about a body of knowledge that's secret by its very nature?"

With the memory of the scent of the incense still hanging in the air, accepting the truth of the supernatural was the easy part. It was one thing to accept that the occult was very real, it was quite another to actually get directly involved. But, as often happens in real life, when extraordinary events happen, the human mind is capable of accepting what it cannot explain, and having accepted it, capable of simply going on with the essential routine business of living.

As it happened, the situation resolved itself, though first

there was a long interlude. At the start, in the few days after that Halloween, Sally put a good deal of conscious effort into searching for a route towards understanding what had happened that night.

During that hectic period, the problem occupied her mind more or less constantly. It was a steady background to her everyday life like a background hum in an industrial plant, so much part of the scene that it eventually was almost unnoticed. Sally followed one lead after another, but eventually, even though her investigations led her to a closer understanding of the local pagan community, in the end she was no nearer to understanding the events. Ultimately, for want of any solid progress, she was forced to let matters lie, in the fatalistic hope that, when the time came, if the time came, a way through would declare itself.

Most of that time was good, the memories of the events faded, as bad dreams will, and there were no more violent happenings to disturb the peaceful flow of village life. The series of nightmare happenings seemed to have stopped. They almost came to believe that the whole episode had been a combination of coincidence and the stress of events.

Sally did not exactly give up the quest for information. It was more that the solution was shelved, to be considered at a future time. As for Jonathan, he lost himself in the everyday practice of medicine, seeing patients into the world as squalling, red, angry bundles of life, and finally seeing them out again. For the time, it was enough and the events of those few days faded from immediate memory, though, each year, as Halloween rolled round, memories stirred.

For a full three years after the night of the Dumb

Supper, there was peace in the village. The Wildes had begun to believe that the nightmare had finally been resolved, and they were content to accept an uneasy peace without being certain of the outcome. Summers came, bringing the regular rush of tourists who clogged the roads and crowded the beaches. Siran grew from a helpless infant into a sturdy, country-raised toddler, ready to attend the reception class in nearby St Mellion.

Sally, with Siran finally consigned to the long process of day-to-day education, found herself, for the first time in years, with free time available to her. The Wildes, to all outward appearances, lived the life of a comfortable middle-class couple. Old Dr Francis did fewer and fewer shifts at the practice, and Jonathan talked of hiring a fresh partner to take on some of the workload. It was a quiet time, a fulfilled and happy time, of gentle living and easy satisfactions, and if there was a hidden undercurrent of unease it was no worse than the normal flow of everyday anxiety that most human beings live with.

Three autumns came and went in a flush of gales that blew in from the Atlantic and three winters were punctuated with Christmas trees that appeared, as if by magic in the village square, courtesy of the parish council, and a crew of four hardy volunteers who laboriously hauled the freshly cut Sitka spruce upright.

The change came, when it came, in the improbable form of an old university friend of Sally's called Izzie Williams. Years before, when they had both been inexperienced, and very recent, graduates, still feeling their way towards a career in the world, Izzie had been a constant in a world of flux.

Emerging from the university experience, with that strange sense of being bereft of the supportive community that had been home for three years, Sally was tentatively beginning to apply her literary background to the shark-infested waters of publishing. Izzie, with a similar background, and a good arts degree, chose instead to apply her not inconsiderable talents to research, on a contract basis, for publishers, authors and film companies.

It was always a fairly competitive field, made more so over the turning years by the then early internet, that, in due time, by-passed a good deal of the spadework and allowed most seekers after truth to do their own background checks. Even so, Izzie had an advantage. No algorithm, even the most advanced of them, could operate on intuition, and that subtle skill was something Izzie had in spades. As a young graduate, she was a skinny, willowy and almost caricature version of a second-generation hippy chick, but underneath the tie dye ethnic clothes and easy going, laid back exterior, was a brain with an almost eidetic ability to retain and order facts, and to detect patterns in events.

Izzie had used her talents to make a reasonable, if not exactly palatial, living out of ferreting out facts that journalists found useful, and writers found essential.

For years, Izzie was the 'go to' person if you were searching for information about the obscure and the exotic. Sally's friendship with her had lasted through the years. It was a friendship conducted mainly at a distance, touching base in person every now and then, and occasionally meeting. Mostly they communicated by email or the occasional celebration card.

Sally had turned Izzie loose on the problem of occult

reference books almost because she could think of nothing else to do. She had already read the usual suspects. Starting with the scholarly Idries Shah's 'Secret Lore Of Magic' she progressed to the excellent Cavendish tome on the 'Black Arts', and the thoroughly unreadable and self-congratulatory Alister Crowley, 'The Great Beast', whose predilection for sodomy and outraging his inanely puritanical mother seemed the major basis for his supposed interest in practising 'Magick'.

The scholarly works were, she found, voluminous and interesting, if rather wordy. The alleged 'practical' works like Crowley's, seemed to Sally no more in the end than the vacuous ramblings of a tedious heroin addict who had built his own desperate fixations into a pseudo-religion.

Crowley did however have a single nugget of information to offer, that Sally first tried to follow up herself, and finally gave over to Izzie to follow up on an 'old pals act' basis, so that, the next time Izzie visited Cornwall, she would try to bring any leads with her, as a payment of sorts, for a few weeks' free board and lodging.

The single lead that she turned up was ostensibly no more than a rumour. During the crazy occult boom and rise of the odd 'magical' societies in the nineteen hundreds, the 'Esoteric and Hermetic order of the Golden Dawn' was run by none other than Crowley himself, and an eccentric individual called McGregor Mathers.

For years those two had been close collaborators, until finally, in circumstances that were shrouded in mystery, they had split and eventually Mathers had fled into obscurity, while Crowley went on to form his own 'Magick' Society, the 'Order of the Silver Star', before escaping England for the more tolerant atmosphere of

Mussolini's Italy to found the 'Abbey of Thelema'. Thus far Crowley was tolerated until, finally, even the fascists had enough and deported him. Later, long after his death, he had achieved brief fame in the counter-culture of the late nineteen sixties.

The split between Crowley and Mathers had not been amicable, and Crowley was as venomous about his old friend as he was about most of his acquaintances, accusing him of making off with an 'ultimate secret' and finally, laying a 'curse' on him. All of that was popular history, but less well known was that, although it is assumed that Mathers was dead by the time Crowley reached the height of his infamy, the exact circumstances of his death were obscure.

The best guess seemed to be that he died in the great flu pandemic of 1918, but his death, like his life, was vague and hard to pin down. There was one major factoid in all that smoke and mirrors account. It was rumoured that Mathers was in possession of a 'Grimoire', a book of 'great power', referred to only in the literature as the 'Well of Dead Souls'. This, it was said, was the 'ultimate secret', that Mathers had supposedly appropriated and vanished with.

A single reference recorded the discovery of documents, supposedly belonging to the Order of the Silver Star, washed out of an eroding sand dune in the nineteen seventies – a cache which did not contain the missing book. There were no other references and the general opinion seemed to be that the 'ultimate book of secrets' was no more than a rumour put about by Mathers himself, after the collapse of his magical society. It was held to be probably no more than a bit of window dressing to bolster his bruised ego.

CHAPTER THIRTY-SIX

When Izzie Williams finally showed up on the doorstep of the cottage one early spring day, Sally had no great expectations of anything other than a pleasant few days of drinking a little too much, staying up far too late, and talking over old times.

But it was the unlikely figure of Izzie, rather overweight, chain smoking Izzie, who set off the final chain of events. Like a tiny spark in a gunpowder mill, they began with nothing and rapidly escalated to a conflagration.

They were sitting in the living room beside a wood burner whose open doors revealed a heart of gold fire and a heap of artfully disposed hardwood logs. Izzie had disposed her not inconsiderable bulk on a Navaho Indian rug, a souvenir of a long-ago trip that Jonathan had taken to the west of the States between postings, some fifteen years before.

Sally regarded her old friend from the comfort of the sofa, while Jonathan, partly out of consideration for giving two old friends a little space, was in the study, beavering away at a long neglected set of paperwork, that was part of the burden that the NHS wished on most GPs in these straightened days.

"I came across Gill a few weeks back," said Izzie. "You know, little Gill? The Biochemist as was?"

"Oh right," said Sally. "How is she?"

"Same old Gill. Got herself involved with an Arab bloke. Not an easy relationship – with the religious differences and what not. Still, they seem happy enough, at least for the time being."

Sally took a thoughtful sip at her drink. "Are you ready for another one yet?"

"Oh, go on then," said Izzie. "I need to take it a bit easy though. My capacity is down on what it was years back."

Sally smiled and poured another hefty slug from the Bacardi bottle.

Izzie said, "Are you going to take one up to Jon?"

"No. He's working. It's endless, the bloody paperwork. You'd think a doctor could get to spend time treating people, not filling in forms."

"Sign of the times, dear," said Izzie rather complacently.

"Are you finding plenty of work?" asked Sally.

"Yeah. It's steady, you know? Right now there's this rather weird woman who wants to know about serial murders."

"Yeah. It's a modern obsession, I guess. Hannibal Lector and all that."

"Look, love," said Izzie, as if that closed the subject of work, "talking of weird, I've got a few leads on your missing book of magic."

"What, Mather's grimoire? Honestly, don't put too much into it. I mean, I appreciate your efforts, I really do, but it was just that… well, something odd happened a while ago, and it came up. I'll tell you the whole story some time."

Izzie looked a little piqued. "Well, if you really don't want to know where the book is, we'll let it go. To be honest, the thing is bloody creepy, Sall. If I was superstitious, I'd say you should forget the whole fucking thing."

"I'm not sure I can do that, Izz. I'd love to, but, well, you know how you start something, and it gets to be a sort of part of your life? I'm sorry I was less than enthusiastic.

It's just that part of me would willingly forget 'the whole fucking thing'. But, if you know where that book is, I'd really like to know."

Izzie stood up. "I've got to take a leak," she said. "Give me five."

"That's not like you, Izz," said Sally. "You always seemed to have hollow legs or something. Some nights you seemed to go all night without a piss. We used to joke about it, remember? "

"Yeah, well it was a long time ago, Sall."

Izzie might not have been exactly sober after four or five large Bacardis, but she still managed the short trip to the downstairs loo with a steady kind of studied care. Presently, she came back and disposed herself in front of the wood-burner again. She sat on a huge scatter cushion and drew up her knees in an almost protective gesture that Sally recognised from years ago.

"It's like this," said Izzie, looking into the flames rather than at Sally directly. "When I started looking around for that book, I just put the word out. I started on the usual contacts, and there was nothing. You know? Not just a few dead ends, but fucking nothing, nada, zilch. Now that is really weird. Often there's not a lot of information at first, that's normal, but nothing? Finally this guy comes out of the woodwork. Came out of the blue he did, cold calling. He said, he'd heard I was looking for a copy of the 'Well of Dead Souls'. He said that I might be lucky. Well, I arranged to meet him in a public place, you know? In this business, you take care who you deal with, if you want to last for long. I met the guy in this scruffy caff in town. It was a transport place mainly, cabbies use it too. Christ! The place put the grease into 'greasy spoon', if you see what I mean? Anyhow this bloke, Sam Collins, his name was, or at least, he said it was. He comes in and right away I think, 'This one is going to be fucking useless. He's a bloody junkie for a start. He had all the signs, the addiction was written all over him. Skinny, pale, scruffy, three-day beard and that bloody thousand-yard stare. So, I'm thinking, 'What the hell? Buy the poor sod a coffee and get the hell out of here.' After all, a hell of lot of leads come to bugger all. Nothing lost, really."

Izzie took a pull at her drink and said, "Well, I was wrong. You know sometimes you get a feeling…? Well, it's no secret to you, I expect, you know how I've always worked. Well, suddenly, I just felt, 'This guy is the real thing. He really knows where a copy of the book is.'

"So, we're sitting there, and he reaches into his coat and just plonks it down on the table in that tatty little caff. It sat there on a cheap plastic cloth, an old book, all mucky around the corners, and bound in, well, honestly, I don't like to think what the thing might be bound in. I reached out and touched it. It was still warm with that ratty little bastard's body heat, and honestly, I felt a bit queasy touching it. It felt like handling a fresh turd, you know?"

Izzie shuddered at the memory, and then she said, "Anyhow, the second I reached out to the cover I knew it was the real thing. I just knew it, the way you do. Anyhow, I said, right then, 'How much do want for it?' and he says, 'Two hundred.' No bargaining, no nothing. It was enough for a few days of Columbian Marching Powder for him, I guess. Now, of course, if you work with a bloody junkie, you don't normally just lay the money over, but I knew it was right. In any case two hundred I could lose in expenses. So I handed over the cash, and he went out into the street, leaving the book on the table. It wasn't quite the last I saw of him – but that was something else."

Izzie took a fresh cigarette from a packet of menthol tipped and went on, talking through a cloud of bluish smoke. "So I took the book and I put it in my shoulder bag, and I stepped out of the place into the sunlight, and, right away I could see this commotion up the street. I'm not a rubber-necker really, but I could see the blue lights gathering a bit up the road, and I was going that way. Well, I got to this knot of bystanders, and I could see a pair of legs, in dirty blue jeans, sticking out from under a big truck. I could see the feet really clearly, they were wearing those yellow work boots, you know, the kind they wear on building sites? There was a big pool of blood and the body was, well, damaged, but I could still recognise the face. The poor bugger never even got to spend his two hundred quid."

Izzie took another heroic pull at her drink, then she went on, "So, I had the book, and Sam Collins – if that was his real name – was dead. So, there's a bit of a problem, cause there's no way to check the provenance of the thing. The thing is, girl, I just feel that it's right. Anyhow, do you still want it?"

Sally drew in a deep breath then she said, "Not really, Izz, not really *want* as such, but I don't think I've really got a choice. Look, how it is, is like this. If I'm asking you to get involved, even in a minor way, it's best that you understand what it's all about." Sally broke off for a moment, gathering her thoughts. "Christ, this is more difficult than I thought. Okay... Well, to start from the beginning, it was just after we moved here. Jon was just getting into the flow of the practice and there was this run of nasty accidents. They came one after another..."

An hour later it was all out, from her suspicions that there was more than a run of coincidence to the weird happenings of the Dumb Supper.

"I suppose that you think I've finally gone crazy. Anyhow, I owe you two hundred, don't let me forget. But Izz, there's something *really* wrong about that old book. Even without actually having it in the flesh, there's something wrong. I just know it. A few years ago, I would have said it was nothing concrete but, well, that was before, and now that things are quiet and we're living a normal life, taking that book feels like waking a sleeping monster."

Izzie shrugged. "I believe you and I don't think you're crazy. In my job, you get to see a lot of odd stuff, and you hear all kinds of stories. Most of it you can explain, some of it you can't. As for the book... well, I understand how you feel. It's all finally gone quiet, why would you want to start it all over? Give me the two hundred quid and call it done?"

Siran, who had until that point been sleeping the sleep that only small children, the financially secure, and those with a clear conscience can achieve, started to grizzle. Her small cries carried clearly via the intercom speaker in the corner of the room.

As it happened, the two friends had no further chances to discuss the book or its weird provenance. By the time that Siran was resettled, and things were quiet again, Jonathan had come back downstairs. He was rather tired from his battle with the practice paperwork, and the conversation was more general, and less interesting. Izzie was due to go back north the following day, and by eight the following morning, Sally was on her way to deliver Izzie to the station at Truro and there was no real chance to raise the subject further.

It was only when Sally was piloting the Jeep back down the long rather ugly dual carriageway that leads from the higher part of Truro to the main part of the town clustered beside the Truro River, that she realised that there was a package sitting on the rear seat. At first, she thought that Izzie had forgotten part of her luggage, and thinking that she might still get back to the station in time to catch up with the London train before it left, she made a long turn round the traffic island at the bottom of the road and headed back the way she had come.

It was a close-run thing, but, as Sally reached the station turn off, she was just in time to see the London-bound 125 trundling out over Brunel's viaduct that carries northbound traffic out of Truro on the old Great Western line.

Sally pulled into the station car park, well aware that it was no use. Izzie was already on her way. Sally got out of the Jeep and walked around to the rear passenger door with that feeling of let down that people always feel when they are irrevocably too late.

The package that Izzie had left on the seat was a plastic supermarket carrier from Asda, bright green and yellow in the company's colours. The bag was folded carefully around a rectangular solid object. Sally picked it up, and knew immediately what Izzie had left for her.

The book was old, ratty-looking, and bound in a soft

skin cover that felt as if it had only recently been flayed from the creature that had grown it. Sally opened the cover, expecting a title. Instead, there was a single line of script that looked brownish, as if it was written in old blood.

Across the page, by way of a title, was the legend: Zasas, Zasas, Nasatanada Zasas.

There was nothing else on that first page, but, leafing through the book, Sally could see that it was closely printed in small font text. Occasionally, there were steel engraved black and white prints, some were complex geometric designs, some illustrating images.

Sally, holding the book, knew what Izzie had meant by the strange feel that it had about it. There was nothing especially odd about the cover to look at. It was just old leather, like thousands of old books that lay untouched and unloved in a million attic rooms. But under her fingers it felt foul, as if it was contaminated with some vile disease agent. Almost unconsciously, she wiped her fingers against her jeans and stood looking at the book as the utterly everyday activities of the station car park went on all around her, in the late summer sun.

CHAPTER THIRTY-SEVEN

Izzie Williams lived in a trendy warehouse conversion in a newly gentrified area of the capital. Once upon a time, stacks of newly imported cotton cloth had stood in huge bales on cast iron racks that stood from floor to ceiling. There were stripped out open areas of blonde honey-coloured pine wood and tall bright white walls with high ceilings that supported industrial aluminium shaded lights. Izzie's flat was cavernous in its minimalism, and stark.

Her walls were scattered with bright abstracts, and the kitchen area, tucked into one corner of the living space, was equipped with sterile-looking equipment that was all stainless steel and digital readout panels. The effect was like a small section of a NASA control room that only people who never cook for themselves could afford.

Izzie regarded the place as not only a place to lay her head, but part of her stock in trade. Working mainly with a trendy – and so self-aware – media savvy group of producers, directors and successful writers, she was expected to live in a particular style. Anything less would have suggested a lack of success, and, working in an area where success breeds success, Izzie Williams was all too well aware of the 'Emperors New Clothes' aspects of her image.

From the start, of course, it has to be said, that returning to an open plan, post-industrial apartment is never going to have the atmosphere of a homecoming to a cosy country cottage.

That night, coming home via the sordid clutter around King's Cross, Izzie was struck, not for the first time, by the contrast between the teeming street life around the station, with its druggies and teenage whores, and the almost nineteenth century bucolic, agricultural feel of the station at Truro, where you could stand and look out at rolling hills all around. Izzie wondered if Sally, her bold, girlhood friend, had not made the better life choices.

Climbing the cast iron staircase that accessed her front door and pressing the switches that illuminated the apartment in hard white light, she was once more afflicted by doubts that this urban chic habitat was not what she really wanted. Coming home from Cornwall, the countryside seemed, in retrospect, idyllic, an oasis of peace, contrasting with this frenetic city that was so obsessed with its own importance. She was still mulling over that rose tinted image as she crossed the floor to the pinging panel of the intruder alarm and fed it the numerical code that silenced it. Sadly for Izzie, the West Country, with its vast silences, holds secret nightmares of its very own, and sometimes they follow you wherever you go. Sometimes apparent peace is really only the quiet of the grave.

She crossed to the cooking area – you couldn't call it anything as vulgar as a kitchen – and switched the coffee machine on. The sound of its boiling water under pressure was very loud in the silence.

It was as she was decanting the coffee, a strong black brew that seemed almost oily as it poured, that Izzie felt that she was no longer alone in that sterile open space. At first, she shrugged the feeling off, dismissing it as the result of Sally's story and the creepy atmosphere that went with it.

"Stupid bloody woman. Acting like the heroine of a

Victorian Penny Dreadful," she chided herself, speaking aloud, but the sound of her voice in the silence seemed to make things worse. Finally, she turned round, sure that something was watching her.

It was no real surprise to see the figure sitting on a sofa just a few feet away.

It was an immaculately dressed, slim young man who had almost the air of a dandy about him. Even in a city, and in an area where people dressed well, his immaculate appearance was exceptional.

"What the hell?" said Izzie, in a small voice, and almost instantly hated herself for sounding weak.

"Indeed, my dear," said the young man. "Most apposite."

"Get the fuck out of my apartment. What are you doing here in the first place?"

"I'm here," said the young man in a level voice, "because you can't keep yourself out of matters that you had better have left unexplored."

Izzie was suddenly furious. She had not, until that moment, realised what depths of anger she was capable of. Once, years before, an oafish work colleague had made the mistake of fondling her arse in public, and the violence of her response, a single open-handed rabbit punch, had left him with a broken nose and bruising that lasted, like a stigma, for three weeks afterwards. She had always remembered that moment of red mist, but that anger had been nothing compared to what she felt now. Now, she was so possessed of the urge to smash and kill, she was hardly capable of speech, such was her rage. She said, "I don't care who or what you are. I'm giving you a chance to leave now. Fucking get out."

"Or what?"

Izzie had owned the ancient shotgun for years. It had belonged to an old uncle who had died and left the relic propped up in the corner of his bedroom. As it happened, it came into her possession at a time when urban rioting was the new pastime among the dispossessed of the capital. There were a few killings, and worst of all, three well reported, and exceptionally brutal, gang rapes.

Izzie, a woman living alone in an area that was becoming gentrified, but still had areas of deprivation, took the old gun home and secreted it, almost as a talisman. In truth, she had very little idea of how to use such a weapon.

She was surprised to learn that while the shotgun itself required a certificate to be legal, anyone, due to a kink in the law, could buy the cartridges from a registered gunsmith. A visit to a little shop near the Portobello Road had provided her with a heavy box of twenty-five fat green cylinders each one marked 'Ely Hymax 00 buck'. She had loaded the gun gingerly, during a night when it seemed that half London was burning, and looting went on less than a mile from her flat, and, ever since then, it had rested in a narrow gap between two bookcases, gathering dust. Now that a possible threat had become actual present menace, she edged towards its hiding place, never taking her eyes off the newcomer.

She was inwardly doubtful if the gun was still capable of being fired. Now, she took up the dusty relic, and pulled the hammers back in clumsy haste.

Her visitor was completely unfazed.

"Oh, my dear," said the young man, sounding as if he were disagreeing with an intellectual position at a dinner party.

Izzie simply kept the muzzles pointed at him, directly at the centre of his chest. He was less than ten feet away.

He stood up in one relaxed, easy, flowing movement.

"I mean it," she said. "I'll blow you apart before I let you near me."

"No," he said in a flat denial, and took a step towards her.

She was hardly aware of squeezing the twin triggers, but the shotgun cut loose with a primal roar. Twin cones of red flame flashed from the barrels and bright red and yellow sparks flew.

Directly behind the young man, a pretty piece of reclaimed wood furniture was torn into bone white splinters, by the twin charge of buckshot. The young man himself was untouched, as undisturbed as if he had been made of smoke.

"Time to die, dear," he said and raised his left hand in a small clenching gesture.

Izzie felt her heart stop. It was as if someone had thrown a switch. Suddenly, a great weight descended on her chest. She clasped both hands to her throat, the shotgun clattered unseen to the floor, fine wisps of blue/white smoke still curling from the barrels, its spurious menace spent.

As the dark swam towards her, Izzie saw through the suave clothing and the manicured exterior, and for the first time, she saw the visitor for what he really was. A slumped, shaggy, red eyed monster was standing in his place. It was all slavering fangs and red eyes. All trace of the suave visitor was gone. She tried to scream, but her voice was trapped in her throat, and suddenly, she was lying on the floor looking up at him.

"Welcome to hell, dear," he said, and his voice was like stones grinding together, and then the dark came for her in waves.

CHAPTER THIRTY-EIGHT

It was a bright early morning in Tregadrew. The sun, even so late in the year, was glittering on a sea that was the colour of a Ceylon sapphire, flecked with pure white. In the Wilde household, the three of them were sitting at the scrubbed pine kitchen table. Jonathan was drinking coffee. Sally was attacking a bowl of cereal and Siran was toying with a strange mud-coloured confection that was claimed to be a 'perfectly balanced, fruit-based, infant food'.

The sunlight streamed through the big sash window, and it carried that golden tinge that comes into the light in Cornwall in September and, with any luck, stays around until it is finally faded by the coming of true winter and the first of the Atlantic gales.

Jonathan Wilde, who was due to take surgery from ten that morning, was in a fine mood. For the last six weeks or so, the practice had produced nothing beyond the steady pattern of minor health care and routine vaccination clinics. Life went along an uneventful and pleasant course. He had recently taken up an offer to act as physician to the local RNLI and a lifeboat pager lay on the table. In the West Country, a lifeboat pager is a badge of honour. He was, he felt, fully accepted in the village.

Presently, cutting into the morning, the phone started its nasal bleep. It was the landline this time, not either of their mobiles, and that, in itself, was unusual.

"I'll get it," said Sally, standing up before Jonathan could react.

"No problem," he said. "If it's that bastard trying to

pretend he's from the tax people, tell him to go forth and multiply, from me."

He found the scam calls immensely irritating.

Sally rose to her feet. From the kitchen, Jonathan heard her end of the conversation, and right away it didn't sound like a routine scam call.

"Yes, it is," said Sally. "Who's calling...? Right, And, what can I do for you?" There was a short pause, then she went on. "Yes, yes, she's a friend, rather than a relative, but she was with us last week, which is why our address is there..." Another pause, then, "What? Christ... I can't believe this. Look, are you sure you have the right woman? Izzie Williams? I see. No, I don't think that she has any living relatives. Her mother was the last, and she died years back. She isn't married, so Izzie is all by herself." There was another lengthy pause, then Sally said, "Freelance, I think. No, I'm sure she was freelance. So, I can't suggest an employer. No, I'm sorry I can't be more useful. What? No, I had no idea she had a gun. Yes. Well, you have this number if you need us. Yes, thank you. Goodbye."

As soon as she came through the door from the hallway, Jonathan knew she'd had bad news, not some minor problem, but really bad news, in the sense of something that changes lives, and turns the pattern of existence upside down.

"What? Sally, love, what the hell is wrong?"

"It's Izzie, Jon." She was trembling with the emotion of it. "Izzie's dead. "

"What? What was it? An accident?"

"They... they found her in her flat. The neighbours heard a gunshot and the police broke in when they couldn't get a reply."

"A gunshot? What the hell?"

"She wasn't shot. The policeman who called me said that she seemed to have blasted a sideboard with a shotgun. They think it was natural causes, but they can't find a relative to contact, and our address was in her bag."

"Bloody hell."

"Jon, I've known her since we were eighteen, for God's sake."

"I know, love. It's never easy when someone goes suddenly."

Siran, sensing the atmosphere, rather than understanding it, began to cry lustily in sympathy. Sally picked her up and held her for comfort. "Shh, darling," she said. "It's okay. Mummy is just a bit upset."

"Do you want me to try to get last minute cover for this morning?" asked Jon.

"No, no, it's okay. It was just a shock. I'll be better getting on with things. The thing is, she was always so full of life. I always thought she'd be there forever somehow."

"I'll make you a drink."

Morning surgery passed in a fog of speculation. Jonathan knew Izzie only at second-hand, a sort of adjunct to the woman he loved, but she had, in his experience, always seemed sane and balanced. Trying to reconcile that woman with someone who fired a shotgun, apparently at random, in her own living room, was impossible. He had intended to keep the problem to himself, but old Eric was far too old a hand at the reading of people in trauma to be fooled, and in the end, Jonathan confided in the older man after the pre-lunch break.

"It's just so out of character, Eric," he said. "I mean,

she seemed dead level-headed and, where the hell did she come by a gun anyhow?"

"That's not hard to explain, Jon, not really. After all, every other house has a shotgun down here. It's part of country life. How often have you gone to a house call and found one hanging in the room?"

"Yes, down here, but in London, for God's sake?" he said. "They aren't exactly infested with rabbits. Besides, they think it was natural causes. But she died after she fired a gun inside her flat. There's nothing natural about a healthy thirty-four-year-old dropping dead is there?"

"Well, that's unusual certainly, but you know full well that it's not by any means unheard of."

"No, no, of course not. I'm sorry, Eric. It's really not a practice problem. I've no right to bother you with this."

"No, at least not in theory, but anything that troubles my partner concerns me. Besides, Jon, after this long, I hope that I can call you a friend."

"I appreciate that, Eric," said Jonathan. "I really do."

"Go home, Jon. Look after your wife. I'll handle the afternoon surgery and field any calls that come in. It's quiet in any case."

"We used to say, when I was working in A&E, that you never say that 'things are quiet', cause it usually makes the sky fall in."

Eric smiled. "Well, if things get desperate, I can always call you. In the meanwhile, go and smooth domestic turmoil for a few hours."

When Jonathan walked through the door, he found Sally sitting in the living room, looking at the old book that Izzie had delivered

"How are you feeling, love?" he said.

"Terrible. The worst thing is that it's troubling Siran. She knows something is wrong, but she doesn't know what."

"It's a nightmare, love. I'm so sorry. Izzie was a good friend. I mean, obviously, I didn't know her as well as you, but she really was, well, she was one of a kind."

"She was that," said Sally. "Still, there's things to do, no matter how we feel about it."

"Sure. Do we know when the funeral is going to be? I'm thinking you'll want to go."

"I was talking to the police earlier. Cause of the way she... died and the gun being involved, it's going to be a coroner's case, I think, so it could be a few weeks before they let us have a funeral."

"She was on her own? Did she have any relatives?"

Sally shook her head. "Not that I know of. I was thinking that three days ago she was sitting here... now all there is to show that she existed is... is this."

Sally indicated the book.

"Is that the one you were trying to find? Mathers' book?" asked Jonathan.

"Yes, well, I think it is. To be honest, there's been too much happening to even think about it."

"Of course. I was only interested."

"I know, love, but don't mind me. It's just that it's all such a shock."

She was suddenly pale and the dark blotches under her eyes were very clear against her skin.

"Can I make you something to eat?"

"No, I'll do it. You still have the bloody practice to run. Is Eric okay with all this?"

"Sure, he's been great. I think it's nice, for a time at least, for him to take charge again for a few days." Jonathan idly opened the book with its cryptic title. "What the hell does that mean?" he said.

"I don't know," said Sally. "I was going to look it up on the net, but, to be honest, it suddenly seems so trivial compared to losing Izzie that way. I'll check it sometime, I suppose."

"Sure. I'm making a drink. Do you want one?"

Twenty minutes afterwards with Sally resting up, Jonathan was alone with the old book in the living room. Siran was building complex models out of bright coloured plastic bricks in a littered corner of the room. Sally's grief had not exactly taken him by surprise but he was at a loss to know what he could do to help.

Idly he opened his laptop and called up a site that specialised in tracing quotes. 'Quotes are Us' it said in cheery multicoloured letters that danced across the screen.

Jonathan typed in the book's title, following the prompts, and the machine began its endless search. It took all of eight seconds, and as he began to think that it was just a nonsense phrase, a learned article flashed up. It was taken from the 'English Journal of Folklore' from June 1962.

'Zasas Zasas Nasatanada Zasas,' it said, 'is a Greek quote transposed almost phonetically from ancient Aramaic. The exact meaning of the phrase is dubious, mainly because of multiple transpositions by a good many interpreters over the centuries. The earliest traceable use is from the Apocrypha where the words are attributed to Adam. In that context, it is said to be the phrase that opens the gates of Hell, allowing the inhabitants to leave their confinement and return to Earth. Wilkinson (1844) in his work on 'The corrupt gospels' quotes the phrase…'

Jonathan Wilde shook his head and shut the site down. Even so, it left an atmosphere of chill behind it as if he had opened the door of a commercial cold store.

CHAPTER THIRTY-NINE

Tall Pines was the rather inappropriate name of a nursing home that stood alone in a well-manicured garden, just west of the village. The pine trees in question were a rough row of Scot's Pines, umbrella-shaped at the crown and twisted by a century of westerly gales. They had once marked a boundary between the grounds of the old parish union workhouse and the common land outside. The building still had the look of the old union, with its dour and austere, Georgian straight up and down exterior and neat brick chimney stacks.

Belying its appearance, Tall Pines was a comfortable, warm, and well found nursing home, owned by an Indian medic who was a consultant at the local hospital.

It was a substitute and, in many cases, a final home, for those older people in the community who found that the mechanics of day-to-day living were finally getting beyond them.

As a care home, Tall Pines was inspected on a yearly basis, but the rather jolly Ofsted inspector who carried out his tick box inspection on a rotating basis was relaxed about it. He had to be – an over-strict enforcement of the letter of the law would be enough to close a home, and then the problem of re-accommodating the displaced residents in an increasingly restricted marketplace would rear its head. Considering the pain that closure would cause to the residents and balancing that pain against the technicalities of the fire regulations, was a Gordian knot. It was impossible serve both the strict limits of the law and the needs of common decency. Cornwall being Cornwall, decency usually won out.

Fact was, that while the home did have fire precautions installed when the act was first introduced in the nineteen eighties, the fire regulations regarding Tall Pines were not strictly enforced.

That laid back attitude was the object of a great deal of censure by the later enquiry, but truthfully, Tall Pines was no better, and no worse, than a good many others.

All of which would have been simply a matter of mild regret if it had not been for Jamie Trenoweth. Jamie was, as far as Tregadrew was concerned, the nearest thing that the village had to 'care in the community'. His birth, twenty-three years before, had been traumatic, and badly managed. Today, the signals of foetal distress would be picked up early in the labour and an elective low section would have avoided the worst of the sequelae.

As it was, Jamie, damaged by reduced blood oxygen levels in the hours leading up to his birth, grew up with a set of psychological quirks that had masked his major problem, and if people noticed that on the nights of the November fire festival each year, he was entranced not by the pretty coloured sparks of the pyrotechnics, but by the glorious crackling yellow flames of the village bonfire, no one thought much of it.

Jamie had started lighting fires when he was twelve and feeling the first stirrings of adolescence. At first it was the odd bit of destructive mischief, a scrubby hedge here, a bale of hay left in a field there. They were small acts of destruction that no one connected with Jamie, not even his long-suffering parents, who thought their son was simply, 'a little odd' as country folk put it.

Eventually, the situation came to a head with the fire at High Antron farm, not a bale or two this time, but a whole barn full of them, and the open sided Dutch Barn had burned for hours, throwing a great plume of greyish white smoke into the night air, and casting a tower of red and gold sparks in a column against the full moon. The flames burned for twelve hours, and the bales were smouldering afterwards for a full three days. Aside from the damage to the hay, the barn itself was a total loss.

Prior to that, the small fires had been written off as bad luck and poor management, but a blaze that big inevitably invited the notice of an investigation team from the fire service. It took only a few days to trace the presence of an accelerant. The conclusion was that some person or persons unknown had poured petrol on the bales and chucked in a match.

The trail of evidence that led back to Jamie was convoluted but absolutely conclusive. He was arrested, tried for arson, found unfit to plead and committed to a secure facility until such time as his compulsion to light fires was deemed cured.

At the end of ten years of talking therapy where Jamie soon learned to parrot the responses that were expected of him, and ten years of a drugs regime that had left him near comatose for days at a time, Jamie was pronounced 'cured' and sent home to the countryside. In Tregadrew, hardly anyone remembered him.

Jamie was certainly not consciously wicked, but in his mind there was a blank spot whose existence even the therapists had never really suspected. Into that small, buried void a very different intelligence now insinuated itself and found fertile ground for its workings.

His father was long dead, but his mother accepted him back into the family home and, while those few villagers who did remember, regarded Jamie with a degree of cautious suspicion, most people accepted him. A strange lad to be sure, but the village was prepared to live and let live, especially for one their own. He even got a job of sorts, as a cleaner in the Tall Pines care home. For the residents of Tall Pines, employing Jamie was a fateful decision.

The winter's night was clear and moonlit. A few odd high clouds were scudding across the sky, but the mass of the countryside was lit in soft silver with deep blue shadows. It was the kind of night that Jamie had always found almost intoxicating. There was something about those winter moonlit nights that made him want to run in the open fields under that silver light. But there was more to it than that. Those same moonlit nights brought to the surface old and hidden urges. They were as urgent, in their way, as the stirrings of sexual desire. In the hospital they had buried those urges deep, but not destroyed them.

Those nights brought not so much thoughts but atavistic images, images built of red and gold and flickering yellow, shot through with the sharp scent of rich burning, like autumn leaves burning on the garden fires in October. In his mind's eye, these images were always laced with a scent. The forbidden tang of petrol was as sharp as a well-honed knife edge.

Finally, there was a night when Jamie knew that, at whatever cost, he must live out the compulsions that he had learned, through the years of therapy, to conceal in that private part of himself that his therapist hardly realised existed. Almost without thinking, acting only on the prompting of an inner voice that he hardly recognised, Jamie found himself, almost unaware of how he had got there, standing under the deep moon-shadow of a tall pine tree. It was bare at the base and the crown above formed a complex umbrella of needles that closed off the sky.

Away, in the middle distance, the rest home reared its mostly unlit bulk against the lighter sky. The dark shape was broken by a single illuminated window that marked the duty office. Jamie, carrying a squat red plastic can of fuel in his right hand, crossed the open lawn like a drifting, smoky shade.

The old basement windows were very nearly at ground level. They had once been the ventilation and light well for the kitchens, and they had thrown a weak, feeble light into a very near subterranean space, where copper boilers, set into brick bases, were used to cook up unappetising food for the unfortunate inmates during the time when the old union workhouse had operated.

Nowadays, the old kitchen was no more than a storage space, holding broken beds, old musty linen and obsolete bits of equipment that seemed too good to be simply thrown away. In the shadows, there were untidy heaps of cardboard boxes, filled with ancient paper invoices that dated from the days before electronic book keeping had made them redundant.

The window was not in the least secure. It was held shut, in fact, only by old dirt and layers of encrusted paint. The thinking was that no one would break into the rest home anyhow, and most of the residents were too dimly aware to try to break out. Besides, the front door was open to anyone who chose to use it, the reception desk in the lobby considered security enough, so who would break in through the old basement window?

The frame gave easily to Jamie's pressure, swinging open in a puff of paint flakes and dried out putty, to expose a rectangle of darkness and release a smell of old must and damp. With that done, as he stood on the very verge of action, Jamie had a moment, just a moment, of doubt. Some part of him, the completely sane part, was saying that this was the start of setting events in motion that were far more serious than a flame and a bale of hay in old Willie Chard's back meadow. The moment of hesitation lasted just as long as it took the inner voice to reassert itself.

Gaining confidence, with his doubts reduced to a vague unease, it was as a passenger in his own skull, that Jamie uncapped the fuel can, fixed the convoluted plastic hose that was intended to allow motorists to transfer fuel to a filler cap, and poured the rich-smelling amber liquid through the open window.

He waited then, for a good ten minutes, savouring the intoxicating cloud of fumes. Jamie was no intellectual giant, but he had a working understanding of fires. The brief interval was essential. Petrol vapour did not so much burn as explode. After a good amount of vapour had built up in the confined basement, he lit a bit of scrap newspaper, enjoying briefly the yellow flare of the flame before he tossed it through the open cellar window into the darkness.

CHAPTER FORTY

Jonathan Wilde was on call that night and when he reached Tall Pines, the situation was already far out of control. The fire service had already declared a major incident and the engines and a turntable platform were already in attendance. It was a big turn-out for a rural area in Cornwall but even so, it was obvious that there was going to be very little that could be done. Flames were already belching out of the ground floor windows and licking up the structure toward the roof. At roof level, the eaves were already bleeding thick whitish clouds of smoke. The whole scene was lit by the flashing beacons bathing the grounds in rotating cones of blue light.

Millie Marsden, the night care assistant had been the first to realise how bad the situation was. Alerted by various smoke alarms bleeping their one note distress call, she had come out of her ground floor duty office, to find that the basement was already well alight. Upstairs, in their various rooms, were seventeen residents of various abilities and mobility.

The rules said that Millie should not have been alone in the house that night, not with seventeen residents, some of whom were confused and three at least who were semi bed-ridden. Two of her care assistants had called in sick late in the day, long after the chances of calling in agency help were gone, and in any case, overuse of the ferociously expensive agency staff was not looked on favourably by her own management. Besides, night shifts at the Pines, especially when most of the residents were in a chemically enhanced sleep, were almost guaranteed to be as quiet as the grave.

So, Millie was alone that night, alone, in charge of a building where the only chance of controlling the fire now rested on the self-closing fire doors that blocked off the separate corridors of the ground floor and the stairway. Through the wired glass port of one of them, the door that led towards the residents' lounges and the dining room, she could see flickering flames gleaming feebly through thick, black smoke.

The alarms sounded their one note warning, causing more problems in themselves, with that constant irritating sound. Alarm notes of that kind swamp the senses of the rescuers, freezing up muscles with the constant urgent need to do something. Reaction, at the expense of thought, paralyses meaningful action, locking people in a deadly cycle of indecision.

Millie was in an impossible position. Evacuating the residents single-handed was impossible, and, through it all, the alarms warbled their one note. There was so little time.

She was standing, frozen to the spot, for what seemed an endless time, though it was really only seconds. There was a distant crump, like a giant belching, and the flames, that had been eating away at the ground floor joists from below, finally broke through.

Millie, all thoughts of rescuing her helpless charges gone, felt the floor under her feet begin to fail in a series of shudders as the timbers broke. Seconds later, she fell twelve feet into a glowing inferno as the fire leaped all around her, feasting on the new source of oxygen. She had just long enough to realise that the cheap polyester tabard she wore was melting, just time to think, 'I'll have to buy another one for the next shift,' before the lack of breathable air took away all thoughts of job problems for ever.

Outside, the first fire engines, alerted by the automatic fire alarm system, drew into the drive. It was all far too late.

Jonathan, by the time he arrived, paged by the emergency cover service, found that he had not a good deal to do. There were three ambulances and an immediate response car on site already, and the casualties they had recovered were already long beyond medical help. Because of the scant emergency cover in the countryside, any major incident triggered a full local response but at a major incident, Jonathan's contribution was really no more sophisticated than anyone else with advanced first aid training.

The jet from the aerial platform played on the roof and washed through the broken and blackened windows of the second floor. Where the water fell, the flames dimmed and darkened, but at the fire's heart, in the guts of the old building, the flames were unaffected. The fire was still feeding on the woodwork of the main staircase, and finding its insidious way to the interior of the Victorian lath and plaster walls, creeping up the voids, turning the rooms into individual ovens.

Dawn crept out of the darkness and destroyed any grandeur that the fire might have possessed by night. Where there had been a picture painted in red and gold, there was only grey ash and dark, ugly smoke. Outside, the rather grand front door where the coloured Victorian glass panels had been, were now glassless voids, letting onto a smoke-blackened ruin. On the gravel, neatly lined up in a mute row, were the body bags. By eight the next morning, a good few of the villagers were gathered outside the front gates, looking on wordlessly, as the final damping down went on.

Jonathan Wilde, redundant as a doctor now, with the main event over and done, could only look on as the corpses were loaded one by one into the undertaker's black vans. 'Private Ambulance' they said in gold letters on the sides, as if there was a chance that the patient inside might suddenly recover.

Sally Wilde with Siran safely consigned to her preschool placement for the day, came to find him at around ten thirty in the morning. By then Jonathan was standing on the periphery of the fire ground along with a few spectators, watching the body bags get loaded with morbid fascination.

"I thought," she said, by way of greeting, "that you might be ready to come home."

"Thank you for that, love," he said. "To be honest, I might as well have been in bed, for all the good I did here."

"You were here. You tried. Sometimes, that's enough."

"Thanks for that." He broke off, seeing her expression. Then he said, "Look, if it's upsetting you, why don't you go home? In fact, we could both go. There's nothing much I can do here.'

"No. It's not that... It's nothing really."

Looking at her pale face, he said, "It doesn't look like nothing. Come on, let's go home."

CHAPTER FORTY-ONE

Later in living room, they took up the conversation again. Jonathan had shucked his smoke stinking clothes, and was wearing jeans and a tee shirt, his regular weekend wardrobe. It was, after all, a Saturday.

He was still troubled by the events of the last twenty-four hours. Even more than the fire itself, he was disturbed by that strange almost fey look on Sally's face as she had stared at an empty space. Before their encounter with the occult, he might have simply been content to put it all down to the stress of the moment. Now he was open to a more troubling possibility.

Settling himself on a soft arm chair next to Sally, coffee mug in hand and with the Saturday paper on the coffee table in front of them, surrounded by the atmosphere of blessed domestic normality, he finally broached the subject. "I really appreciate that you came to collect me, love, but if it's really still upsetting you…"

"It's not that, Jon. It's just that, well, when I was standing there, with them loading the bodies. I saw… well, at least I think I saw… No, it's no good, I saw her as clear as day. There was nothing ghostly about it."

"Who, love? Who did you see?"

"I saw Hannah, Jon, as clear as daylight, right down to that daft tie dye kaftan she always wore, and she nodded to me, as if she was telling me something. It's all happening again. She promised that when the time came, she'd warn me. Now she has."

Sally had been shocked by the apparition. She felt that, after finally putting the strange happenings behind them and beginning to lead a normal life, she had suddenly been jerked back to face a reality where nothing had changed. The past few years seemed to have been no more than a cruel illusion, a temporary peace and no more, and Sally was inwardly certain that the fire at Tall Pines was the harbinger of a fresh assault.

For his part, Jonathan was exhausted after the night's events. He was really too tired to talk through Sally's fears that morning. With Sally's revelation done, there seemed nothing more to do. Finally, with a few comforting words that were well intended but meaningless, Jonathan took himself off for a hot shower and bed with the promise that they would talk properly later in the day. Sally, for her part, was content to delay discussing her increasing fears with Jonathan.

Despite her modern day ideas on a woman's role in a marriage, Sally was determined that her role was to protect her man. In the back of her mind was the idea that his denial of the occult, even after the proof that they had experienced, might be a fatally dangerous chink in their defences. Always more open to ideas of the spiritual, she was still determined to do whatever she could to prepare against further attacks. She cast about for a concrete course of action, and finally, reluctantly, turned to the book that Izzie had produced.

From the moment it had come into her possession, Sally regarded the book with disdain. Everything about it seemed wrong in some way that was almost visceral. One part of her wanted simply to be rid of the thing, but an inner voice cautioned against throwing away something that might prove vital. The book was stored between the wall and the taller books of their collection, hiding behind such innocuous volumes as 'Seventy Walks in Cornwall' and 'The Book of Home Repairs'.

Sally took the book out of its hiding place, wincing again at its slippery half tanned cover. Something about that leather binding suggested that the hide it was made from was not from a farm animal.

The typeface was strange, uneven as if the type was hand cut and there were areas of annotation in a spidery hand which had faded over the years to the colour of dried blood.

By way of an introduction, on the first page there was a preface of sorts. With an inner shudder, Sally read.

The forces that operate in the plane known to occultists as the outer circle mean no good for mankind. They are agents of chaos, and they intend only total annihilation for the ordered structure of the macroverse.

Powerful as they are, these beings are constrained as everything is constrained. To effect their will on our plane of being, they must operate through the agency of human beings. All that is needed is that a human allows them entrance. Such events are not common, and there may be times when the forces of chaos seem quiescent, but, in reality, they never sleep.

Feeling the echo of her own fears, Sally put the old book down with a shudder of revulsion and inwardly cursed Hannah for involving them in this nightmare.

Hannah's old house was still trapped in a legal peculiarity. Such things are far from unknown in Cornwall. Often properties stay in the same family for many generations and transfers of ownership are frequently informal and unregistered. As a system, that works well enough until family lines end and proof of title is needed.

Hannah's cottage was a case in point. At her death, she had not left so much as a will. Her distant descendants, living far away from the scene, found themselves unable to dispose of her property without first registering their title. Because there were no papers regarding the old place, the only certain data point was an ancient parish record of eighteen fourteen, when the old estate that had then owned the cottage was taken over for debt.

The result of all that was that, while some of Hannah's household goods that were easily portable and had a monetary value, were taken away, legally or not, the old place stood mostly untouched for the years immediately following her death. It gradually took on the air that all abandoned houses take on. It was a sad proof of the laws of disorder. Perhaps the most depressing physical principle ever proposed, those laws of entropy that state that the degree of chaos in the universe must always increase.

Hannah's old cottage demonstrated that principal admirably. The windows gradually clouded with ancient cobwebs as enterprising house spiders set up home. Odd tiles slipped from the roof in the winter gales, and damp penetrated the upstairs floor, in disfiguring patches that grew dark mould on the pale plaster. Presently, the local children put about the idea that the old cottage was haunted. Of course, as it happened, they were exactly right.

Isolation, in the sense of being far away from the centres of population and power is a two-edged sword. Cornwall has long been a rural backwater, surrounded by the sea, and blessed with a mostly equable climate, but in the years after the second world war, that isolation, and low population density, was seen as an asset by the powers that be, in very different terms.

In 1945, with the whole of Europe still smouldering from the after effects of the war, things were done in the name of the national interest, that might, in better times, have been less acceptable.

When Germany was overrun, and German assets, especially defence assets, were seized by the victorious allies, a small scale, and rather exotic chemical plant, in the west of the country was commandeered and dismantled. It was taken as a prize of war along with the plant operators, and a small research team who were still in residence when the allied troops arrived. Those elite few were given a choice of either co-operating with the victorious allies or facing trial for war crimes and certain execution. Given the meticulous records of their activities captured at the same time, the research team had only one realistic choice.

The chemicals that this small factory produced rejoiced in the name of Alkyl-phosphono-fluoridates. Those outside the tiny, enclosed world of research chemistry, simply called them 'nerve gases'.

By the time the Americans destroyed Hiroshima and Nagasaki, the world order had changed, the parameters of the Cold War were already emerging, and the victorious western allies created a protocol among themselves to oversee the development of war gases, and weaponised bacteria, against the time when the Russian bloc did the same. A multinational agreement for the development of such weapons was put in place. America, as the major paymaster, developed the bulk of the manufacturing capability for war gases at Fort Detrick in Maryland. They would also provide open air space at the Dugway proving ground for field tests. The British would broker the use of open air ranges at Medicine Hat in Canada, and, as the junior partner, they would also provide research facilities. These were into germ warfare at Porton Down in Wilshire, and at a certain isolated ex-radar station in the far South West. This outstation, where the old German nerve gas plant finally came to rest, was intended to test manufacturing methods on a small scale, and it was established as CDE Nancekuke in Cornwall. The thinking was that it was far from centres of population, and the winds usually blew offshore, out to the open Atlantic, offering an elegant solution to the problem of possible leaks.

This system worked well enough, at least as well as any such system could be said to work, for the best part of half a century.

There was, however, a weakness in the official thinking. Nancekuke was a small scale production facility, only there to test manufacturing processes, but the nature of this diffused set of assets meant that, somehow, fifty gallon drums of finished product needed to be transported from Cornwall to Porton Down on a regular basis.

Various solutions were suggested. Air transport was considered too risky, though it was seriously suggested, as the Cornish site did have a runway left over from the forties when the site had briefly served as a dispersal base. Being on the coast, sea transport via the tiny harbour at Portreath was suggested. It was simply not practical, dismissed as being too slow and too uncertain. In the end, in the great British spirit of 'use what you have to hand', the finished gas was simply transported by a twelve-tonne army truck through country lanes and along the desperately busy A38, going northwards towards Porton, and mingling with the tourist traffic as it went. Fifty gallons of liquid VX – the most frequent cargo – weighs in at more or less 190 kilograms. The fatal dose for VX or, as the literature so delicately puts it, the 'level of guaranteed lethality', is more or less five milligrams. Thus, each drum transported by the ad hoc delivery system, contained enough poison to kill about two million people.

Nancekuke is just twelve miles from Tregadrew, perched on a clifftop and referred to on maps as 'RAF Nancekuke', named for the old radar station that was there before the MOD took over the site for altogether more lethal operations.

The army transport corps, who were responsible for shuttling those heavy containers, has a great many good points in its favour, and due care in selection for racial balance is one of them. After years of being castigated as 'male, white and prejudiced', the army's selection process is nowadays strictly based on order of merit. Thus it was that Asrad Mohammed, a second generation Afghan immigrant, and a qualified HGV driver, trained on driving everything from six wheeled all terrain trucks to Scammel transporters designed to recover tanks, happened to be assigned to the Nancekuke run.

Asrad was not, by any standards, a devout Muslim, still less was he an extremist. He found the ravings of his more fundamentalist ex-countrymen annoying, and essentially ridiculous. He had learned the basic tenets of Islam from his grandmother, who had been imported under the dependant relatives scheme to the UK and her version of her religion was gentle and peaceful, as most religious belief is, in the very old. Even so, Asrad soon discovered that prayer five times a day and strict dietary restrictions were not to his taste, or for that matter, terribly compatible with army life.

In any case, by the time he had applied for basic training, Asrad was essentially a westernised and unexceptionable young man who lived his life according to right as he saw it, and he was more God acquainted than God possessed as they say.

It was his misfortune to fall victim to quite another kind of possession.

CHAPTER FORTY-TWO

By the time the Woodstock generation came of age, and began to operate tourist businesses in Cornwall, a trend developed for staging festivals. Emulating the national success of Glastonbury, and tapping into a market that consisted mainly of middle class, middle aged customers reliving the youth that they thought they had had in the seventies, one town after another set up a temporary pyramid stage in rough fields and ran in a generator set to produce enough power for a music system.

The only other requirement, aside from a camping ground, was a line of blue and white portaloos, set discretely away from the designated residential area. The arrangement made for sanitary inconvenience, but, at least, it limited the smell. All that was needed then was a festival theme, ideally one with a link to the venue. Surfing was a popular choice of theme, especially early in the summer, before the autumn gales raised the waves too far, but there were also festivals celebrating folk music and cider, sea food, jazz and even the opening of the oyster dredging season.

Tregadrew was too small to host a festival of its very own, but the South West 'Harvest Home' festival was held not three miles up the road. It filled a few fallow fields, and clogged the roads with the festival goers for a few days. They pitched hundreds of bright tents that were usually left abandoned when the music was done. A few enterprising locals made a modest income from reclaiming and selling them on.

The locals regarded the 'Harvest Home' event with

some amusement, and a little perplexity, but as it was held in late September, it pulled in late season punters and the site was well away from most villages so the noise level was kept to a tolerable level.

This was no Worthy Farm. The camp-ground was no more than five acres or so of rough grass, and the stage was stripped down to a skeleton for most of the year. It was waterproofed and covered, for a few weeks before, and a week after, the actual event. The marquees, offering fortune telling, vegan burgers and other such delights, were erected by Aussie marquees, a few days before the actual event. For the rest of the year, the festival site was pastureland, tussocky and silver grey, blotched with patches of brighter green.

The one thing that was guaranteed, every year, were the crowds who drove west to the site like migrating birds and camped out under the stars. It worked very well for eight years out of ten, though it must be said that the Harvest Home Festival was the last major event of the year. As a result, the weather occasionally threw a spanner in the works, and caused a last minute cancellation.

That year there were no such problems. It was one of those glorious Septembers when it seemed that summer would go on forever. The days were golden, sunlit, and not too hot, the beaches were uncrowded, the sea was blue, and the restaurants and cafes were well pleased with the late season rush that would help carry them through the long, lean days of winter.

The actual festival site, Pentual Farm, was situated in a wide valley that ran down towards the sea. The campsite was in a hollow in the ground that levelled out at the bottom to provide a clear, flattish grassy area. As a festival ground, it was very nearly ideal. Years ago, when the land was farmed for dairy, the valley was a notorious frost hollow, not that that was much of a problem in the West Country where frosts were a rarity. All the cold air in the area funnelled its lazy way down through the valley and flowed like an invisible river towards the sea. It would have made for a cold camping ground in the winter, but the Harvest Home festival was held in late September and, for most of the time, late summer weather persisted through the month.

CHAPTER FORTY-THREE

At Nancekuke, the actual military presence was small. In army circles it was regarded as a soft posting. The site was well fenced on three sides and on the other side two-hundred-foot-high cliffs fell away to the ocean. Security was not really a problem.

Asrad Mohammed had joined the army when other careers seemed limited by his Asian heritage and the military was making great efforts to show itself unprejudiced.

He was a gentle easy-going man with an aptitude for things mechanical and the transport corps suited him admirably.

As that long summer crept into autumn, he had begun to notice intrusive thoughts. It was as if a second personality was starting to intrude more and more into his daily life.

Normal procedure would have been for him to report to the MO to remove himself from active duty in the ticklish area of transporting the lethal product from Nancekuke to Porton, but Asrad knew that disqualification on psychological grounds was likely to remain on his record forever. So he simply said nothing and went about his work as normal.

Each day that passed, while he remained outwardly normal, he began to feel less and less in complete charge of his body. After three weeks or so, he was virtually a passenger in his own head. More and more of the time, that second personality took over his life, until, eventually it crystallised into a course of action. By then it was almost a relief. By the time his free day rolled round, he knew exactly what he had to do.

On the high ground, looking down into the valley facing the stage, Asrad was doing a thoroughly discreet professional reconnaissance. As a professional soldier who had been taught basic strategy in training, he recognised that the low-lying ground of the festival ground was an indefensible spot where whoever held the high ground of the walls of the valley above, could dominate the terrain with a very small force.

He was troubled. The intrusive thoughts that became more and more part of his thinking seemed to be taking over his whole life. There were bonuses. Each night, as he drifted towards sleep, the inner presence manifested itself as a woman, and every desperate, febrile fantasy of sexual fulfilment was satisfied. With such advantages as a willing succubus on offer, fighting for his identity seemed less and less important as the time passed.

Looking down into the valley, he noted that a couple of machine gun nests could have dominated the whole terrain. To his left, a quick scout around had located a tiny quarry cut into the side of the valley wall, where, years before, local farmers and builders had blasted out useable rubble stone blocks for building works on the walls and farmsteads.

The level quarry floor was perfect for what Asrad had in mind. A canister of VX nerve gas planted up here, and released, would allow an invisible cloud to flow like a liquid. VX being heavier than air, it would run down the natural slope of the hill, funnelled by the quarry entrance towards the currently empty valley floor below. That same valley floor was dominated at the eastern end by the skeleton of the stage where a team of industrious riggers were working away at cladding the structure with heavy sheets of PVC coated cloth, while the roadies were beginning the work of wiring up the sound system.

In two weeks' time, with the festival in full swing, assuming that the weather held, the valley would be full of festival goers, all of them distracted by the music. According to the website, the bookings were pretty well sold out. The last event of the summer was always a big draw. It was a seasonal thing, a last gasp of summer, before the crowd withdrew back to the cities to hunker down for the winter. According to 'Bookers', the website handling the tickets, twelve thousand people were expected. It was a good house, considering that the big headline acts were still to be announced. Asrad reckoned that, whatever happened, twelve thousand would be plenty.

Back on the base, he went about his preparations meticulously. Canisters of war gas are tough old things and the only filling and emptying point was a valve that needed a complex algorithm code entered on a keypad to open it. The walls of the canister themselves were titanium steel, one of the toughest materials on earth. They were lined with borosilicate glass to limit corrosion from within. The whole issue weighed in at nearly ninety kilos, empty. For ease of transport, the container came in a sturdy steel frame that protected it from impact and came on wheels so that it could be simply shifted.

Tough though it was, the protection was intended to resist accident damage, rather than an attack with deliberate malice. Even the valve system was intended to prevent accidents during transfer of the contents, rather than resisting direct attack. But Asrad was a soldier, and before he had joined the transport corps, he had served as an engineer, and there, he had learned a great deal about the use of explosives.

Just slapping a charge against the container and blasting it would probably not compromise the contents, but generations of explosives engineers over the years had developed shaped charges for just such toughened eventualities.

A shaped charge effectively squirts a jet of high-pressure gas in a given direction. Those gasses emerge from the casing of the charge at many thousands of bar pressure. The gas is mainly evaporated heavy metal, and, under such circumstances, the toughest steel slices like a hot knife sliding through soft butter.

The standard military shape charge that Asrad had in mind was a flexible plastic-coated rope called lead linear. Wrapped round the container of VX and detonated, it would slice the elaborately constructed containment, nearly in half, and release the contents into the air.

Naturally, such materials are not customarily available to the public, but Asrad had the code to the keypad on the camp explosives magazine. Sure, the contents of the secure store were rigorously checked every three weeks or so and any missing material would trigger all kinds of investigations. The magazine was in a separate, guarded, little blockwork building. The electronic lock on the steel door registered the identity code for every single person who entered, but the next check was twenty days off and Asrad himself was due to stand a night-watch guard on the magazine three days hence. There was a chance that he might be caught out by a snap, unscheduled check. But the chances of anyone inspecting the guard inside the main compound at night were low, an acceptable risk. By the time the next audit was scheduled, it would be far too late for it to matter.

That night he slipped into the magazine. It was dark in there, and he couldn't risk a light. The explosives were stacked in neatly labelled separated bays and the walls were lined with white painted fibreboard. There was also a padded fibre floor covering under his feet, intended to protect against stray sparks. It was purely a legal requirement, a hangover from the days when explosives had ignited that way. That time was long gone.

After a few minutes searching, he found what he was looking for. Thick coils of bright orange, plastic-covered cord coiled around heavy cardboard tubes. He selected a stray, three-foot length of lead linear, left over from a training project the previous week, and from a separate bay, he took a simple electric detonator cap, packed in its own plastic box and nestled in foam padding. With it wrapped up under his uniform poncho, the bulge hardly showed. Just for a moment he imagined what might happen if the charge went off right then. He supposed it would slice him into two separate sections, but, right then, he didn't really care.

At that point, Asrad was a passenger inside his own head. Each time that an obstacle came up that might destroy the insane plan that had taken over his life, it seemed that it would magically dissolve. Certainly, the voice inside his head, the intelligence that was driving his body the way a good engineer will drive a heavy piece of machinery, had all the answers, and the real Asrad, the essentially gentle, cultured human being, was effectively dead by then, in any case.

As the day of the festival approached, the new schedule for the regular run from Nancekuke to Porton was published on the duty roster board that admin used to communicate with lesser mortals. The day of the transport was the day before the Harvest Home festival was scheduled to start. Such serendipity was almost magical. It seemed to Asrad that it was as if some power was guiding events.

CHAPTER FORTY-FOUR

The Wildes were not aware of that particular gathering storm and in any case they, like most of the population of South Cornwall, knew what Nancekuke did, at least in general terms, but it was hardly a matter of concern in their daily lives. They had far more pressing matters to deal with.

"You are sure?" said Jonathan. He was sitting opposite Sally in the living room.

Sally took a sip from her mug. "Do you really think I'd have said anything if I wasn't sure, Jon? The thing is, I always half expected something like this. It always felt, to me, like unfinished business that eventually we would have to go back and complete."

"But why now?" objected Jonathan. "It's been quiet for ages, and, until the fire at the Pines, everything had settled down. And as for that fire. Well, it was dreadful of course, but, well, I hate to say it, but if you put a load of old people with low grade dementia in a big old house there's always going to be a risk of something like this. It's just a sad fact of life. I reckon Tariq, who owns the place, did everything by the book, more or less. In any case, I think that, in the end, it will turn out to be bad luck."

"I'd go along with that, except for Hannah showing up."

"You are really certain it was her?"

"Yes, I'm sure. It's strange, you know. Even talking about it feels weird. Five years ago, neither one of us would have given a second thought to the possibility of a visit from a long dead local witch. Oh, okay, I was brought up on this sort of story. That's the price of an Irish childhood I suppose, but, when it happens in real life…"

"You think we really have to do it all again?"

"I think Hannah will tell us what to do. She did last time."

"Hannah," said Jonathan, and he made it sound like a curse. "It all comes back to that bloody woman. Christ's sake, what happened to the time when the dead left the living alone to get on with life?"

Sally said, "I think, my love, that it comes from living here. In Cornwall, I mean. This place is very old. No, I mean everywhere is old in one sense, but Cornwall has a history of being close to the other side, and here in Tregadrew, history has a way of coming back to haunt the present."

"I'm not even going to argue," said Jonathan. "I said once that arguing with the facts isn't rational. It's just cant. The fact is that last time Hannah showed us how to lay the 'restless spirit', I suppose you call it, of a long dead witch, and we did it. Crazy as it sounds, it happened, and we really did it. Last time, I saw enough to make me think that if we don't take an active part, events will just shove us aside. It's like trying to stand against a hurricane. You just can't do it. But, and it's a big 'but', last time we got involved in this kind of thing, we had help. Hannah showed us how and where to go. Hannah told us where to start, and there was all that stuff in her work room to help. Even if she was willing to help from wherever she is, how could we reach her?"

"Her old cottage is still empty," said Sally. "Maybe we should start there. The estate agents handling it has changed since Julie Raines went broke last year, so no one is going to think it odd if we ask for the keys again to take a look. Maybe there will be something to give us a clue. Besides there is always the 'Well of Lost Souls' that Izzie found. Maybe there is something to help there."

Jonathan, remembering a misty figure that carried an air of dreadful malice as it swam through the air towards them, shuddered. "Can't we think of a better way?"

Three days later, on a damp, misty Saturday morning, they were once again at the door of Hannah's old cottage. As Sally had predicted, the new estate agent, a smooth young man who looked as if he were new made from a mould, had made no objection to giving them the keys, though he had suggested that they 'take care', as the 'structure of the old place might not be as solid as it once was'.

Hannah's cottage was actually much as they had last seen it. There were the same piles of bright coloured junk mail inside the front door, some of it faded with age and sunlight now. There was a pervading smell of damp and the same air of absence, as if this was a place long deserted by the living.

The kitchen was as it had been, though now with empty shelves, and a few rusting tins. A jar of strawberry jam was still on the table with its label in a wrinkled ribbon of paper lying round it. The contents were shrunken to a blob of rubbery jelly and the top surface was dull green and fluffy with mould. The dresser was just as they had left it. No enterprising intruder, relative or estate agent, had discovered the cache, it seemed. The old hinges screeched against the clotted dust of misuse and the edge of the dresser scraped a clean groove into the dust on the floor. The power was off. Someone had either finally decided against paying the standing charges to keep the connection going, or maybe they thought that the old wiring, left to itself to deteriorate, might burn the cottage down, and so the electricity had, long ago, been disconnected. Jonathan's torch threw a cone of bright white light that cut through the dimness that seemed almost solid.

On Hannah's old work table, the mortar, the pestle and the jars of dried plants were the same, though now dust covered everything in a grey brown carpet, and webs were everywhere. Sally had no great love of spiders and when a largish, long legged, bristly-looking house spider scuttled along the table, Jonathan saw her shudder.

"Don't worry," he said. "It's harmless," and he knew bloody well that made no difference.

The spider, big, but not freakishly so, insinuated itself into a gap between the dusty and scattered tools of Hannah's trade, and vanished from view. Jonathan batted at it, intending to scare the creature into moving to a less inhabited part of the house, and, as he did, he saw the folded envelope.

It was right in the middle of the worktable. The envelope was bright white, clean in contrast to the background of dereliction all around it. If the lights had been working, they would have noticed it at once. Written across it in Hannah's neat handwriting was 'Sally'.

Jonathan picked it up gingerly, as if it might carry a low-grade electric charge. It did nothing of the kind, of course. He said, "Well, I think that's your answer. She left you another message."

"You know what?" said Sally. "When this is done with, I wish this place would burn, like Tall Pines. Fire cleanses, you know?"

For the second time, Sally was holding a letter from a dead woman, but this time, even so long after the event, the paper looked fresh. Before, the note had been flattened with age as if it had been within the pages of the book where it was found for a long, long time. This missive was clean, as if it was fresh this morning, this though Hannah had been dead, and her cottage deserted, aside from visiting relatives, for years. Sally was almost reluctant to open it. It felt as if that was the final, irrevocable step. Instead, she tucked the sealed envelope into her pocket.

It was only once she was sitting at their own kitchen table while Jonathan brewed a drink that she ripped the envelope and took out a couple of sheets of paper covered with Hannah's neat script.

As Jonathan poured a hot drink, she began to read.

'*So, maid,*' it began and Sally could almost hear the soft West Country burr in Hannah's voice. The letter continued:

You finally have come to me, come for the second time. Don't worry, the last time pays for all. But now matters are very dangerous indeed. You have no idea how much this letter means, how difficult it is to communicate with you. Reaching across time is very hard, even for the dead. For me to contact you is to tear the fabric of space and time and that will have consequences that even the great ones cannot foresee. It is allowed, just this once, because, though the risks are great, the risk of not acting is infinitely greater.

The monster that has plagued this place for five hundred years, as you understand time, knows, full well, that its allotted span is coming to be short now. Such creatures have limited foresight. They exist only in a frantic hatred of the present, but it knows that its ending is near. It must either do what it was made to do or return to the plane of existence it came from, forever, and there it will suffer in ways that you cannot understand, and you should be glad for that ignorance, maid.

Only one thing can save its miserable being. It must be a crime so violent, so dreadful, that the Lords of Disorder will forgive and allow it to live on, as far as such things can be said to live at all.

The world, Sally, the world as you know it, has lived on the edge of a razor for seventy years and more. One good push in one direction or another might finally tip the balance towards war, and war, as you would fight it today, could mean the end of all your carefully tended civilisation. You might climb back, given a few hundred years, but the damage might be so great that there would be no chance, even for that. That is what the demon seeks, a world unmade, and all men reduced to beasts, with all that is good in humanity destroyed.

This demon seeks to ignite a great conflagration, and it has the means to do just that. The man that it has taken for its vessel is a poor victim. He is guilty of nothing more than being available, but he must be stopped, even if you need to kill him, because, if he does as he intends, then humanity itself will be imperilled by the consequences. The event he intends is small in the great scheme of things, but it is as if a small stone dropped in the right spot triggers a mighty rockfall. The consequences of allowing that to happen are beyond your comprehension.

So, last time pays for all, Sally. Use Mathers' book to call up the demon. Face him for what he is. I say 'he', child, but this monster has no real sex. You must dismiss him in due form, Mathers' book will tell you how. Send him back to the abyss he came from.

His name, his secret name, is 'Asgaroth'. The Lemegeton gives him the rank of Duke. Call him to face you, and dismiss the scum back to the primordial fires that he came from. There will be dangers. This monster is powerful. He will do all he can to thwart you. He is fighting for his very existence, but remember, this creature deserves no pity from you. You must dismiss it finally. Between his kind and humanity there can be only enmity and will always be so.

You must use the stone circle, Sally. The old circle is a lens of power, your forbears knew that, and they will help you when the time comes. They will lend their powers across the centuries, but you must be there, to funnel and to direct that power. Call the monster, and best him, and remember, a single candle flame is more powerful than all the darkness in the world.

Blessed be, child, and may the old Gods go with you.
Your friend,
Hannah.

CHAPTER FORTY-FIVE

Asrad, alone in his quarters, looked around him, taking in a room that was as austere and sterile as it was possible to be. White walls, a simple single bed, whose covers were taut enough to bounce coins on, the top sheet turned down in a ruler straight line, and the pillow, just a single pillow, plumped up into a creaseless pad.

Opposite the bed, on the other wall, was a simple laminate desk, with a plastic covered chair tucked against it. The top was bare, aside from a single sheet of paper resting between the wall and the top of the desk like a white tent.

It was, in its way, a simple suicide note, couched in the usual crazy pseudo-religious language of martyrdom to the cause of Isis. It also contained a single line of code words that had been roughly agreed between antagonist states years ago so that they could sort the real communications from terrorist groups from harmless, but extremely disruptive, wannabees. It was a system that had developed during the troubles in Northern Ireland to lend some degree of authenticity to real warning calls regarding bomb threats. Since then, it had developed and spread, covering a good many sponsor nations. The codes had evolved to allow a rough identification of the originator and this particular code sequence was only used for communications from the Islamic Republic of Iran. Given the current fuming insanity of the Gulf State politics, and the creeping dominance of the religious right in the west, the note, coupled with a mass casualty event, might well serve as an excuse for a pre-emptive strike among the more rabid western politicians.

The world had lived on a knife edge for so long that people almost regard it as a normal situation but times were increasingly dangerous. No western power could ignore a mass casualty attack. Nine eleven had taught that lesson well. They would have to retaliate, and the Iranians, innocent in this case, would regard such a Western attack as simple, unprovoked, aggression. The secret nuclear development projects that had borne deadly fruit in the dark spaces of the desert land, would finally be tested in real life. Certainly, the republic had no ICBM system capable of delivering a nuclear bomb. Making missiles is a good deal more difficult than producing a simple warhead, besides, the 'iron dome' defence system made directly attacking the western allies uncertain at best. But there are other ways to deliver such a payload, especially if there is no time pressure to transport the bomb. Under deep cover, the insane religious fringe had long ago laid plans against the time when events would allow them to strike. Ships, for example, visit ports all around the world, and there are a million places on a freighter to conceal a bomb the size of a large packing case. The ports of Galveston, or Southampton, London, or New York would catch fire. Tel Aviv would burn and the world would fall into the flames. Dominoes would fall, one after another. The old Cold War model would finally be proved right. This time, the dominoes would really fall, not in the sweaty jungles of South East Asia, but in the empty, arid desert plains, that had once long ago been the site of a largish hill called Meggido or, as the west translated it, Armageddon.

Asrad was only dimly aware of any of this, though he was suffering a constant low-grade unease as if something amorphous and deadly was threatening. Inside his conscious mind he feared the consequences of his actions, He was no battle strategist but only a fool could ignore the growing international situation. In the end, he was sure of what he was going to do.

The insistent demand for action was too strong to ignore. Reading through his suicide note, his last conscious missal to the world, he felt a strange mixture of exhilarating involvement in a great noble cause.

In the morning, he was assigned to drive the transport from Nancekuke to Porton, leaving at ten thirty or so. He would be escorted, front and rear, by ministry Range Rovers, both of them containing men armed with H&K MP40 machine pistols.

There were no scheduled stops. He would have a co-driver/navigator aboard the truck, in this case a rather taciturn Yorkshireman called Gerry Monroe who was also armed with an H&K. Asrad himself was not officially carrying a personal weapon, though he had other ideas about that.

Out on the narrow roads of West Cornwall, the festival goers were starting to trickle in. Some drove respectable and conventional vehicles, family cars co-opted for the job. Some drove the inevitable orange and white VW 'splitties', mainly hired for the occasion, and not a few arrived in roughly home converted vans with camper units replacing their manufacturers flatbed bodies. Others, either lacking motorised transport, or eschewing the polluting internal combustion engine, simply stood beside the roads, and hitched a lift.

As they reached the show ground, those scattered trickles, like the tributaries of a mountain stream, became a steady flow, until, finally, near to the festival site, the flow became a flood. The local police regarded the event with a sort of bemused tolerance, only paying real attention to those few devotees to the 'Magic Dragon', who were foolish enough to smoke more or less openly, thinking, wrongly, that the festival was a tolerance zone.

It was a fairly typical influx of the young, the silly, and those older people who ought really to have known better. In Tregadrew, the populace regarded this invasion with a mixture of bemused surprise and tolerance. By the morning, at the same time that Asrad was going through the pre-movement checks on his truck in the sterile area at Nancekuke, a bit of bureaucracy that army regulation insisted on, the festival camp ground was already filling.

At exactly ten thirty in the morning, the little convoy set out down the long sloping private road that led towards the village of Portreath on the valley floor. From there on, the route that the convoy would take was a long twisting passage through roads that followed the lines of ancient cart tracks and old mine haulage-ways towards the main spine road that led through Cornwall towards the north. The lead vehicle, an anonymous dark Range Rover with heavy privacy glass in the rear, led off, creating a gap between it and the following truck, while keeping a close view on any possible traffic that might get in the way.

There was a fair bit of that traffic about on that sunny morning. The Harvest Home festival had contributed some of that, and, as it happened, the date coincided with the end of the season for the Showman's community, so that huge, lumbering, custom converted trucks, hauling articulated trailers of fairground rides, acted as rolling roadblocks as they headed toward their overwintering park in South Devon.

CHAPTER FORTY-SIX

It could not be fairly said that security around the Nancekuke loads was sloppy, at least not initially. But systems, no matter how tightly designed they might be at their inception, decay, and the lead vehicle in the chaotic traffic conditions was much further ahead of the truck it was supposed to be guarding, than it really should have been. Eventually, the heavy truck, carrying its lethal cargo, was well out of sight of the lead escort vehicle, and the tailing Rover was still around half mile back on the Cornish express way over Bodmin Moor.

Asrad had been gradually becoming more tense as the time for action approached. He drove the big truck one handed, resting his left hand on the wheel while with the right he fondled the grip of the nine millimetre Browning inside his body warmer.

Gerry Monroe, his escort, was as near asleep as makes very little difference. Having spent the previous evening in the Rashleigh Arms, he was 'delicate' that morning.

Asrad slipped the pistol out of his waistband, pointed it with careful precision at Gerry's head and took the shot. The Browning is not a huge gun. The shot was hardly louder than a child's cap pistol might have been, but the hollow point round at three feet range was instantly fatal. Gerry, all thoughts of his hangover abolished forever, slumped into his seat.

Around a half mile ahead, the road forked right, bypassing a section of the old original roadway that stood, forlorn and semi-deserted, while the traffic rumbled past, behind a windbreak of conifers, that had been intended to give high sided trucks some protection from winter gusts blowing over the open moorland. Asrad pulled hard left, picked up the microphone to the comms net, and pressed the transmit switch.

"Escort Two," he called. "This is Courier to Escort Two, come back."

The response was almost instant, at least they were awake back there. The voice from the speaker said, "Go ahead, Courier."

"Escort Two, I have a breakdown problem. I'm pulling off onto the old section of the A38 near the Treglowan Top. I'll wait for you there."

"Roger that, Courier. What is the problem?"

"Gearbox bearing by the sound of it. I thought I'd best pull into somewhere to secure the cargo. Can you cover security for me?"

"Roger that, Courier. We'll be with you in ten. Out."

Asrad slipped from the cab and took Gerry's H&K from the gap between the seats. He held the gun, muzzle down, close to his body so that it would be hard to see from a distance and stood near the stationary truck. Presently a Range Rover rumbled into view. Asrad crouched beside the trailer hitch as if he were examining the transmission case. The Rover pulled in. Two hefty blokes, built like fire plugs and dressed in fatigues climbed down. They weren't expecting trouble. Why would they be? In defiance of standing orders, neither one carried his personal weapon. All that fire power was resting on the Rover's back seat. The guns might as well have been on the moon. Perfect. Asrad waited. They stayed close together as they strolled towards him.

The man in the lead started to say, "What happened,

mate?" before he saw the splash of blood and brain on the truck's passenger side window, and realised that Gerry was sprawled in his seat with a bullet hole in his head. He had just enough time to say, "What the fucking…?" before a traversing burst from the H&K cut both him and his partner down where they stood, the gun fully sound moderated, and the shots hardly louder than a heavy canvas sailcloth ripping in the wind. Asrad crossed to them, and put another single round into each man's head. One of them twitched, just once, at the impact.

Then, working fast, but not in a panic, he hauled the bodies to the roadside ditch and dumped them. It would not conceal the crime for long but, then again, he didn't expect to need long.

Preparations done, he reached into the truck's cab, rummaged under the dashboard for a few moments, then tore a bundle of wires loose. At that moment, the truck vanished from the satellite tracker that hovered in geostationary Earth orbit far above.

The road to the Harvest Home festival ground was a twenty-minute drive away, using cross country tracks. The big all terrain truck would handle them nicely. He was humming to himself as he started the engine. After a few moments' consideration, he got out, unloaded Gerry's body, and hauled the limp form over to the impromptu burial site in the ditch to join the others. That done with, he drove away, leaving the Range Rover where it was. In the west, the sun was passing its zenith and beginning the long journey towards the night.

CHAPTER FORTY-SEVEN

Jonathan and Sally were spending that late afternoon in preparation. There was a need, they thought, for a degree of discretion, if not exactly secrecy. Mathers' ritualistic formulae called for various exotic supplies, but almost all of them were easily available from Hannah's collection. Somehow after all that had gone before, the matter of illegally holding a spare set of keys seemed very small beer. The logistic problems were one thing, the practicalities of carrying out a ceremony of ritual magic in a public outdoor space was something else, though. In fact, the problem solved itself, albeit in a rather strange fashion.

The Nine Maidens stood in a flat area of tussocky grass not far off the rough road that once led from the village towards the old Wheal Fortune mine.

The stones were just rough shaped uprights of good local granite. The circle of nine uprights enclosed a patch of ground around eighty feet across, and beyond the circle the terrain was deserted heath land, fit only for rough grazing. It was not a place that was frequently visited, not because there was any reason to avoid it exactly. It was simply that the circle was a little off the beaten track, and dog walkers and hikers tended to follow the coastal path, rather than divert inland into an area that was not especially inviting. Even so, the Wildes were well aware that people from the village did pass by the circle, with fair frequency, and being seen there in the gathering dusk, burning braziers of strange scented incense, and marking out patterns on the ground in white tape would certainly cause comments. It was not something that a respected

GP could undertake publicly, even in Cornwall, where openly pagan rites cause no real surprise or comment.

Even so, from the moment that they laid out the triangle of manifestation, at the north point of the circle, things began to change. At the start, a couple of walkers following the little used pathway that led past the stones, came over the rim of the shallow hollow that contained the circle. Jonathan had a brief moment of panic, but then the strangeness started.

The walkers were a pretty average couple, the kind of people that you might see any time slogging along the long-distance footpath. They were wearing heavy hiking boots over woolly, bright-coloured ankle socks, with large, heavy-looking rucksacks on their backs. They were headed right towards the stone circle, and they could hardly miss the preparations that the Wildes had already carried out, but just as they reached the top of the hollow, they turned abruptly aside, as if suddenly repelled by an invisible barrier.

At the same moment, the solid, prosaic, figures of the hikers became less real. The bright colours of their hiking socks faded to a sort of sepia monochrome, like an old photo. Presently they turned away, heading down the track towards the pointing finger of the Wheal Fortune engine house, dark against the sky, and were gone into the gathering dusk.

"I thought," said Jonathan, as the hikers vanished into the distance, "that we were going to be very embarrassed then."

"Yes," said Sally, "but they didn't see us, did they? Not really. I think that they couldn't, somehow. I think something is already happening."

"God. This gets stranger by the minute."

"I think we aren't 'there' in the same sense that they are. I reckon we're in the same place as we always were, but maybe on a slightly different plane of existence. I don't think that anyone can interrupt us now, at least not for as long as the ceremony takes."

"Well, that's the least of our worries out of the way," said Jonathan. "Now all we have to do is summon up and get the better of some kind of other world monster, and then we can all bugger off to the Seychelles for a break."

"It's serious, you know, Jon, really serious."

"Yes, I know that, and God, I wish it wasn't."

Sally opened Mathers' book and consulted the details.

"Okay," she said, "now we wait for moonrise. Once the moon is fully up, we can start."

In the little quarry, the truck occupied a good part of the floor. It was like a performing elephant trapped in a ring too small for it.

Even so, it was only obvious at ground level from the access road, and then, only along a narrow line of sight.

The search for the missing truck and its lethal cargo was all the more frantic because it had, to a great extent, to be kept under wraps. When Escort One, running far ahead of the missing truck, had lost contact, protocol called for it to retrace the route as far as possible until contact was re-established. Retracing as far as the Cornwall Services, a full five miles beyond any expected position for the missing truck, Escort One, having made no contact with the convoy, radioed base and reported the loss of cargo to higher authority. That in turn demanded a satellite fix, and all that did was to confirm that the tracker had ceased transmission some ninety minutes before. The tracker from Escort Two was stationary at Treglown Top and the crew were unresponsive to radio calls. At that point, higher authority, who were inclined, as always, to regard such complications as probably just a communications issue, began to take matters more seriously. Escort One was ordered to re-check on the ground, and then report back as a matter of urgency. It was just a half hour later that they found the bodies, along with the empty Range Rover. Of the truck, and its lethal cargo, there was no sign. At that point, mild alarm shifted abruptly to panic, and a long unused emergency plan was activated.

The stone circle was old, and it was very far from the first time that ceremonial magic had been performed there. The preparations were simple enough, no more complex than following a recipe. The spell was prescriptive and the only major problem was that they had no way of knowing which parts of the detailed instructions that the old wizard had left, were vital.

They worked out the orientation first. The triangle of manifestation had to be at the north of the circle and, with the help of a pocket compass, they found that easily enough. The triangle itself was marked out in a broad crimson red silk ribbon.

In the centre of the stone circle, they laid out a second circle twelve feet in diameter and within that an inner circle, precisely a foot inside the outer rim. Then the pentacle was constructed. That took a good deal of measuring to make sure that the five-pointed star was true and accurate, so that the intersecting points of the star rested where they should. In the end they constructed a small, pentagonal enclosure to work in. Mathers claimed that that space was proof against any occult attack. At each point of the five-pointed star, they placed the ritual objects, a smouldering pot of incense and five multicoloured candles from Hannah's secret store. In the valleys of the star, they placed Mandrake roots, carved as if the root had itself grown to resemble a naked human figure. Three were female, two male. With all of that done, and the circle purified with sweet smelling smoke and water from a pure freshwater spring, the moon rose impassively into the sky, looking down on the scene and bathing it with bright white silver light. The time for the summoning was come.

After the loss of the cargo transport there followed the muscular equivalent of a panicked howl of anguish as every possible source of information was activated. The problem was that, at first, the whole business had to be kept 'under the radar', and the road system in the search area was already blocked up with slow moving traffic. Eventually, as the sun sank below the western horizon, ending a long, long, day of ineffective activity, the local police were finally informed that an army transport, driven by a man who must be considered armed and dangerous, was at large. The orders were that, if it was spotted, no one was to approach. They were simply to locate and report. In the gathering dark, the chances of any such report were vanishingly low.

CHAPTER FORTY-EIGHT

In the quarry, Asrad was going about his final preparations. The evening breeze was coming up, the offshore breeze that blows over Cornwall each day, as the land cools and the warm sea creates up currents at the coast.

From where the stolen truck was parked, the track of that prevailing wind would blow straight from the quarry site towards the tented gathering of festival goers in the valley below. Now, on the opening night, with the addition of the intrepid, un-ticketed few who had slipped past security to join the throng in the valley, there were eight thousand two hundred and sixty-three people gathered on the festival site.

Lead linear is a most effective way of explosively slicing metal, but the effect is highly directional. On the plastic sheathing of the charge, marked in bright red against the casing, was a broad line. The line marks the position of the fine lead cord that would vaporise and produce the cutting jet when the time came.

Outside the stone circle, something stirred. It was as if a vortex of whirling air was surrounding it, though the grass was completely untouched. From time to time, shadows moved at the boundary. They were twisted and distorted, completely insane, like images from a madman's nightmares. Sally intoned the ritual words of consecration, sealing the circle within the ring of stones against attack, calling on the guardians of the four cardinal points to protect against evil approaching from the outside. According to Mathers, the circle so constructed was a barrier against a visitation from the dark one himself. They could only hope that he was right.

Asrad coiled the cord around the wall of the cylinder, pulling it tight against the metal and taping it closely with silver duct tape so that, when the time came, the cutting jet would have no chance of dispersing. When he was satisfied that the charge was held against the cylinder wall, he took the detonator cap from its grey foam nest and taped it tightly to the free end of the cutting charge. Now, all it would take to fire the charge would be to connect the lead of the detonator to the battery of the truck.

As he was considering this, a rattling clatter from the west gave away the presence of an approaching helicopter. The truck was not that obvious from the air. It had been camouflaged by experts, like all army trucks, a paint job designed with avoiding air surveillance in mind. And the engine, after five hours standing, was long ago cool, so infra-red detection was going to depend on finding Asrad's own body heat. Dropping the detonator wires for the time being, he slipped under the truck, hiding under the bulky body, where its mass would conceal his tell-tale heat signature from above.

The chopper flew a search pattern that took it right over the quarry, but from where he was lying in the cool grass, Asrad was not seriously troubled. He waited, and after a few minutes, it rattled off into the middle distance. Down below him, the festival pyramid stage was illuminated like a ship at sea, an island of light against the darkness around it. The tented village was a softly illuminated fairyland of colour and light as the various tents were lit from inside.

The music was loud enough to reach him quite clearly,

and Asrad sat, listening, enjoying what he expected would be his last experience of music. Down inside him, in the basic levels of his personality, something recognised that music, recognised its association with more innocent times, and screamed at him to stop, while there was still a chance. Then it was as if a greater being than his own personality shouldered his objections aside, and asserted its own will.

Asrad was weeping, as he took the cable in his hand, ready to strip the plastic covering from the ends of the command wire. He found himself grieving for his own dear, lost self, and for the dreadful nightmare that was to come, but tears were of no use now. It was all far too late. The time for action was come.

CHAPTER FORTY-NINE

Back in the stone circle, that sense of dislocation from the present was complete. Outside the stones, the darkness had gathered, and it was full of whirling, half seen shapes that circled them like a party of marauding native warriors, circling a wagon train drawn up on the veldt. None of the shapes were visible in any detail, but the small visions that presented themselves were dreadful.

Sally opened Mathers' old book. It was full dark by then, aside from the moonlight, but the pages seemed to nearly glow with their own spectral light.

"Asgaroth," she said in a clear voice, "Duke Asgaroth, you are summoned by the rites and rituals of magic to stand before us now in the triangle prepared for you. You cannot disobey. Show yourself in pleasing form and answer my questions. You are bound by the words of power Tetragramaton, Eloh, Eloi, Vacheon. Come, Asgaroth."

As she spoke, it was as if something took over her voice, at first hesitant, and a little diffident. As she spoke the names of power, she began to sound stronger, imperious even, as if there could be no denying her.

Jonathan, in his turn, took over the incantation. Within the triangle, mist was gathering, but it did not cross the lines marking the boundaries. Something was certainly forming there, but there was one last part of the ritual to perform. Addressing the triangle, and the swirling shape in it, he said, "Zasas, Zasas, Nasatanada, Zasas," in a loud voice that was not quite his own, and the gates of Hell were opened.

Asrad was having trouble stripping the wires to connect his detonator cap. It was ridiculous to be bulked at this stage by a simple bit of vinyl plastic. It was something he had done maybe a thousand times before. Always before he had simply nipped the end of the wire between his teeth and pulled the sheathing off, exposing the bare wire inside. Now, no matter he tugged and bit at the thing, the vinyl sheath refused to yield. Finally, he took a lighter out of his pocket, and touched the flame to the sheathing, It blistered and blackened, sending up a tiny cloud of stinking black smoke and exposing the bare wire inside.

The smoky shade inside the triangle was becoming more solid, taking on form as they watched, and the throng of half seen monsters capered around the edge of the stone circle, flying like a shrieking vortex around an oasis of calm.

Presently, in the triangle, a young man stood there. He seemed perfectly solid, nothing ethereal about him. He was dressed in rather old-fashioned evening clothes, and he looked like a merchant banker ready for an evening out at one of the more formal nightclubs. His hair was jet black, swept back in the same rather elegant but old-fashioned style, but when he raised his head, his eyes were like nothing human. Hell itself lived in that gaze.

"Duke Asgaroth," said Sally, addressing the thing inside the triangle. "Your business here is finished. You must trouble this place no more. You are commanded to return to the realm prepared for you. I order you to leave this place in the name of the great rites and rituals of magic. Go, Duke Asgaroth. Your charge is completed. You have fulfilled your promises as best you can, now go."

The voice that answered her was cultured, soft and slightly amused, as if the conjuration were the most amusing thing that the creature had ever heard.

"And if I do not leave, conjurer...? If I will not 'relinquish my charge'...? Then, what will you?"

"You cannot defy the laws that are, Duke Asgaroth," she said. "Even you are bound. Leave us now and trouble this place no more."

"And if I take your fine young daughter with me as the price of my dismissal, what then?"

"You cannot. Your power is spent. She is protected by the rituals of high magic. Now leave us in peace, Asgaroth. I order you by the names of power: Araish, Arish, Tetragrammaton, Elohim."

The thing in the triangle winced as if she had struck it with a whip.

It said, "Stop, while you still can stop, woman. You cannot imagine your fate if you do not." There was very little of the urbane young man left now, the demon stood there in all its unlovely, grotesque horror.

And again, Sally spoke in a voice that was not quite her own. "The time for you to threaten is over, demon."

"Threats?" said the apparition in the triangle. "Is that what you think? Watch then and believe."

In the air, a picture formed, an image of a room that they recognised, a pleasant nursery room where Siran was asleep in the corner, and, in the vision, something vile was standing over the sleeping child. It grew larger as they watched, stretched great tenebrous wings that cast a shadow over the sleeping infant who whimpered at their shadow.

Jonathan Wilde said, "No. It's just a trick. It's not real.

He lies, the way that shit like him always lie." He spoke with no forethought, working on instinct alone, and he thought, even as he said it, that, if he was wrong, Sally would never, ever, forgive this night's work.

Sally took a handful of dried leaves and powder from a pouch. It was a very special potion that Hannah had made years before. Using it, was to put her faith in the dead woman, but somehow, at that moment, it did not seem that Hannah was really dead at all. Trusting her friend, Sally made her leap of faith.

"This is your last chance, demon," she said.

"I think not, conjurer. You are pretending to a power you do not have."

Sally said, in a borrowed voice, "You do not face the woman alone, demon. Your prescience has failed you. Still, the last time pays for all, monster."

Sally threw the powder in a cloud towards the triangle. As it contacted the demon's body, the apparition screamed.

It writhed, losing shape and cohesion, and raised its arms above its head in a gesture of submission, throwing its face once more onto shadow.

As it faded, something else was there, something of tenebrous wings and hungry eyes, but it was ruined, completely broken and destroyed.

Even knowing it for what it was, Sally felt a moment of pity, at the utterly lost and despairing look in those inhuman eyes.

CHAPTER FIFTY

Asrad was ready, finally ready. The battery on the truck was mounted outside the cab in a heavy plastic box bolted to the chassis rail beneath the tangle of tubes that carried the brake lines. They were bright shiny plastic, bright blue and bright yellow. He touched the first bare wire of the electric detonator to the positive terminal of the truck battery, and he was rewarded with a tiny blue spark. With a smile on his face, he took the second lead and reached towards the negative terminal.

In the stone circle, matters took a turn for the catastrophic. The thing in the triangle was changing even as they watched, losing its shape.

Each aspect was more vile than the one before. At one moment it was reptilian, plated with scales, and with glowing green eyes with vertical pupils, then it was formless, no more than an amorphous cloud of malice, that quivered in the triangle, and all the while the droning voice went on.

"Know this," it said. "For what you have done today, you are Hell's enemy. There is war between you and yours and Hell forever. Until the end of time, we will follow your line through all eternity."

And Jonathan, even before he knew he was going to answer, said, "I would have matters no other way, monster. Now leave us."

That last command carried an authority that he never knew he had possessed. It was as if something older, and infinitely stronger, spoke through his voice.

And just like that, it was gone. The vortex that had hidden the countryside around the circle flickered and went out. The heath was once more just the same moonlit heath that it had ever been.

Jonathan said, in the new silence, "Is that it? Is it really done?"

And there was an answer of a kind. A figure stood in the centre of the stones, a familiar dumpy figure in a multi-coloured kaftan.

"You have fulfilled your bargain, my lovers," said Hannah. "More than fulfilled it, and you have carried out a greater work than you can possibly understand. Hell might yet try to trouble you, but you will never be alone in the fight. There are more forces than those of chaos in the universe. For now, you have completed your charge. For the time, be content with that."

"Siran," said Jonathan. "She is okay?"

Hannah smiled a sweet calm smile with ancient wisdom in it. "These monsters cannot harm those who are truly innocent. That creature showed you a false vision. It reached for the one thing that might trouble you most."

Then, quite suddenly, the stone circle was empty again and the smouldering pots of incense were no more than burning plants, as innocent of power as a bonfire. Outside the boundary of the circle, the open countryside stretched towards the sea, open and windswept and cleaned of malice.

"Is that it?" said Jonathan again. "Is it really done?"

Sally, who inwardly doubted that such events would ever really end, said, "I suppose that's all we can hope for. At least for now. That thing has gone, forced back to wherever it came from. I think that for it to come back would take another dreadful event like the original witch burning to open the door. Anyway, for now, I think that we've done all there was to do."

In the little quarry, Asrad was suddenly, finally, fully aware of what he was doing. He looked down at the stripped wire that he held and threw it harmlessly away as if it were a poisoned creature that he had, inadvertently, taken up. He pulled the detonator cap from the lead linear charge, making it harmless.

He felt suddenly empty, without direction or purpose, and tired, so desperately tired. He realised, all too well, what he had nearly done, but the voice inside, the voice that had been the real instigator, had gone. Without it, he was like a driverless car, impotent, and incapable of independent action.

Grief for his lost life, regret for what had so nearly happened, guilt for the innocent lives he had taken, washed over him in a great, grey wave of depression. He crossed to the truck and took the 9mm from the door pocket. It was a well-cared for gun, and the magazine was still half full. The muzzle tasted of oil and metal against his teeth and tongue.

'Last time pays for all,' he thought inconsequentially, and squeezed the trigger.

There was very nearly no outward fuss around Asrad's death. Officially, he was another victim of PTSD. It was a convenient, easy label to explain the suicide of any serviceman, even though he had never served in an active combat zone. As for the transport from Nancekuke, the system was tightened. The old, lazy ways that had grown up since the first tentative shipments in the nineteen fifties, were swept away, and eventually, in the fullness of time, Nancekuke itself was closed, decontaminated and forgotten. Only the empty bunkers, on a lonely, windswept clifftop bore witness to it having ever stood there.

AND AFTERWARDS

People, of course, have short memories, but the Wildes remembered the truth, and part of them was forever on guard. At the beginning, in the first few months after the event, on winter's nights, when the gales swept the peninsular and the other world seemed close, the burden of that memory was great, but humanity is infinitely adaptable, that is both our blessing and our curse.

By the time that Christmas rolled round again, they finally began to relax, as normality returned. Sitting in the firelight with the TV playing banalities in the background and Siran allowed the rare privilege of staying up to witness the coming of Christmas Day, it finally seemed that everyday life could be not just good, but could be a thing of wonder.

For some, Cornwall is a paradise on Earth... for others, the reality is darker, and, for all of us, wherever we are, the darkness gathers constantly around the small circle of light where we live, but, always, the truth is that ignoring the dark, cannot make the circle vanish. Only the light can do that.